ELLIOTA

ELLIOTA

Paul F. Halloran

VANTAGE PRESS
New York

Published by Vantage Press, Inc.
516 West 34th Street, New York, New York 10001

Manufactured in the United States of America
ISBN: 0-533-11189-7

Library of Congress Catalog Card No.: 94-90337

0 9 8 7 6 5 4 3 2

ELLIOTA

Chapter 1

It is difficult to determine the beginning and end of any story, life, or event. When is the alpha? When is the omega?

When did the Church begin? Was it at the cross on Calvary? Was it at Pentecost when the Spirit came in tongues of fire upon the apostles?

Whence does one begin the life of Christ? At the manger in Bethlehem? At Cana with his first miracle? At the Annunciation by the angel sent to Mary?

Should the beginning be traced to King David as Matthew suggests? To Abraham, the original Hebrew, who received the promise on which he based his faith? To the first Adam?

Perhaps this story should begin at an earlier date. Maybe its alpha should be much later. Whatever is correct, I have decided the proper commencement is April 9, 1804.

On that date, in Woonsocket, Rhode Island, Ezra Elliot was introduced by proud parents to friends, neighbors, and relatives. At birth he weighed twelve pounds, eight ounces. This very large baby was to become a very large man.

Ezra's immensity was solely physical. He disliked institutions. Time spent in school or church, in his case, could best be described as "spent." As far as he was concerned, there was no return on his "time" invested in desk or pew.

Life is full of reciprocity. Only his schoolmaster was more pleased than Ezra when the lad played hooky, for any or no reason, in his pursuit of happiness.

The reverend knew it was more a pursuit of pleasure than

1

happiness that moved the boy to fishing and hunting. Like the teacher, the preacher was only too aware that Ezra's presence meant mischief. The pastor secretly gave thanks when young Elliot played his pranks elsewhere, rather than on clergy and congregation.

Ezra Elliot could read the signs of nature. He knew what portents led to which weather. He couldn't read or write, but he could outthink a trout and outsmart a fox.

At fourteen he went west into the wilderness of what one day would be the Midwest. "Yes," his father would explain to the neighbors, "Ezra has gone to the frontier. He loves adventure."

"That's right," Ezra's mother concurred. "He loves excitement. He wants to be where the action is."

"Who are we to put limits on the boy? He loves the freedom nature offers. He has never appreciated the enslaving chains of society," they agreed.

The truth was that they had no idea where Ezra was. He hadn't said a word of farewell. There was no explanation on his part.

He was their son, so Elijah and Sarah Elliot didn't talk to neighbors about their child except in glowing terms. The extent of their boasting was limited by the area's knowledge of the lad. The couple never discussed the real issue for two reasons: first, it was too painful, and second, it was too obvious. Ezra Elliot was antisocial. He was totally void of social graces. Their rare moments of wonder as to his whereabouts and hurt over his unexplained sudden departures were salved by the constant hope he might never return.

"You work hard as a cobbler," Sarah often reminded Elijah. "You make good shoes for satisfied customers, and your prices are always fair. It isn't your fault Ezra isn't a good son."

"That's right," the cobbler would respond. "Ezra had every opportunity to be a good, hardworking individual. We've both kept our noses to the grindstone. What more could we have done?"

They constantly absolved one another for the fact that their own flesh and blood was somewhere wasting his life doing nothing. They both agreed, "Ezra is solely responsible for his total lack of responsibility."

The failure of the system (the parents, the church, and the

2

school) actually was attributable to a conversation Ezra had overheard when he was a child of nine. The conversation was between two Indians, who were lazily making their way through town heading west.

"This is no place for us. Civilization is not good for the spirit. We need to move away. The white man speaks new words. He speaks of wilderness and wild. To us all is friendly. Nothing is wilderness. Nothing is wild until the white man comes with guns."

"The stranger in our land says we are no good. We do not work. They use our way of life for only a moment and call it vacation. They work hard for such vacation, which we enjoy all the time."

"We give them the best of our way. In return they give us the worst of their way—alcohol. No good for them; no good for us."

"Let the white man work; he invented it. We move on."

Ezra had thought of those words often: at home, in the shop, in church, at school, and as he headed west to follow the Indians and their ways.

The many appetites of the white man drove the center of population slowly but certainly toward the Mississippi. It ate the forests and plowed new lands. Lonely cabins grew into villages. Villages needed protection, so forts were built. The Louisiana Purchase said to the French, the British, the Spanish, the Americans, and the Indians that this land was U.S. property. It was a vacuum that demanded settlement. The concept was understood and accepted by all save the Native American. The purchase had cost the white man mere coinage. The price paid by the Indian was blood or slavery or both.

Ezra had the best and the worst of two worlds. At times, he was the white man in the red man's world. At times, he was the red man in the white man's world. It was in the latter moment that he one day entered the frontier town of Elyria, Ohio, on a return from Illinois country.

*   *   *

Rebecca Aldred was the daughter of the Reverend John Aldred and Sarah Mack. John was the pastor of Elyria First Baptist Church. His piercing eyes commanded such attention that

3

people were generally oblivious of his very handsome face. He wore a full beard and mustache as though there was something that needed camouflage, which was certainly not the case. His whole bearing would bring to mind the vision of what Samson must have been before he met Delilah.

John's wife was no Delilah; she was innocence personified. Her Mother Hubbard apron covered her slight silhouette at all times except when she was in the church for Sunday services. She played the organ and had a beautiful soprano voice. Sarah was a cheerful person with a constant smile, which she could quickly erase in the presence of her rather stern spouse. They loved each other dearly, and each would do anything for the other's happiness.

Sarah had only one complaint, which she dutifully kept to herself. Whenever Pastor John wanted something that he feared might upset her or something that she might not understand, he would always say, "Remember, this is for the Lord," or, "In His service, this seems necessary."

Why, she thought to herself, *does he say those things? Can't he discuss them with me? Does he think I'm stupid? Does he think I would disagree? Is he so busy we can't discuss it? Doesn't he realize that I am not fooled by his ruse of blaming God?* But she would bite her tongue until she could voice assent: "Yes, the Lord has need of it!"

Sarah educated Rebecca in reading, writing, and 'rithmetic. From her pa, the Reverend John, Rebecca received a deep knowledge and love of the Scripture. Every step she took was in the light and shadow of Holy Writ.

The pious couple sent their daughter back east to a small, private women's college for the refinement seldom found in the frontier, except in homes such as their own. She returned a polished young woman. She had studied music and education. Soon after her return, the reverend and his daughter opened a private academy for the greater honor and glory of God and His people.

It was at this time in the life of Ezra Elliot that he first saw Rebecca. She was walking past the Bird Dog Saloon on her way from the general store to the parsonage. Ezra lowered the stein from his lips and slammed it on the bar. "My God, who is that good looker?"

"That is the Reverend John's daughter."

"And who is he?"

"He's the Baptist preacher."

"Preacher?"

"Preacher!"

Ezra walked slowly out of the saloon into the sunshine. "Maybe gettin' religion ain't all bad," he pondered aloud. "I never had the benefits explained to me 'cause I never listened. Maybe I'm ready to listen. Gettin' religion might be all right."

He started walking in the direction Rebecca had been heading when he had seen her through the smoke-darkened glass window of the saloon. Suddenly he stopped and perched on the philosopher's bench in front of the Star Hotel. "I ain't in no shape for religion. I got beer breath. Ain't shaved. Need a bath. Gotta get out of these rags."

These were all new problems for Ezra. *How does a fella move from skunk skinnin' and liquor into Bible readin' and salvation?* he asked himself. He chuckled over his condition. *One thing is for sure. Ain't nothin' I have to forget to become a Baptist. I ain't never learned nothin'. Wouldn't this kind of talkin' jolly my folks?*

"Hey, boy, where's the church?"

"Which church?" asked the young lad, looking quizzically at this unlikely fugitive from somewhere south of hell.

"How many Baptist churches are there?" asked Ezra.

"Just one. But there are others," said the lad.

"Other whats?"

"Other churches." The youngster chuckled.

"No, there ain't. No, there ain't," stated Ezra emphatically.

"Well, then, you just go up this street to that harness shop on the corner. You turn that way," the boy pointed to the right, "and go until you get there."

"You're a good boy," concluded the man hell-bent on salvation. Ezra entered the hotel. *No one ever called me a "good boy,"* he reflected. *They'da been liars if'n they had.*

The hotel clerk, Jeremy Jones, eyed Ezra with fear and said to himself, *I don't want anyone of his ilk staying here.*

"Gotta place for a bath?"

"You going to put the same clothes on again?"

"You're a thinker, ain't you?"

5

"It doesn't take any thinking to know that a bath wouldn't do you any good if you put *those* clothes on again," countered the clerk.

"Ain't never worn nothing but buckskin since I left home. Could you point me to a real clothes place?"

"Just the other end of the next block. You can see the sign from here."

For a moment Ezra forgot his Baptist intention, grabbing the clerk by the shoulders and raising him so they touched nose to nose. "Don't you poke fun at me or I'll bust every bone in your body. Don't point to no signs to me. You know I can't read," Ezra sneered. The frontiersman dropped the frightened clerk.

"I'll take you there; I'll take you there. I'd be happy to take you there," the clerk chattered as he ushered Ezra to the clothier's.

The clothier measured his prospective client's muscular frame with deep admiration. In his entire professional career he had never seen such a fine physique.

The suit was delivered to the hotel on Saturday morning. Ezra bathed. Ezra shaved. Ezra put on the fine garb. Ezra was ready to meet Rebecca and God!

Ezra was the first to arrive at church on Sunday morning. He knew only one thing about church, and that was that he didn't know how to act properly. He waited outside for some kind of divine intervention. It came in the form of the hotel clerk and his family. The clerk hoped his wife's presence might serve as needed protection. Ezra tapped the clerk on the shoulder, this time with a much lighter hand. "I'm going in with you," he announced definitely.

"This is Ezra Elliot," Jeremy said, introducing Ezra to his family. "This is my wife, Mary, and these are my children."

The wife's terrified countenance evidenced her knowledge of the incident at the hotel. The children weren't sure if they needed to enter the church to find God. God couldn't be more powerful-looking than Papa's friend Ezra Elliot.

Jeremy sat at the end of the pew. Next to him sat Mary. Next to his mother was Jeremy Junior, and next to him was the newest prospective parishioner. The other three children, all girls, filled the rest of the pew.

The Joneses' pew was number one. It was immediately in

front of the pulpit. The organ was to the right of the pulpit. Rebecca was the organist at the service.

Mary handed Ezra the hymnal and whispered, "Number 238." She turned ashen as she remembered how her husband had explained the incident at the hotel. *Dear God, he can't read. Save me!* she thought as her knees sagged and she slumped slowly to a sitting position.

Ezra clutched the book. He hadn't heard Mary. His total attention was directed to that ethereal being playing heavenly music at the organ.

Reverend John ascended the pulpit at the conclusion of the opening hymn. "I see that Jeremy and Mary Jones have a guest with them this morning. Jeremy, would you honor me and the congregation with the kindness of an introduction?"

Jeremy rose slowly to his feet. He motioned to Ezra. Jeremy knew Ezra's full name because he had written it in the hotel registry so that Ezra could place his *X* next to it. "Pastor John, fellow believers, I want to introduce my good friend Ezra Elliot to you."

"Thank you, Jeremy. Mr. Elliot, would you want to tell us something about yourself." The bearded pastor smiled.

Ezra had never seen such commanding eyes before. It was as though they literally raised him from his seat.

"Face the people, if you will, Mr. Elliot!"

Ezra had always been uncomfortable in church, but nothing like the present moment. He began slowly. "I ain't never been much for church. I don't know nothing about God, so I'm here to learn."

Ezra's nervousness intensified seeing that every eye was glued on his personage. He was the only one present who failed to recognize that while he was speaking he had bent the thick hymnal in half from top to bottom. He sat down.

The congregation was awestricken. Pastor John recovered enough to bow his head and say, "Let us pray."

It seemed forever before the pastor continued. "God, our heavenly Father, we thank You for the presence of Ezra Elliot in our midst. He has already taken that first step to Your glory in faith. He has admitted he is a sinner. Let not the blood of Jesus, Your Son, be shed in vain in regard to our new friend in the Lord. We pray for him. We encourage him. We befriend him. We accept him as one of us. Lord, help us guide and direct him that he may know the joy of Your friendship and fellowship. Let us all say amen."

With one voice the congregation of believers responded, "Amen," in unison and applauded their new member.

After the service there was fellowship. Ezra shook everyone's hand. The pastor embraced him. Together they seemed to form pillars capable of relieving Atlas of his terrible worldly burden.

Rebecca was intrigued by Ezra. Both hoped the reverend would make introductions, but her pa seemed content with Ezra's introduction to religion and not to her. In fact, the reverend's every instinct said to keep them apart. The instinct became apprehension as he observed their obvious interest in one another. Rebecca maintained a constant watch on Ezra's visage. Ezra, on his part, was embarrassed and pleased by the distant attention. He would steal a glance, meet her eye, and quickly look away.

Again he turned to the aid of his friend Jeremy. As before, Ezra put his hand on the hotel clerk's shoulder. "I want to meet her."

Jeremy knew who "her" was. He had noticed the pastor had not made the introduction and agreed with the pastor's discretion. The big hand slowly began to tighten on Jeremy's still bruised shoulder.

"Indeed. Indeed. Follow me."

They walked across the room. "Rebecca, I want you to meet my very good friend Ezra Elliot."

She flushed. "Happy to make your acquaintance."

"If you ain't the prettiest thing I ever did see," he stammered.

"We were so pleased to have you with us at the service this morning. It is always an inspiration to witness someone coming to Jesus," she said, gradually overcoming her embarrassment.

Ezra wasn't sure what *inspiration* meant, but the way she said it made it a positive word.

She continued, "We love to sing at worship. You didn't sing. You didn't open your hymnal."

He had opened the hymnal momentarily but wasn't sure whether it was right side up or not. He quickly shut it to avoid discovery. Now, in his confusion, he spoke the truth.

"I ain't never learned to read. It didn't mean nothin' before. I ain't got no books. I sing songs I know, but if it takes reading, I'm out of luck."

The pastor stood at a distance from which he could hear the conversation without becoming involved. His initial impression became more confirmed. He didn't trust Ezra and was afraid for Rebecca. He said nothing.

Rebecca was overwhelmed by Ezra. She had never seen anyone so virile and handsome. But he was ignorant. His ignorance was so abhorrent she wanted to flee, but her upbringing as a Christian challenged her.

"Would you like to learn how to read?"

"Ain't much I'd druther," he responded.

"We have mostly children in our academy, but there are some adults. Would you want to join us? We begin at 8:30 in the morning."

"I know when morning is, but I can't tell time either," he admitted.

"There is no problem. Jeremy can waken you in plenty of time," she persisted. "He does that for guests at the hotel all the time."

The next morning Ezra was at the school. He began learning the alphabet and his name. He wanted to learn, not for his sake, but for hers. She was so pleased with his every accomplishment that it was a great satisfaction for both of them.

The pastor became more alarmed with every improvement. "Don't you think we have done enough? We can't afford a nonpaying student. He is faithful on Sundays, but he doesn't contribute there either."

"Papa, we must offer him some kind of employment. I know his profits from his fur sales are low. He applies himself so well at his studies."

"How can he have a job when he is in school all day?" asked the pastor, hoping that a job might force Ezra out of school.

"Let's take one thing at a time. First the job, then let us worry about it conflicting with his education."

"Well," said the Reverend John, "I will do everything in my power to seek work for him."

Before the end of the day, the pastor's search was rewarded.

Work was available at the sawmill for a healthy, strong, ambitious man.

Work, thought Ezra, reflecting on the conversation he had overheard between two Indians many years earlier. *I left home to avoid work. I ain't never—no, I don't use* ain't *anymore—I don't want to work.*

He approached his schoolteacher concerning his conundrum. "If I work at the sawmill, what will happen to my learning?"

"I've thought about that," she replied. "What we must do is tutor you at night."

"Tutor?"

She chuckled. "That means the same as *teach*."

An inward smile crept across his mind. "You mean that you and I would be together every night?"

"I don't see any other solution."

"Then I'll take the job right off." He was relieved, somewhat because he did feel awkward with the little people who were his fellow students, but much more because he needed the money to remain in Elyria to learn as much as he could about Rebecca and God.

The reverend was furious. "I will not let you spend every evening with him. You need time to prepare the next day's classes."

"Papa, I will have more time to do that than Ezra will. He works long hours and studies hard."

"You're spending too much time with him. We don't really know him very well. Where is he from? What's his history?"

"Papa, we should be interested in his future, not his past. Jesus tells us to make disciples of all. Are you doubting the words of Jesus . . . or my intentions . . . or Ezra's?"

"Not the Lord's or yours. I'm not sure of his. I'm not sure either if you or I know where your head or heart is in this matter."

"What do you mean? I am a teacher who wants to bring Christ to everyone," she said. She was not sure just what her intentions really were.

"How do you feel about Ezra, not as a teacher, but as a person?"

She had asked herself the same question many times but had avoided any answer. She knew she needed an answer now.

10

"I feel a deep admiration for his strength and physical appearance. I feel pity because he is unschooled," she stated.

The pastor had recognized her admiration and pity for Ezra from the beginning. He hoped nothing had changed. He wanted to make sure.

"Rebecca, my child, admiration and pity can both lead to love. When admiration is for the total person, love must follow. When it is merely for the physical, real love will never be present. Your admiration is admittedly physical. Pity is just as much a problem. Sometimes pity becomes frustration and future hope is dimmed as far as love is concerned. In this case, pity has become a bond.

"You are successful in teaching him. There is great satisfaction with each success. What happens when such success ceases, because he either refuses to or cannot learn more? Then comes the truth. Pity never suffices for love, real love."

"But, Papa, he is changing. As he gains in wisdom and knowledge, he can earn my total admiration and there will be no need for pity."

"Rebecca, are you dreaming of how you can change him or of whether he will change?"

"What is the difference?" she puzzled.

"When a man loves a woman, he says to himself, 'I love this about her . . . I love that about her . . . she is wonderful in every way. May she never change.'"

"Isn't that good?" she asked.

"Yes, except for one thing. She will change, either really or only in his mind. But she will change."

He went on, "But on the other hand, the woman will say of the man before marriage, 'I like this . . . I like that . . . I'll change this . . . I'll change that.'"

"Isn't that all right?" she questioned.

"It would be but for one thing. He won't change and she can't force him to change. It is as simple as that. A man wants his woman to never change, and she does! A woman wants her man to change, and he won't!"

The pastor knew his message was truth. She'd always heeded the truth in the past. He prayed she would accept his admonition as truth.

He wanted to say it, but the timing was wrong. He'd heard it

11

somewhere, maybe in the seminary: "That is why a woman's mind is so clean; she changes it all the time."

Rebecca pondered the message and tried to compare it with the reality. It all seemed correct except for one thing: Ezra was changing, and it seemed to her that he wanted to change much more.

On his part, Ezra really wanted just one thing to change. As the pastor had stated, Ezra didn't want to change in any way. The only change he wanted was a change for Rebecca. He wanted her name to become Rebecca Elliot.

She was at a disadvantage. He knew what he wanted and was in no great hurry. This was the first time he'd had a goal in life. He wanted a woman and she was the woman.

She wanted so many things. She wanted him to be educated. She wanted him to have gainful employment. She wanted him to be a responsible Christian. She often thought of all the things she wanted for him. Occasionally, she thought she might want to be his wife.

No one could possibly believe that Rebecca, with all her education, might ever entertain such thoughts. If Jeremy Jones had ever thought it, he would have warned her that Ezra was not at all her type. The hotel clerk was grateful that it never entered his head. He was satisfied never to see his "dear friend" again, except in church. He didn't want his shoulder blade touched by Ezra the fourth time. Three times had been enough.

His lack of social amenities was Ezra's greatest protection. He didn't know how to propose anything, especially marriage. He would see her every evening for tutoring. He would see her in church on Sundays. He knew she didn't have time to date anyone else. Each moment with him was a challenge for Rebecca. She attempted satisfying his obvious needs. They never discussed that in which he wanted satisfaction. If she could have read his mind, as she could read all those books, their whole relationship would have been terminated quickly. It was the challenge he offered that kept her interest. It was the thought that in marriage she could have more time to respond to the challenges that intrigued her. The fact that there was no human reason for her marrying Ezra indicated to Rebecca there must be some divine purpose. Even though her father argued otherwise and to no avail, Rebecca seemed unable to do otherwise. She was a crusader with a crusade: "God wills it."

Despite all his resistance, the pastor one day found himself standing in front of Rebecca and Ezra. Her father had pleaded with her that it be a small wedding. In his own mind, he saw no reason why money and embarrassment should be risked over a marriage that had no saving quality.

Rebecca and her mother wanted a large wedding and were making the plans when Ezra let it be known, in no uncertain terms, that he agreed with the reverend. For a short period in their relationship, the two men were in agreement. The reverend was almost ready to admit that Ezra wasn't such a bad fellow after all and maybe the marriage would work.

For the time, the reverend discounted embarrassment but went along with his future son-in-law from a financial point of view. Little did anyone realize that Ezra's real motive was what generally drove him: his antisocial makeup.

The wedding was small, simple, and short. *After all, the real test of a marriage is not the wedding, but the marrying couple,* thought the pastor. Ezra and Rebecca were married.

Ezra, like Rebecca, had been too busy with education for anything else. Now, in marriage, the regimen of work and study began to deteriorate. It was no longer necessary to set a time for the next lesson. Any time would be all right. As with everything, any time quickly becomes no time or never.

He remained an attentive, if not a loving, husband. She attributed his inability to love to innocence on his part. In her innocence, she was not capable of helping him.

Once the educational programs were scrapped, all conversations became difficult, while some became impossible. Too late she discovered that they had absolutely nothing in common. Nothing, that is, until she became aware of her pregnancy.

Rebecca's disappointment with the marriage gave way to the bright promise of an offspring who might save the relationship as education had nurtured it. Hope is never a substitute for love, but she could at least hope a child might open love's door.

She was correct in her conviction that Ezra would never be unfaithful. He was faithful because he couldn't introduce a conversation with a woman on any subject. His interaction with females was limited to mental activity, and very little of that.

Rebecca lost the baby in the sixth month of pregnancy. Ezra was unable to fathom the situation. In his confusion, he retreated to the Bird Dog Saloon.

The usually even-tempered pastor's emotions exploded with righteous wrath when he was informed by various parishioners and nonparishioners of his son-in-law's slip from grace. Ezra accepted the outburst with patient humility. His sorrow had never been greater. He was sorry he was a failed parent, a recalcitrant husband, and an occasion-of-sin son-in-law and that the headache accompanying his hangover needed silence. The anger he had formerly known for his teachers, parents, and pastor was rekindling. The bad memories of civilization were suddenly as overwhelming as the past incidents themselves. Once again, the choice seemed obvious between fight and flight. He would flee.

"Rebecca," he began, "think of all the wonderful times we had when you were teaching me about reading and writing. I never knew God until you introduced Him."

"Those days were good," she said. "You listened to me and we grew to know the Lord; we grew together."

"I want to see you that happy again," he offered.

"I would be if only you would be more attentive to me, Ezra. Let us forget your recent failing and return to peace and happiness," she suggested.

"I'm not sure if that is possible. My friends in Christ are quite upset with me," Ezra replied.

"All you have to do is work hard, support me, and sing loudly from the front pew in church. You can show them."

"Then," he said slowly, as though by a sudden but certain inspiration, "I want you to be happy. There are dozens and dozens of people, white and Indian alike, who need you to teach them as you taught me. I don't think you can be happy knowing that and not helping."

"I can be very happy right here in Elyria, praying in our own church, singing with my own people, teaching children about the Lord and life. There is no force can change my mind."

She set her jaw. Ezra shrugged his shoulders. He had planted the seed. It would take time. Meanwhile, he would do all she asked. This was her moment of victory. His moment would come.

It was nearly eighteen months later when Ezra and Rebecca were reading Scripture together that Ezra was amazed by the words of Paul to the Ephesians: "Wives, be submissive to your husbands in all things."

The next day, after work, Ezra stopped at Reverend John's house. After the usual formalities, Ezra accepted the invitation to sit and talk.

"How are you and Rebecca doing?"

"Fine. You have a wonderful daughter."

"I know. I know."

"I only wish I were a better husband and son-in-law."

"You will be if you remain faithful to the Bible. Is there anything else on your mind today?" asked the pastor.

"No, not really." He hesitated. "Yes, as a matter of fact there is a spiritual help I'd appreciate. Actually, it pertains to the Bible."

Grateful that the help was spiritual, the pastor spoke eagerly and earnestly. "Anything. Anything at all."

"Have you ever preached on Ephesians 5:22?" asked Ezra.

"Not in recent time," acknowledged Reverend John. "I used to preach on that text regularly. I developed a real—excuse the expression—'barn burner' on that Bible reading."

"I'd like to hear the best you have to offer on it," Ezra requested.

"You'll hear it this very Sunday," promised the clergyman.

Ezra was pleased at the prospect of Sunday's sermon. The results could have a profound influence on the rest of his life.

The pastor was pleased his son-in-law was finally showing such avid interest in the Bible. He would reward Ezra with his best effort from the pulpit.

From the organ bench, Rebecca listened attentively as her minister father waxed eloquent. He was outdoing himself. If she hadn't known better, she'd have thought her mother had upset the beloved pastor and husband.

Rebecca studied the happy features of Ezra as he listened. He was holding the hymnal loosely but carefully. She was so pleased that all was right with the world.

John Aldred always looked overpowering, but when he stood in the pulpit his physical and moral strength could not be chal-

15

lenged. He had given the sermon on the wife's subservience to the husband many times. It was memorized. Since there was no faltering, the talk was all the more persuasive and dogmatic.

He had admitted to Ezra that he hadn't given the sermon for many years. He had last presented it the year of his marriage. His wife had insisted it never be voiced again from either his place in the church or her place in the home.

Now he had had a specific request. Now he had been challenged. He would meet the demand. He was in charge, after all, of God's message, and it must be presented.

One more time. He meditated. *One more time and I'll promise Sarah, again, never to preach on the subject.*

"My dear friends in the Lord Jesus Christ," the reverend began, "of late I have had numerous requests to speak concerning Paul to the Ephesians, chapter 5, verse 22, and following.

"I have just read that sacred Scripture which had been handed down from the earliest Christian times. Since it is God's word, we must not only preach it, but adhere to it with every fiber of our being.

"The Apostles' works are not without a tradition that goes back to the very beginning, as we find testimony in the Book of Genesis. The crowning glory of God's creation is man, Adam. He had given man dominion over all other creatures.

"God knows it is not good for man to be alone. None of the world's creatures is a suitable partner for Adam, so God casts a deep sleep upon man, takes from him a rib, and forms it into the woman.

"You see that man does not come from woman, but woman comes from man. She was created from her man for his satisfaction, not hers. The Bible does not say it is not good for woman to be alone, but man should not be alone. Woman was made for man. On that Genesis is very clear.

"Satan tempted Eve rather than Adam. She, in turn, tempted the man. It was through woman that sin entered the world. The devil knew her to be weak. He knew also that the man would be more tempted by her than by his wiles.

"To the woman, Eve, God speaks sternly in Genesis after the sin: 'I will multiply thy sorrows and they conceptions: in sorrow

16

shalt thou bring forth children, and thou shalt be under thy husband's power and he shall have dominion over thee.'

"Elimelech, of the tribe of Judah, had two sons, Mahlon and Chilion, by Naomi. One of the sons married the Moabite woman named Ruth. In Moab, Naomi lost her husband and both sons. She encouraged her two daughters-in-law to return to their families. Orphah did as requested, but Ruth remained with Naomi and was true to her husband even though he was dead. She spoke the beautiful words by which we remember her best when she responded to Naomi in Ruth, chapter 1, verse 16: 'Be not against me to desire that I should leave thee and depart; for whithersoever thou shalt go, I will go; and where thou shalt dwell, I also will dwell. Thy people shall be my people and thy God, my God. The land that shall receive thee dying, in the same will I die and there will I be buried.'

"Paul, the Apostle, speaks to this when he urges all women to worship with heads covered, since this is their crowning glory. Thus he speaks in his First Letter to the Corinthians, chapter 11, verse 3 and following: 'I would have you know that the head of every man is Christ, and the head of the woman is man, and the head of Christ is God. Every man praying or prophesying with his head covered disgraces his head. But every woman praying or prophesying with her head uncovered disgraces her head for it is the same as if she were shaven. But if it is a disgrace for a woman to have her hair cut off or her head shaved, let her cover her head. A man indeed ought not to cover his head because he is the image and glory of God. But woman is the glory of man. This is why the woman ought to have a sign of authority over her head.'

"The Apostle Peter is in agreement with Paul as he writes in chapter 3, verse 1, and following: 'You married women must obey your husbands, so that any of them who do not believe in the word of the gospel may be won over apart from preaching, through their wives conduct. They have only to observe the reverent purity of your way of life. The affectation of an elaborate hairdress, the wearing of golden jewelry, or the donning of rich robes is not for you. Your adornment is rather the hidden character of the heart, expressed in the unfading beauty of a calm and gentle disposition. This is precious in God's eyes.' The holy women of past ages used to adorn themselves in this way, reliant on God and obedient to

17

their husbands. . . . For example, Sarah was subject to Abraham and called him her master.

"The Muslims, in their worship service place all the men in front and the women to the rear. They are appreciative of the Apostles' message and take the extra mandated precaution of not allowing a woman to be a distraction in prayer by coming between them and Allah.

"The Old Testament always considered women as minors. The women's role is to work, to obey her husband, to bear children, and to please. The Mosaic Law gave women a low social status. They had no right to inheritance. They needed to be faithful to the husband but had no right to his fidelity in return. He could divorce her under the slightest pretext.

"The New Testament insists both spouses be true to one another. Marriage is a holy covenant through which God assists the husband as head and the wife as the heart of the family.

"Paul indicates the relationship desired in marriage by the Lord. Let me read again what he says: 'Let wives be subject to their husbands as to the Lord because a husband is the head of the wife, just as Christ is head of the Church, being Himself savior of the body. But just as the Church is subject to Christ, so also let wives be subject to their husbands in all things.'

"It behooves us to rejoice that the Founding Fathers of our most wonderful country were driven by principles which are God-fearing and just. There is no place in the Bill of Rights or the Constitution which allows for women's suffrage.

"A wife's place is not in the political arena, nor in the professions. The woman's physical being does not allow competition with man but, rather, compliance. Her place is in the home tending the children and the hearth.

"There are painted women who don't understand their role. They don't understand that even in nature the male bird is beautifully feathered while the female, by God's design, is feathered so as to blend into nature's surroundings for her own protection.

"Therein is the lesson. God will protect the husband and the wife as long as each maintains the proper role. God, Paul, Peter, and nature have so decreed. The Bible proclaims it and as believing Christians we accept it. So all together now, let us show our assent to these words with a loud amen!"

With varying degrees of enthusiasm, the congregation proclaimed aloud, "Amen." Without a moment's hesitation, the pastor announced the next hymn.

For the first time since beginning the sermon, he stole a furtive glance at his wife. At the conclusion of his greatest sermon, he knew he shouldn't have given it.

Chapter 2

People react to the same sermon in different ways. After hearing this one of her husband's sermons, Sarah Mack Aldred became absolutely cold to him. She continued serving his meals. She shared the same table. Every meal, however, was a time of stony silence.

He had vowed to her he would never give that sermon again. He had lied to her. Now she was determined to prove what they both already knew, but he had occasionally forgotten, that she was the strength in the household. Never again would she bless his bed with her presence. He knew she would if he were to ask. She knew he would never ask. Breaking his vow, for all practical purposes, was tantamount to taking another vow: the vow of celibacy.

Tragedy continued in another form for the pastor and his wife. On Wednesday evening the church hosted a potluck supper. Ezra Elliot and his wife, Rebecca, were in attendance. The son-in-law came forward and grasped the hand of the pastor with enthusiastic congratulations. "The best sermon I ever heard in my life. Everyone should hear that talk at least once a year. You said it like the Bible says it!"

The pastor took the compliment with downcast eyes. He avoided everyone's gaze, but especially that of his wife. Everyone, especially the men, joined in the praise. The minister was certain his own personal Armageddon had arrived.

Ezra's treachery kept unfolding. "Next Monday morning Rebecca and I will begin a new and adventurous journey together. As an obedient wife, she has agreed, as did Ruth in the Good Book, 'Whither thou goest, I will go.'"

For a seemingly eternal yet really brief moment the pastor peered into his daughter's countenance and saw the agony there. Sarah ran over to embrace her only child. Any pretense of joy was unmasked as the two women stumbled blindly toward the preacher's house. Neither husband made a move to follow. Instead, the victor again clasped the hand of the vanquished. "We aren't sure, really, where we are going, but you have my word as a born-again, faith-filled Christian that I will love your daughter even as Christ loves the Church, willing to give my life for her."

The Reverend John Aldred was dazed. In one sermon, encouraged by Ezra Elliot, his son-in-law, he had lost his wife and his daughter.

"Just sit where you are, Pastor. I'll get food enough for both of us," Ezra told him. "This is a time to celebrate. The message of God has come alive in me through you. May He ever be praised."

The people weren't quite sure whether this was a time of celebration or not. To cover the embarrassment of their uncertainty, they all responded with vehemence, if not conviction, "Amen."

Ezra wasn't finished. His unbelievable orchestration continued. "Go ahead, everyone. Grab your food. I know you are happy for Rebecca and me. I know you want to share in our joy. With the pastor's permission, the elders will take a collection now and another at the Sunday service to help outfit us for the journey. What do you say, Reverend?"

The pastor made some very earthy sounds that seemed to spring forth from his very bowels. Everything was happening so fast. It was as though he had been caught up in a cyclone and slammed harshly back to Earth.

The enthusiastic son-in-law slapped the pastor heartily on the back. "That's the spirit. We all know you couldn't deny your own daughter. Elders, you heard your pastor. Give the people the opportunity they all want. Take the collection."

After the festivities concluded, Ezra sauntered to the parsonage to take his hostage, Rebecca, home. She came submissively, according to the dictates of her father's sermon.

Reverend John Aldred walked aimlessly in the darkened streets. Then, totally exhausted, he unlocked the church, entered, and slept fitfully in the back pew. If ever a man wanted to be struck dead, the pastor was that man.

21

The Sunday service, for all intents and purposes, was a funeral ceremony. Only the collection made it otherwise. Parishioners weren't sure whether to fill Ezra's pockets with their money or to refuse and somehow save Rebecca.

This was her farewell appearance at the organ. It was farewell to parents and the town. It was farewell to the community who loved her and whom she loved.

The Reverend and Mrs. Aldred were not present when Ezra and Rebecca moved out of town to the West, as they were unable to countenance the situation. At daybreak, a few people heard Ezra shout at the horse he was riding, then shout at the horse that was pulling the cart that carried his wife. They heard it, rolled over, and went back to sleep.

It was a short procession. In the lead was the husband astride his mount. A rope knotted to the back of his saddle was used as a lead for the second horse. Rebecca slumped uncomfortably on the cart's seat. Ezra accepted her token resistance to his authority in refusing to take the reins. This was an empty victory for the woman who was allowed the luxury of one trunk filled with her connection to civilization. The cart was otherwise filled with tools, guns, and ammunition.

The same procession concluded with a family cow. Ezra had wanted no part of the animal but condescended when told it was a gift. Under his breath he muttered, "I guess it is meat whether one shoots it or not."

The present generation never understands why they are called the good old days. It listens attentively. It knows why they call them old. Why they are called good is a mystery. The older generation talks at length on the hard times of yesteryear. Everything was difficult; nothing was easy. It is as though the repetition of trials and tribulations proves the speakers better people than the listeners could ever be. And when the last greatest hardships are described in minute detail and all the reminiscing is concluded there is needed just one phase: "They were the good old days."

Ezra Elliot knew the good old days were full of heartaches and sacrifice. He also understood them to be part of everyone's life in every age. What he never comprehended was that he was more often the cause of the troubles than the solution.

He claimed he couldn't countenance crowds. He felt better in the wilderness, where he could be alone with nature. He felt pride that he was a leader who dared move into the unknown. In reality, he found it easier to move on than to communicate with others. People allowed his ruse of rugged individualism to camouflage his total lack of social grace.

Ezra boasted that he could see God in rocks, trees, streams, lakes, and mountains. His Creator was obvious in nature. Ezra failed to see God in the creatures that were made in His image and likeness.

People have the power of God. They know and they love. They have free will, which is the requisite of love. Ezra's free will found more acceptance and acceptability in the world about him devoid of humanity.

Rebecca had her free will also. Ultimately, it had been her choice to marry Ezra. Her father had taught her to love people and use things. She, initially, was unable to comprehend that Ezra loved things and used people.

So it was a mystery to all that the beautiful Rebecca Aldred could ever fall in love with such a man. Women were outnumbered nearly five to one in the area and could afford to choose carefully. "Opposites attract" seemed the only answer, but it wasn't logical or an accepted one.

Ezra was so hopeless and helpless in society. Perhaps he provided a challenge for Rebecca. Maybe it was her challenge from the Almighty to change this pagan into a Christian gentleman. Also, she deeply admired the strength of Ezra. To her, he was a handsome, unspoiled giant who merely needed the taming of education and etiquette. He was, indeed, a challenge she was convinced she could not only meet, but overcome, not as an adversary, but as his wife.

Despite warnings from parents and friends, she pursued the transformation of Ezra. It was generally conceded that each change of his character and personality was evidence of her success.

Rebecca loved people. She appreciated neighbors. She needed

a place where there was a church and a school. Consequently, the mystery merely deepened when it was learned she would accompany her husband to what would be the Minnesota Territory.

With aching heart she left the comforts of Ohio. He had assured her the separation would be temporary, but she felt from the beginning that was not his intention. Before reaching their destination, she ascertained she was pregnant and begged to be allowed to return. With his refusal, she knew there was little likelihood she would ever see her beloved Ohio again.

The journey was horrendous for Rebecca. The winter journey was difficult; she had never seen so much snow. In the spring of the year the crossing of the Mississippi was especially fearsome for her. Never had she prayed as she did then. The snow melt had brought flood and treachery to the river. The raft constructed by Ezra wasn't adequate for the crossing. A huge tree struck just as they approached the shore.

It was a miracle that the two horses and the cow survived. The tools and the guns sank in shallow water where they could be retrieved. The chest containing all Rebecca's special mementos floated quickly out of sight.

Rebecca was thrown clear of the raft and the tree. The icy water caused such shock that she had no realization or care for the trunk and its treasures. Ezra pulled her to the shore. He built a fire to dry themselves. He erected a temporary shelter so she might rest.

Up to this point it had seemed to her a terrible dream. Suddenly it was a nightmare. By their assessment, the baby should be born in six weeks to two months. Now, under these terrible circumstances, she began to deliver.

Both used the name of God, she in prayer, Ezra in cursing. Neither knew what to do. Fortunately, her words were answered. Three Indian women had seen the accident from the bluff tops. They had witnessed the rescue and the building of the fire. They seemed drawn like insects to the flames.

They delivered the boy child and placed him in Rebecca's arms. In the midst of sadness and terror she experienced joy. His name would be Joshua. The year was 1831.

She was a gentle woman, a caring wife, and a dedicated mother. She missed her family and friends. She missed a loving husband. All her energies necessarily turned to her child as her only defense against self-pity. This infant son was more than her offspring. He was her strength, her life, her sanity.

Ezra was a patient person. He knew a successful hunter or angler had to be patient. He was in no hurry to clear the land and plant the crops. He understood that all took time.

He was painstakingly careful in building the cabin. Each stone for the fireplace was chosen with special care. It couldn't be rushed and be right. These things Ezra understood. He didn't understand Rebecca's moods. He didn't understand her three miscarriages. He didn't understand why she needed the boy with her as though he were a daughter rather than a son. There were less than occasional moments when Ezra seemed to appreciate her tenderness, but he didn't understand that either. For him, there were better characteristics to be found in a woman than tenderness.

Ezra worked hard. He played hard. His ingenuity was such that success should be guaranteed. Consequently, when success was his, it was totally his. When failure was his lot, the blame was always on her shoulders.

Despite the fact, or because of the fact, that it upset Ezra, she told Josh often about the good old days in Ohio. The lad loved the telling. He urged her to tell more. He delighted hearing of happy places with happy people. He listened attentively about doctors and lawyers, schools and churches, opera houses and mercantile shops, newspapers and elections, Sunday clothing, and a day of rest.

Even more wonderful for the boy was to watch his mother's eyes sparkle and dance as she was transformed by recounting the good old days. She promised that one day she would take him back to Ohio so he could experience it all with his own eyes.

He remembered everything she told him. He remembered what she taught about reading and writing. He remembered her stories from the Bible. He remembered the night she died trying to give him a little brother.

Josh never forgot his father digging that deep hole at the top of the hill. The boy watched the box being built and saw his mother and his little brother for the last time.

Josh was eighteen in 1849 when he helped shovel the dirt over the box. He remembered. He remembered how his dad told him of his pride in having such a hardworking son. And Joshua knew that his father's pride could never replace his mother's gentle, loving tenderness.

Despite Ezra's attempts to "make a man of" Josh, the lad became more and more the dreamer. He shared little of his dad's interests. The attraction of the good old days in Ohio was constantly beckoning him. His daily visits to his mother's grave confirmed his resolve to go East.

Much had changed since the three had settled in their cabin. To the south, Irish and German families claimed homesteads. To the north, Norwegians, Scotch, and English did the same. Most of the Indians had moved farther to the west. Ezra was getting restless. He would soon follow the Native Americans.

For Joshua, that was the wrong direction. If only for a short visit, he wanted Ohio. Ezra knew he would push on alone. He took his son, now twenty-two, to the Recorder's Office and placed all his holdings in Josh's hands.

Sometime in the night, without a farewell, the father left. Josh hoped that Ezra might have spent a few moments at Rebecca's grave. Somehow, he knew he hadn't.

Then preparations were made for Josh's departure. A recently arrived Irish family moved into the cabin with the understanding that it would only be temporary. In return, the Carolans gave assurance of protecting Joshua's holdings and caring for Rebecca's grave. He let them know that he would return.

Josh rode southeast through the hill country. He knew about the Mississippi and the role it had played in his birth. He decided to stay a few days in the well-established city of Dubuque.

While there, he heard that a stage line was about to open between Dubuque and Saint Paul. On further inquiry, he was told that Burr Oak and Mantorville were the only projected stops at the moment, but other intermediate stops would be necessary.

Immediately he went to the stage office. When shown the proposed route, he recognized quickly the advantageous location of his property.

Letters of application had already come from Carimona and High Forest. He made a proposal for a stop to be located at his place, between Burr Oak and Carimona. The officials were impressed by his personal visit.

26

That night he was unable to sleep. If acceptable, what would he call the stop? Elliot would be a name after his father. Not that. No stability. His mother was the one who had wanted buildings and streets. Rebecca? No. His father was always so proud of his manliness. Why not give the stop a woman's name? Elliota? Josh thought his mother would like that.

By the next evening Josh was informed that Elliota had been selected as a stagecoach stop. Hurriedly he retraced his steps back to his homestead. The entire area was excited by the news.

Men volunteered their services for the construction of the inn and stables. It was 1853 and Elliota was on the map. Josh told the volunteers that anyone who wanted to establish a business in Elliota would be given the necessary building sites for free.

As if by magic, the buildings his mother had described seemed to rise out of the very ground. When he visited her grave he knew all this would have pleased her. She never returned to civilization. Civilization had come to her. All her tales of the good old days was reality right in the hollow where he had first heard them.

Josh married for love. His wife, Julia, was the cobbler's daughter. Her father had instilled a good business sense in the girl. She had the excellent homemaking instincts of her mother.

The daughter Julia presented to Josh was a reincarnation of his mother. She was the new Rebecca Elliot: beautiful, tender, and loving. Fortunately for Becky, Josh inherited parenting skills from his mother rather than his father.

Julia was a natural as the innkeeper's spouse. She kept the books. She hired excellent help for the comfort of the traveler in regard to room and board. Life in Elliota was good for Josh, Julia, and Becky.

It was heartwarming for Josh to have a church in the village. The Methodist pastor was strict but kindly. Whenever a death occurred, Josh would look back to the lonely death of his mother and her burial. Now people here had a preacher during sickness and in death.

In gratitude, Josh donated a large area on the hill for the cemetery. In its center, a newly cut marble stone marked Rebecca's grave. Now she and her stillborn child were no longer alone.

A beautiful iron fence was shipped from Ohio to encircle the land. The local blacksmith created the words *Elliota Cemetery* above the iron gate. Josh could think of nothing more he could do in his mother's memory, and he was proud.

Elliota was a quiet hamlet cradled in the hill country. It was located on the Minnesota-Iowa border, but it nestled completely on the Minnesota side.

Bountiful springs made it generally unnecessary to dig wells. Magnificent hardwood trees provided needed lumber, fuel, and shade.

Besides the Stagecoach Inn, there were two other inns and two very impressive hotels. The village boasted one cobbler, a harness maker, and two blacksmiths.

Since there was no mill, it was necessary that each farmer make an annual three-day trip to Prairie du Chien to have his wheat ground. Three general stores vied for trade. The produce house provided ready revenue for chickens and eggs.

Anthony Gossman, reportedly the richest man in Iowa, made it unnecessary to have a bank. He kept his money in cream cans in his basement. All knew it was there, but he was never robbed.

His farmhouse was the bank. He never charged interest but would accept a gratuity for his service. He never kept records; no notes were ever signed. Business was done by a handshake. He trusted everyone and everyone trusted him.

There was only one church in town, Methodist. It was painted every three years without fail. It literally glistened. It was the heart and the center of the town geographically, spiritually, socially, and politically.

The parsonage was humble in size and appearance. It wasn't befitting the most powerful person in the community, its pastor. There were always plans to build a more respectable and acceptable home for him.

From the square, flat-topped steeple one could look up the hill to the east and see the Methodist cemetery. It was presumed that every citizen would be of that persuasion, so it was unnecessary to call it the Elliota Methodist Cemetery. Even though it was a Methodist smithy who fashioned the tall posts and huge arch over the gate, high enough for the tallest carriages, it merely read in large letters: ELLIOTA CEMETERY. Catholics, who were generally latecomers to the community, prayed and found their final resting place at Saint Agnes, two miles into Iowa.

Chapter 3

As a primary stop on the Dubuque Trail, Elliota had a promising future. Suddenly, it all changed. Like many happenings, it began with rumor. Everyone had known the age of the stagecoach would come to an end. The Iron Horse was a threat to the future of the town, as it was a promise to the nation. The trail, so prominent in many lives, would soon be history. That which had brought people, news, merchandise, indeed life, was to be a matter of memory.

The townspeople knew the stagecoach was their umbilical cord. They also knew the railroad from Dubuque to Saint Paul would logically follow the Mississippi. The river banks would be easy travel, with their gradual lowering to the Gulf of Mexico. The bluffs around Dubuque and the hills of northeastern Iowa provided difficult terrain for the Iron Horse.

Josh went to the president of the railroad in Milwaukee. He knew a proposed track was scheduled to run two miles north of Elliota from east to west. Couldn't it come just that much south to save the town?

Then he went to the state legislature. There was no financial or political way to change the railroad's plans, nor was there any way the stagecoach could compete.

The lifeline was cut. Elliota would die. Town meetings, no matter how well attended, no matter how logical, were useless when the real decisions were made in Chicago, Milwaukee, and Saint Paul. The decisions were not made by governors, judges, politicians or financiers. They were being made by an altogether new institution: the railroad.

Continued life for Elliota demanded its migration to the tracks. The citizens, despite protestations from Josh, decided in favor of continued existence. Within days, the moving began.

Huge jacks raised whole buildings up on large supporting beams. Large iron wheels were placed on axles holding the beams and buildings in place.

The procession moved like so many ants scurrying in a long line with every worldly possession. The horses, mules, and oxen pulled the structures up the hill past the cemetery. Shortly beyond the graveyard, the caravan turned due north for two miles, passing by the Olson, Young, and Ryan farms.

Then the buildings were lowered onto new foundations as close as possible to the place where lengths of iron tracks and wooden ties were being wedded by the Milwaukee Road.

Behind was a myriad of open cellars, stone foundations, and the cemetery. Ahead was the railroad with its promise of a new and greater town. Anticipation for the future was evident. Like a phoenix, Elliota was being born again.

The exodus from Elliota was not without incident. All did not go according to plans. Supporting beams occasionally slipped from beneath burdens or even cracked and needed replacement. Sometimes the structure's weight would shift as progress moved up and down the hillsides. Such occurrences were surprisingly rare.

Tragedy struck most horribly for the Courtneys, who owned the largest saloon in Elliota. Their son, Jim, was a handsome, many-talented young man who showed much promise as an artist. He painted many of the leading figures of the village. Occasionally, an Indian would pose for him.

Jim was very popular. He was a favorite with the girls. Many would postpone engagements with the hope that the young Courtney might pay them special notice. It was suggested that perhaps he was opposed to marriage. To counter that possibility, he painstakingly carved a perfect heart in a tabletop in his father's saloon. In the top half of the heart he carefully inscribed his initials. Below the initials, *J.C.*, he added the word *loves*. The implication was obvious. Jim Courtney was looking for the right woman, and no initials would be added until the engagement announcement was reality.

Jim was the sole fatality of the migration. The Courtney saloon was edged between its neighboring buildings ever so slowly by the men and the oxen. Then jacks raised it from the beams and the erection of the foundation was continued. Young Courtney was carrying stone for the masons. Once the mortar was set, the jacks slowly lowered the saloon to the stone. The artist was making certain the building and the foundation were in proper alignment. Suddenly the jack release gave way and the young man was crushed to death.

For a time the Courtneys maintained the saloon. They closed off table number three, where their son had inscribed the heart, and placed a glass over it so that no one could mar the heart and letters.

Since the saloon was a constant reminder of their loss, the Courtneys sold and moved to Rochester, Minnesota. One of the conditions of the sale was that while table number three could be used, the protective glass would always remain in place.

The young man's burial was in the Elliota cemetery. It was now all that remained of that once proud village. Joshua appreciated the fact that the residents of the new location would always use the cemetery.

For Julia, there was no decision to be made. She knew the Stagecoach Inn also had to be moved. As much as Josh was a sentimentalist, she was a realist. When the inn was moved he refused to accompany it. He followed at a distance as though he had changed his mind. Then he entered the cemetery to spend a brief moment with his mother. From the hill he could look down on what had been his town, her town. Now it was rubble and open holes. It was as though Sherman had marched through with his army.

Josh walked amid the rubble. His mind was numb, but his memory was clear. He remembered that once this desolation had been a holy, untamed place where he and his mother had spent hours of happiness. He had invited the merchants and the money changers to utterly destroy this hallowed ground. For the first time in Josh's life, his father made sense.

How to recover? Then it struck Josh. Why not? After all, he had provided everyone free land in Elliota. They must have some appreciation. Let them show it by naming the new town Elliota.

He asked for a town meeting, and it was readily granted. He

addressed the assemblage. "You have abandoned the building sites that were so graciously given you. Together we made the village of Elliota a thriving place. In its place is rubble and ruin. I am not asking much in compensation. In fact, what I propose will cost absolutely nothing for anyone. Would you consider naming the present location Elliota?"

Much to Josh's dismay, they rejected his request:

"We gave up all claim and rights to the land when we abandoned it."

"Elliota gave us many good memories, but the final memory is of failure."

"A new town, a new name."

"Why should we name a boomer like this with the name of a town that couldn't make it?"

"That's right; this place is a boomer, not a bust."

"I think what I'm hearing sounds great. Let's call our new and successful town Boomer!"

"I'll second that and call the question."

"All in favor of naming the place Boomer say, 'Aye.'"

All shouted together, "Aye!"

"Those opposed, same sign."

Not even Josh raised his voice. He walked up the street past where the new school was being built, past the foundation for the town hall and across the street to the new location for the Stagecoach Inn. Julia was hanging freshly ironed curtains in the windows.

Josh stood in the doorway. "Well, the name of the town will be Boomer, instead of Elliota."

"That's nice," she said, paying him no heed.

"After all we did for them, you'd think they would call it Elliota," Josh continued.

"Will you hold the other end of this rod so I can hang the curtain on the big window?" she asked.

"Not one person voted for my proposal," he whispered.

"The old sign—should we leave 'Elliota Stagecoach Inn' on it or should we change it to 'Boomer Inn' or just drop the word *Elliota*?" she asked.

In Elliota, Josh's counsel had always been honored, his ideas met with agreement, his requests granted. That night, at the town meeting, the people had stripped him of all power. He couldn't muster the strength to cast the sole vote against naming the town Boomer. He was alone.

He had hurried home, but suddenly it wasn't home. The one he loved was more interested in hanging curtains than in offering consolation. It wasn't home. It was just a house.

At the meeting he was made to feel helpless. Now he felt hopeless. One is alone when there is no strength. One is lonely when there is no understanding.

When the whole world disagrees with me, I'm merely alone. But when my very source of love and understanding ignores me, I am lonely, he thought to himself as he sat in stunned silence.

No matter how young a person is, if all he can talk about is the good old days, he is old. By the same token, no matter how old a person is, if he speaks of the future, he is young.

Now Josh could talk of nothing but the good old days. He was so much in the past that Julia and Becky didn't understand him anymore. His good old days were not those of his mother in Ohio. His good old days concerned worrying about the Indians when his father was on a hunting foray, not seeing another human being except his mother for weeks on end, being without church and school and having only his mother to teach him about God and people, the cabin burning to the ground in the dead of winter and him and his mother moving in with an Indian family, crop failures, burying his mother and little brother, and all the hell of the good old days. And the implication to his wife, daughter, and anyone was there: "Without my good old days, you wouldn't even be enjoying life."

So the man, Joshua, without any future, walked south to all that was left of Elliota. He opened the cemetery gate and walked over to Rebecca's grave.

Only she really knew him. Only she could reach out with consolation for her son. He needed to be close to her. His tired body needed rest. His tormented mind needed peace. So often had he come to this spot to share grief and sorrow, joy and happiness, sometimes standing, sometimes kneeling, sometimes stretched out, and sometimes sitting. Somehow she always gave him answers, and he accepted them.

Now he sat with his back resting on the magnificent marble monument. "Mother, I am alone and lonely. From my birth you have been my strength. You held me. You taught me. I was your life."

Julia was concerned. He had left the house at ten while she was hanging curtains. He hadn't come home all night. She and Becky hitched the horse to the buggy and drove south to the cemetery. They found him there.

Josh was buried beside his mother.

Chapter 4

The Stagecoach Inn was moved to Boomer and placed on a new foundation one block to the east of Main Street across from the town hall. When Josh died, his widow and daughter maintained the inn.

Competitive hotels were relocated on Main Street and near the depot. Business was not good enough for survival, so the widow Julia sold the original holdings at Elliota to the Carolans.

When Julia's daughter, Becky, married Jason Gossman, they were the innkeepers until the size of their family dictated otherwise, as every room was needed for the offspring. Even a traveling Mary and Joseph would have been turned away.

Jason accepted a job at the local livery stable. The ancient sign that had advertised the Stagecoach Inn was chopped into pieces and burned in the family stove.

Descendants of Josh continued living in the home. In the fifth generation, James and Joanne Jacobsen brought a most beautiful baby girl in the world. They named her Helen. Helen was interested in family history and was proud of the Elliot name and the Elliota tradition. As a teenager she decided her first daughter would be named Elliota.

Helen and Bill Burton named their baby Elliota. Ellie was a charmer from the very beginning. Her ready smile spread not only over her face, but to every face she countenanced. At any moment she could erupt into boisterous laughter that would have seemed absolutely unladylike for any other girl. Flushing cheeks betrayed a refreshing innocence appreciated by all who knew her. She had the total confidence of her parents. It was unbelievable that one so attractive could be so unspoiled. Her coal black hair could not shade the sparkle in her large blue eyes.

Ellie was a grand combination of pleasant personality and impeccable character. She was a better than average student and possessed average athletic ability. She sang with a mellow alto voice in the chorus and the choir and played first violin in the orchestra.

Ellie was not without ambition. She observed that the only residents of Boomer who seemed to have a future were those who left or were the children of farmers, who had a hope of inheritance. A college education, even for them, seemed a necessity.

Despite the fact that she was much loved by the people and she in turn loved them, she was anxious to leave the village. Ellie's childhood ambition was to be a nurse. In her teen years, she decided she should move to Rochester, become a nurse, marry a doctor, live on Pill Hill, and raise happy children.

Rochester was a mecca of medical miracles. It attracted the sick and those wanting to dedicate themselves to the care of the sick. The miracle of Rochester began with a tornado on August 21, 1883. It was the year that Sitting Bull and his braves killed the last large herd of bison in America that had escaped the planned slaughter by the white man. It was the year the U.S. Mint first coined the Liberty-head nickel.

On that sultry day in '83, the citizens of Rochester looked hopefully for relief to a dark cloud moving in from the west. Doctors Will James and Charlie Mayo noticed the rolling clouds as they drove north to the slaughterhouse to obtain a sheep's head they could practice on for eye operations. Suddenly the rolling clouds formed a funnel. They watched buildings being sucked into the air. Immediately after the two had crossed the Zumbro River bridge, it was taken from its moorings into the sky. Whole boxcars were thrown from the tracks to descend as slivers. The doctors' mare broke loose from the buggy when the corner billboard of the Cook House Hotel landed on the dashboard of the vehicle.

Twenty-six people were killed by the storm. Many more were injured in a city without a hospital. Many of the injured were brought to the motherhouse of the Sisters of Saint Francis. Mother Alfred now saw the wisdom in words addressed to her by Archbishop Ireland a few weeks before the storm. He had suggested that her religious community should consider building a hospital in Rochester. At the time of the conversation her sisters were all dedicated to teaching. The money required and the fact that she had no nurses allowed his suggestion to go unheeded.

The nearly one hundred members of the Order were "home from teaching" in August. The elder Dr. Mayo approached Mother Alfred with the request that she appoint sisters to supervise people who had volunteered to care for the injured in makeshift hospitals. He reasoned that if the sisters could organize youngsters in a classroom, they could certainly put order into the chaos that was so rampant among the volunteers.

When the last temporary hospital was closed, Mother Alfred visited with Dr. W. W. Mayo. Should a hospital be built in Rochester? The doctor had many practical objections but let her know the idea was to his liking.

At her insistence, Dr. Mayo consented to draw up plans for the hospital the sisters would somehow finance. So it was that Saint Mary's Hospital was conceived. By frugal living and money-producing endeavors the plans moved toward reality.

On July 26, 1887, the Congregation of Our Lady of Lourdes voted to build the hospital. Four months later, nine acres of land were purchased west of Rochester for $2,200. The sisters paid the amount in cash.

The Doctors Mayo traveled the eastern United States searching for the best that could be in a hospital. The architect designed what the Mayos wanted.

Dr. William Worrell Mayo had come to Rochester in 1863 as an examining surgeon for the Union Army Enrollment Board. He remained in Rochester after the War between the States. By 1892, the number of patients coming to Rochester was too great for the father and his two son doctors, William James and Charles Horace, to administer. Other physicians were added to the staff. The words *Mayo Clinic* became synonymous with Rochester, and they included Saint Mary's and Methodist Hospital. Anyone wanting to be part of medical advancement, be he or she rich or poor, could find no better organization in the world than the Mayo Clinic.

No one questioned Ellie's ability to become a nurse. Even less did anyone question that she would marry a doctor if she wanted. Everyone readily agreed she could marry any man she wished.

At the conclusion of her training in Rochester, Ellie donned her nurse's cap and remained at Saint Mary's Hospital. Because she was so attractive and had no regular boyfriend, she had no difficulty finding male companionship. Sometimes she would be treated more as an object than a person, and she resented it. She never accepted a second date with that kind. Her sense of humor drove her to keep a diary containing the different approaches she encountered and how she countered them. On her occasional visits back to Boomer she would bring the diary to amuse her parents:

*   *   *

"I want you to know I can have a hundred women in this town. Do you realize that?"

"Yes, I realize that. Do you realize you can't have a hundred and one?"

*   *   *

"You don't expect a man to buy a pair of shoes without trying them first, do you?"

"Given a choice, that would be better than accepting a pair every tramp has used."

*   *   *

"Are you afraid of AIDS or becoming pregnant?"
"Not at all. And I don't intend to be afraid."

*   *   *

"For me, sex is a prerequisite to marriage."
"For me, sex is a prerequisite after marriage."

*   *   *

"I can't control myself."
"And you can't control me either. Lust is the desire to control another when you can't control yourself."

*   *   *

"Do you understand how important my passions are?"
"I only know they aren't as important as my principles."

*   *   *

"If you really cared, we would make love."
"Love is sharing totally with another as long as you both shall live. Lust is for the moment. I strongly suspect I've not yet met my husband. He will control himself for me as I control myself for him."

*   *   *

"Would you want to view a film that would turn us on?"
"The Song of Songs says: 'Do not arouse yourself and stir up love before its time.'"

*   *   *

"Aren't you concerned about my needs?"
"I think you are more concerned about your passion than my principles."

*   *   *

"Can we discuss sex?"
"Why not? It is a noble subject. Let's be sure it stops with talk."

*   *   *

"What do you think about sex?"
"There are many aspects, the spiritual, the physical, and the psychological. All are important. Unfortunately, some consider sex equivalent to barnyard morality."

*   *   *

"Don't you want to make love? Are you normal?"
"I want to share love, not make it. Sharing love is what normal people want. Counterfeits aren't acceptable."

*   *   *

39

"Are you afraid of men?"

"My dad is a man. My uncles are men. My husband will be a man. I'm not afraid of anyone I love."

*   *   *

Her dad studied her. "Is that all young men think of today?"

She jested, "You mean all young men or all they think of?"

"Either way, the question is valid," he replied, smiling.

"Actually, Dad, many of my dates are really nice fellows. I'm in no hurry, though. I want to make sure we are right for each other," she added.

Ellie Burton was a happy person. She was a good nurse and loved her vocation. Someday she might meet the right person. If she didn't, she could live with that, too. She attended to her patients; they loved her. She helped the doctors; they respected her. Ellie was happy.

Chapter 5

Boomer lived up to its name. Every expectation for the thriving town was not only met, but surpassed. There were three churches: the Methodist building that was moved from Elliota, the Catholic church built immediately after the town was chartered, and later the Presbyterian church.

Eventually, the same preacher served both Protestant congregations. Their members decided it would be wise to unite the two parishes to save on electrical and coal bills as well as repair expenses. It seemed easier for the minister to serve one place rather than two. Consequently, one of the original Elliota buildings, the Methodist church, became a duplex. Main Street was thusly named for obvious reasons. All other streets were named after trees except one. It was called Methodist Avenue. Now the only avenue in town no longer had the church for which it was named.

Main Street had a harness shop where shoes were sold and repaired. The street also contained one of the two produce houses, and four grocery stores graced the street. One of them, the farmers' store, also sold clothing.

Ford Motors had a dealership in Boomer. A bakery, a bank, a millinery shop, a bowling alley, the *Boomer Star* weekly newspaper, the meat market, the post office, the drugstore, the telephone office, the hardware store, the lumber company, and three well-patronized saloons filled both sides of the main thoroughfare.

The original frame school was replaced in 1904 by a brick building. In 1926 a new and larger addition was built. The three hotels thrived.

Farmers drove their livestock to the local yards. Some sold on the spot. Others would accompany the animals by train to Chicago or South Saint Paul. The two feed mills and elevators did a thriving business. There was a creamery and a cheese factory.

Right next to the track, connected to one of the elevators, were the coal bins. The patrons had a varied selection of the black material. A dray hauled coal for those without horses and also delivered packages to and from the various places of business. Among other materials delivered by the dray, from the train to the post office, was the U.S. mail.

The train known as the Milwaukee Road ran twice a day each way. It carried soot-covered passengers as well as freight. During the depression, youths from especially poor families would hurl stones at the engineer and the fireman. Generally, the volleys were returned in the form of coal, which was hastily garnered by the youngsters to keep the home fires burning.

The local nursery would ship many railroad cars of trees to various parts of northern Iowa and eastern South Dakota. The nursery had several full-time salesmen and a crew of sometimes up to forty people digging, balling, and carrying the trees.

But Boomer was a borrowed town living on borrowed time. The Great Depression forced the bank's closing. With that failure, people who had lost their life savings began to move out. The newspaper was one of the earliest victims, followed shortly by the greenhouse, the cheese factory, and the creamery.

In the early thirties a new U.S. highway skirted the town. Now passengers began riding clean buses instead of dirty coaches. Trucks became the common carrier rather than freight cars. Time, energy, and money made the train part of history.

The train had left Elliota with nothing alive but the cemetery. The same train that had birthed Boomer was gone. Tracks and ties were removed, and property was sold to farmers whose land adjoined the roadbed.

While Prohibition did away with many taverns, saloons, and bars, it, interestingly enough, had a different effect on the Boomer establishments. Boomer became a bootleggers' and boozers' haven. When Prohibition was a memory in America and nearby towns had legal liquor, the consumers migrated to newer establishments for refreshments. The Boomer saloon keepers retired.

Farms in the area began following a national trend. Getting bigger or getting out seemed the only two options. Farmers would rather consume one another than help each other. The population was quickly diminishing.

For a time people retired to Boomer. As shops closed and services became limited, existence became difficult for the elderly. Housing costs were reasonable, but the cost of commuting to work grew. Cheaper groceries and goods in other towns balanced the cost of transportation. The high school closed; only the grade school remained.

In the middle of the twentieth century another force came upon the scene. The Amish in many areas of the eastern United States began selling their very expensive land for exorbitant prices. In turn they bought relatively inexpensive land in the Boomer area. No farmers could match their offers. Farm after farm was in Amish hands.

Hitching posts were again evidenced on Main Street. The odor of horses filled the air. Buggies and wagons provided the traffic. Bearded men and heavily frocked women felt at home.

Any Rip van Winkle of Elliota, after fifty years of sleep, would have thought his slumber only a moment in duration. Except for frilled buggies and curtained windows, all was the same.

As an aged person gradually assumes the fetal position in preparation for death, Boomer seemed to revert to ancient Elliota. Houses in which electricity and running water had been removed smelled heavily of kerosene lamps. Windmills and all sorts of ancient contrivances held youngsters spellbound.

The once proud Boomer school district, which in its day had devoured the neighboring country schools, was forced to merge with a neighboring town. The strength of a once proud village seemed totally sapped.

An Elliota stillness filled the land. People asked the same question over and over. Had the Amish come in time to save the town, or had they come just in time to celebrate the funeral?

In some instances, whole buildings and houses left Boomer as they had entered. They were again pulled one by one to be placed on new rural Amish foundations with the same old horsepower.

More buildings awaited an undeserved demise. The antiseptic Amish would dismantle them board by knotless board. Each

43

piece would be carefully placed on a wagon and, for the last time, carried a few yards or miles to the north. Once more, like the phoenix, they arose as barns or outbuildings on Amish land.

The sounds of stagecoach and drivers had long been stilled, but the sounds of cattle and sheep abounded. Most precious of all, the voices of children were heard throughout the land.

Of the original Elliota edifices, two had survived best. One was the saloon originally owned by the Courtneys. The other was the hardware store. The latter was the first moved from Elliota. From its completion, the second story was living quarters for the owners. In Boomer's heyday, the business thrived.

When the lumber company began merchandising nails, twine, and steel posts, the hardware store began to fade. The lumber people added paint to its sales, and the hardware store went bankrupt. Then it was abandoned. The bank owned it and was eagerly searching for a buyer. It seriously considered the value of the store as not worth the taxes. Certainly the building didn't justify the time spent at the bank's board meeting discussing its future.

Courtneys' Saloon changed hands several times. During Prohibition, from all outward appearances, it became a restaurant. Common knowledge was that it was actually a booming bootlegger's bonanza. After Prohibition it became a three-two beer joint with ice cream and hamburgers for fare. Teenagers met there as the official place where something might happen. Time thus spent usually ended when a parent or friend would offer a ride home as the reward for patience.

The frame building was twenty-eight feet wide and fifty-four feet long. It was facing east and abutted the sidewalk. The roof was tin. The foundation was stone.

The neon signs in the windows hadn't worked since before the advertising breweries had failed. Rusty snuff and cigarette signs protected the storefront from any need for paint to protect the lumber.

The huge door was original, and the owner proudly displayed the one and only key its lock had ever known. A child couldn't enter the doorway without the aid of an adult. That served as an accidental safeguard against youngsters being present without a parent.

Older citizens, aware of the actual or legendary history of the place, were pleased with the heavy door. Everyone knew the place as a safe haven.

The south wall was covered with six-foot, perpendicularly placed boards. Above the wood was some kind of composition material that obviously could not be repaired but pleaded for replacement.

Originally the customers had sat at tables. In the thirties, booths had replaced the tables. The old chairs were discarded, but the tabletops were used in the new arrangement. The initials and carvings, which in many instances dated back to Elliota times, were thus maintained long after the inscribers were gone.

Booth number three was the mystery booth. On its tabletop was the perfectly inscribed heart with the message: "J.C. loves." It was the favorite booth. The history of young Jim Courtney chiseling the heart and his initials within the heart was lost. No one knew who "J.C." was or whom he or she loved. That heart demanded such respect that no one ever carved or whittled while sitting there.

Some of the brass coat hooks on the booths were broken off, but one could still hang caps on those that remained. Generally, people just threw their coats on the seats to serve as cushions.

Running the full length of the ceiling was a single row of fluorescent lights. As far as anyone could recollect, they had never been used. If there was a switch for them, it had been covered over for some time.

The choice between glaring lights and soft darkness was all too easy. It wasn't that there was anything that needed hiding; it was just that there was nothing to see.

In the forties there had been a jukebox. Each booth had a lighted box for the coin and buttons to push for the desired tune. Instant noise was available for anyone with the proper coin. The company that owned the machine failed. Since no customer knew how to maintain the juke box, it was junked. Most patrons preferred the quiet. However, the boxes remained in each booth, making it unnecessary to have any other lighting on that side of the establishment. Reflected in the plate glass window, the lighting effect in the booths offered a Halloween-like reflection.

The only other lighting in the building was from some forty-watt bulbs above the plate glass mirror behind the bar, the pull-string lights in the rest rooms, and the often burned-out light in the exit box.

The ceiling was designed in hammered tin. One could not, with such lighting facilities, ascertain what the original color had been, but any change in color was not the result of paint.

Chapter 6

In the summer of 1991, a product of Boomer coined the phrase *Minnesota nice*. In a talk given in Minneapolis she explained why the people of the Land of Sky Blue Waters were "Minnesota nice."

Many Germans who had come to the state had left the fatherland to escape militarism. They were peaceful.

The Norwegians had left a beautiful but harsh land. They brought their beauty and left the harshness behind.

During the potato famine, the Irish had raised enough food for themselves, but by the time the English had exacted taxes in the form of that vegetable, there was nothing left for a people who weren't allowed to fish their own streams or hunt their own game. In coming to the States they knew if anyone was to be free, everyone had to be free.

Minnesota weather demands cooperation. In the early days, barn raising was a neighborhood task. Threshing and haying were neighborhood projects. A person was aware not only of the size of his own woodpile, but of the neighbors' as well.

The winter demands a slower pace. Each blizzard proved one's own inadequacies and gave pause to consider the sick and the elderly, who constantly bore the storm. It allowed preparation for one's own old age.

Such times of forced meditation told the Minnesotan there is enough harshness in the world, so be gentle; be nice.

There is something about a Minnesotan that is somewhat akin to ancestor worship. In other states, when a person is asked where she or he is from and who he or she is, the answer is: "New

York," "Florida," "California," etc. In Minnesota, one says, "I'm a Norwegian Lutheran Republican" or "an Irish Catholic Democrat" or "a Scottish Presbyterian Independent." When one wears his nationality, religious persuasion, and political preference on his sleeve and in his heart, he has no choice; he has to be nice.

So the people in Boomer were always nice. They believed all crazy fads started on the East or West Coast and lost momentum as they moved to the heartland. They looked on the gangs in their cities as spin-offs from the coast. They even hoped that if you were nice to the worst of people, they would learn to appreciate the beauty of nice in return.

With rare exceptions, Minnesota politicians are nice. They represent those who are helpless and downtrodden. Minnesotans are people who are proud of who they are and what they are and can earnestly pray that a good government will make it possible for all to be as happy, gentle, and nice as they.

In such a climate one is allowed to be a character. Boomerites appreciated the Babe Ruths of baseball's past, when a person could speak out without being fined. They loved the Jimmy Durantes who could poke fun at themselves and laugh all the way to the bank. Boomerites recognized the importance of being one-self and being loved for it because one is understood.

The smaller the town, the higher the percentage of characters. In Boomer everyone was a character. Personality is who you are. That can't be changed. Character is what you are, and what you are is up to you. So the people of Boomer respected free will and what one chose to be.

Sean Carolan was born and raised in the Boomer area—in fact, in Elliota Township. His parents, Brian and Molly Carolan, were part of the Irish group who settled to the south. They were farmers.

When Josh Elliot began his return journey to Ohio, he had placed the Carolans in charge of his property. When he returned to establish Elliota, the Carolans remained. At Josh's death, his widow sold the property to Pat and Sadie Carolan. Brian, their grandson, was the third generation to farm the property.

Everyone knew, except Brian and Molly, that they were not good farmers. They loved the land and they loved the livestock.

The problem with loving the stock is you remain small. You can love ten or twelve cows, but you can't love four hundred. You get big and you love dollars instead of cows.

The pair never picked all the corn. They always left some rows for the deer and pheasants. The fences were in bad repair but were kept in place so the birds and small mammals would have homes.

Brian and Molly never used poisons on the land. Why should anyone poison what he depends on? If it kills the weeds and the insects, he kills something of God's creation.

The pair may have been frugal, given the chance, but if you live on the bank's money, you're not frugal; you're poor. They worked hard, but nothing was so important that it had to be done on Sunday. It wasn't that God wanted the world to stop on Sunday. Rather, the pair looked upon the day as a time to pray and meditate so the rest of the week would be more acceptable to the human race and its Creator.

Sean hated the farm. He hated hard work. It didn't take a genius to figure that his folks' kind of farming wasn't long for this country. Anyone but his folks could see that you don't protect rabbits that destroy the apple trees.

The son saw no reason for delaying the inevitable. The day after his graduation from high school he was apartment hunting in Saint Paul.

Sean never thought of himself as college material, so he decided against further education. Such a decision made it unnecessary to seek the funds a college education would have demanded. His marks in the years of grade and high school evidenced, at most, an average intelligence, so no scholarships would have been offered. His high school records indicated that even if his parents had the available cash, it wouldn't be wise to invest it in a college education for Sean.

Initially, he moved from job to job in Saint Paul. Finally, he decided being a salesperson in a men's clothing store was his niche. For the first and only time in his life he worked hard and was prompt, courteous, and somewhat successful.

The real attraction was not the work or the salary. Sean loved clothes, and the job allowed him any choice of merchandise at 25 percent off.

Sean was six feet, two inches tall. He had a full head of hair. He was happy with his ability to grow and sport a neat, impressive mustache.

Even though he was not muscular, he looked strong and in excellent condition. Sean was one of those rarely blessed people who could eat whatever and as much as he wanted; it never turned to fat.

It was generally acknowledged that Sean was indeed a very striking person, who wore clothes magnificently. He was considering a rather attractive job as a male model for a well-known and respected company when his parents, Brian and Molly, were killed in a car accident.

The funeral at Saint Agnes in Plymouth Rock was well attended. Many came because the couple was genuinely loved. Some came to be seen by Sean so they could use the occasion to drop the hint that they were interested in buying the quarter-section farm for cash. Sean appreciated both groups' support and presence.

The next few weeks Sean spent at the farm arranging the furniture and machinery for the auction. He knew nothing had any value, except sentimental, and bemoaned the fact he was not a romanticist.

Before the holy water sank into the graves, offers to buy the farm were accompanied with monetary figures. Sean thought how sad it was his parents hadn't sold the land themselves and enjoyed life. Then he would shrug his shoulders with the knowledge that they would never have sold. Unfortunately, they had always been happy on the land.

The farmer who offered the most money was a neighbor. Sean's farm was worth more to him since it adjoined his own. He wouldn't have to run his machinery on the road. He could easily tear out all dividing fences, which took so much time, energy, money, and land.

When Sean returned to his apartment in Saint Paul a letter was awaiting him from the First Boomer Bank. Actually, the first bank had failed during the depression in the thirties and it was seriously joked that the new bank should be called the Second Boomer Bank or the Last Boomer Bank.

The letter explained the availability of the old saloon building and the hardware store on Main Street. It didn't quote an asking price but assured the reader it was very negotiable.

The bank had clerked the farm auction. Also, the check written for the farm's purchase was drawn on the same institution. Consequently, the bank was quite aware of Sean's financial condition. The author of the letter wanted some of that cash for the two Boomer edifices lest Sean might spend the money foolishly on something else.

Sean read the letter carefully. He called his girlfriend and they discussed it. The next day she was seeing Boomer for the first time. They inspected the buildings in the company of the banker. All three agreed that neither building was a prize. Yet there was something about the living quarters above the hardware store that intrigued Colleen, Sean's girlfriend. It had real possibilities. Colleen liked it.

Sean had never asked her to marry him. But if he wasn't serious, why would he want her input? By instinct, when she said she liked the place, they both knew they were engaged. After all, if he bought the place, no one else would ever live there. The logical conclusion for the pair was that they would abide above the store.

Within the week they were married somewhere in Ramsey County. He quit his job and they loaded their clothing in the car and headed southeast to a new life together in Boomer.

At first, Colleen was disappointed with the apartment. In the time between her first inspection and eventual arrival, she had perused catalogs, visited showrooms, and mentally furnished the place beyond its limitations. The drapes and furnishings she had pictured somehow hadn't materialized in the windows and on the floor of the barren quarters. Momentarily she was homesick for Saint Paul. This could not be anyone's dream place for a honeymoon. She wished she was home, or anyplace else in the world.

Sean's assistance was worse than nothing. "Buy what you want. Do what you want. Put it wherever you think it will look best," he offered.

"The odds are we won't entertain here anyway as long as we have the place next door. No one else is ever going to see the place, so do what will make you happy," he concluded.

His realism was never timely. His words of support left her cold with the possibility that she might never have friends or fun in an out-of-the-way second-floor apartment on Main Street in Boomer, Minnesota.

Sean Carolan maintained his well-trimmed mustache. His thick hair was graying, but not due to work or worry. His only gait would be best described as leisurely.

He never scheduled his days. They were always ordered for him. He fit in wherever it was comfortable and convenient.

The fact was, Sean was controlled by his environment rather than controlling it. He didn't have an alarm clock. It saved him having to wind and set the instrument used by most people. He depended on his wife for his morning start.

Colleen was an attractive woman with beautiful auburn hair. Her coloring or high blood pressure must have been responsible for her flushed cheeks, since nothing embarrassed her and she rarely drank.

She carried too much weight for her five-foot, five-inch frame. However, it seemed like most of the weight was where it belonged. Most important, she was content with whatever excess she bore.

Friendly, astute, intelligent, ambitious, and determined were all the qualities that made Colleen the perfect wife for Sean. She was kind enough to accept him as he was. Most of the changes in his life after he came into money were in his apparel.

Breakfast was always served at seven-thirty. Her only demand was that he would be ready to eat when it was served. He ate what she prepared without comment. An occasional smacking of the lips was always accepted as an unintended compliment.

After breakfast Sean would remove his robe, then shower and shave. He dressed meticulously. His shoes were always shined. His trousers were subdued in color. His trademark was the Donegal tweed coat that covered his vest. If there was color in his otherwise drab clothing it would be his vest.

Sean would peer through the front window across the street as he enjoyed his third, fourth, or fifth cup of coffee until the people who always waited patiently for the mail each morning would come pouring out of the post office like so many bees intent on securing the day's nectar. Sean would put away his cup, walk down the stairs, saunter through the store, unlock the door, back out, lock the door, and walk across the street to meet all the citizens he knew better than did anyone else in the whole town. His mail was kinder than most people's because he always paid for his merchandise when it was delivered. It wasn't that it was better business to do this. It was because a lack of bills in the mail allowed his breakfast to settle better and the day could start on a higher note of optimism.

Sean would wave at Colleen standing in the vantage window he had left shortly before. Then he recrossed the street to his place. He ascended two steps, picked up the newspapers from the stoop, opened the door, and walked behind the bar to read the *Star Tribune* and the *Pioneer Press*.

After a casual perusal, the papers were placed neatly on the showcase for the benefit of anyone wanting the latest in the written word. That concluded, the operation was open for business and the spoken word.

From all outward appearances, it seemed that Sean Carolan was a person in control. There was never a donnybrook in his establishment. The truth is, there was hardly so much as a mild disagreement.

It wasn't called Carolan's Saloon, Carolan's Bar, Carolan's Café, or Carolan's Restaurant. It was just "Carolan's." You could get beer and setups there. Sean scooped large cones for a more than fair price for the children. He wanted the adults to enjoy themselves without any hassle from their offspring. There was soda pop, ready-made pizza, and things similar that took little labor. It was like something for everyone and not much for anyone.

Carolan's never had anyone waiting on the people in the booths. One came to the bar, ordered what was wanted, waited, then took the food to the booth. If a person couldn't make it to the bar to get another beer, the odds were it wasn't needed. When a booth was vacated, Sean would bar-rag the surface whenever he had time. Occasionally, too much in the way of bottles, cans, glasses, and napkins would accumulate. A sort of time-out would be called so everyone could bring the same to the bar for needed care.

On rare occasions, Sean would be interrupted by someone who wanted something from next door at the hardware store. The real strength of that establishment was parts. Anyone owning an obsolete lawn mower or kitchen appliance had a fair chance the needed parts could be found there. The shelves contained merchandise that had long since failed to catch the fancy of Boomer's

53

population. There is a great time distance between utilitarian and antique value. The goods in the store were in the middle of that distance.

At Carolan's, interruptions gained little attention. Most drank slowly and had no need to go on with any other business of the day. It was like an official time-out in a pro football game. It could be considered a necessary evil, but it seemed altogether unnecessary.

Also, Sean wasn't altogether necessary for all the conversations. If he knew his absence might be lengthy, he would call Colleen. Most of the patrons preferred her personality and charm to Sean's small talk.

Chapter 7

Bob Burke was born and raised in a suburb of Washington, D.C. His dad, Richard, was a doctor who had studied at Johns Hopkins in Baltimore. Bob's mother, Maria, was a graduate of Georgetown University Nursing School. They met at Saint Agnes's Hospital in Baltimore, where Dr. Richard was an intern and Maria was a nurse.

Dr. Burke joined a staff of doctors at a small clinic in the nation's capital immediately after internship. Shortly thereafter, Richard and Maria were married at the National Shrine of the Immaculate Conception. Robert was the first and only child born of their union. Dr. Burke and Maria were convinced they were the happiest couple in the world because of their great love for one another. They shared the conviction they were the luckiest because their baby was so beautiful, totally healthy, and thoroughly good.

The son wasn't sure how much he actually remembered his dad or how much was merely knowledge garnered from watching videos and viewing pictures of his father. It was never certain whether the man who entered the doctor's home was merely a burglar or if his intention was to kidnap the five-year-old child, but the results were as certain as they were tragic. In an attempt to thwart the man's purpose, Dr. Richard Burke was killed. In spite of what seemed like mountains of evidence, the murderer was never arrested and the case remained a mystery for the District of Columbia police.

One of Dr. Burke's associates, an elderly doctor, spent much time with Maria during her bereavement. He did much to ease the pain and help her cope with her terrible loss. Dr. O'Donnell had a son, Jim, who was a priest. Father Jim not only shared his dad's concern for Maria and Robert, but gradually became the father figure in Robert's life. As a result, the lad decided from an early age to become a priest. Father O'Donnell explained how much he would have to study to be accepted in a seminary. Consequently, the youngster from that moment worked at being an ideal student. From the beginning of his education he applied himself to every area of learning.

Young Robert was blessed with a photographic memory and could remember everything in minute detail with one reading. His particular loves were languages and the sciences. His special dedication was to chemistry.

The loss of his dad was an ongoing tragedy. It was not just being deprived of a father's love and guidance as much as having a mother who felt such continuing sorrow. Looking through her eyes, Robert saw a world pregnant with loss and void of happiness and pleasure.

Despite urgings from Father O'Donnell that she recapture her spirit of joy, Maria chose another avenue as the best solution. She decided the best grief therapy was to throw herself into her work. She took refresher courses and began nursing as many hours as Walter Reed Hospital would allow.

Because the boy was deprived of both parents, he was sent to boarding schools. His circle of friends was generally from wealthy families, and he lost touch with any other reality except through Father Jim, who often visited him at school. When the priest couldn't come at least once a week, he would write Bob a letter or phone him. Upon graduation from high school Bob was accepted in the minor seminary.

The priest's attention was the studious lad's salvation. In Father O'Donnell, he faced a resurrection from the books in which he was otherwise buried. A real bond grew between Father O'Donnell and Robert Burke.

Burke was tall and more than thin. He seemed emaciated. He took little delight in food. His clumsiness precluded any possibility of participation in sports. Bob resented periods of recreation, as it generally provided him with nothing but embarrassment. He would take an occasional walk and a less occasional bike ride.

The young man's genius allowed a blind spot concerning personal care. Father Jim explained to his friend that while cleanliness was not necessarily next to godliness, it was, nonetheless, of value, and certain habits, like combing hair and brushing teeth, were worthwhile to cultivate. Happily for them both, the youngster accepted correction from his friend with graciousness.

"Bad breath shouldn't bother anyone as long as I'm in the pulpit and they are in the pews," Bob joked.

"That's correct," responded the priest, "but your arms aren't long enough to distribute Eucharist from the pulpit."

Then they could both laugh and be happy; they shared much camaraderie. Bob knew that Father Jim was his mother and father, brother and sister, friend and confidant. No one else shared Bob's joys and his sorrows so completely or with such total acceptance. He longed for the day he would be Fr. Robert Burke.

Burke's melancholy moods were often translated by faculty and students alike as a necessary part of his genius. His hazel eyes were often red from reading. His bushy eyebrows seemed to be nature's way of protecting his eyes from the viciousness of lamps.

His thin face and slight body seemed always to punctuate his height into something less. Even to him, it seemed he sat so much that his full stature was rarely attained.

In the seminary, his quiet manner and studious nature found a natural setting. Bible study was especially enhanced by his photographic memory. This group of young men, his fellow seminarians, was much to his liking. An environment built on pride in past schools now became a situation in which humility was the constant uniform of the day.

Robert Burke found the seminary the closest thing he'd ever known to "home." Everyone seemed like family. These were happy days, and he thrived.

As endemic as the seminary was to Burke, so was it hostile to the person who sat next to him in classes, at meals, in the prayer hall—indeed, everywhere. Tom Burns, from Minnesota, found his whole being smothered by the rituals of study and silence.

"Are there numerous aborigines in Minnesota?" Robert asked Tom one day.

"You mean Indians?" responded Tom.

"Yes, Native Americans."

"We don't have many in the diocese of Winona."

"Winona. What kind of name is that?"

"It's an Indian maiden's name. She was the daughter of Chief Wabasha," volunteered the Minnesotan.

"Thought you said there weren't any Indians."

"Massachusetts is an Indian name. Many Indians there?"

Tom had finished philosophy at Saint Mary's University in Minnesota. Now he was studying with seminarians from all over the United States at another Saint Mary's, this time in Maryland. Burke had taken his philosophy studies at the Catholic University in Washington, D.C. Now he and Tom were together at Roland Park in Baltimore.

Burke knew nothing of the Midwest. He thought everything beyond Philadelphia was West. Now part of the West was Midwest. Burns was more ignorant of things in the East. Both realized that since rooms and desks were assigned alphabetically, they should be close friends.

Except for the desire they shared to be priests, the two had little in common. Indeed, they were exact opposites. While Burke loved studies and had no time for sports, Burns accepted his courses as a necessary hurdle to ordination. He never tried to camouflage that he enjoyed athletics much more than academics. Tom knew much more about farming and nature than about Canon Law, and he felt comfortable that way except at test time. Burns and Burke preferred their own way of life, yet each had a certain envy concerning the other.

"I wish I could remember things by reading about them just once," Tom complained. "I don't remember after studying them three or four times. I think athletics is the one area I can be a good mentor." Then, more jocosely, "Wouldn't it be something if your bishop were to send you on your first assignment to teach in a high school and be the athletic director there also?"

"One really doesn't have to die to enter hell, does one?" joked Robert as he mentally tugged at a fictional Roman collar and sweat beads of perspiration generated by ignorance.

58

For the first time, young Burke became serious about sports. "I've considered myself fortunate. The things I haven't understood don't interest me at all. As for sports, I know that *fan* is short for *fanatic*. Why should anyone be a fanatic about anything that has the common result of exhaustion, whether one wins or loses?"

"The only concern I have is that so many Catholics are Irish and a Notre Dame victory is some kind of salvific bonding. I'm Hibernian. The term *Fighting Irish* suggests pub pugilists rather than a televised public exercise between goal posts in honor of Holy Mother Church."

"But, Bob, don't you understand that some Catholics want a Notre Dame victory on Saturday afternoon more than a learned homily on Sunday morning?" joked Burns.

"I understand it is a fact," Bob said, serious for a moment. "I can't comprehend how it can be so. Do you think Saint Peter knows the score?"

"Sure hope he does," laughed Tom. "Fact is, I'm depending on it. Anyway, Bob, I'd better start explaining different sports to you for your own benefit. Some people won't think your ordination is valid if you're not a sports enthusiast. At least, that would be the case in Timber Wolves, Viking, and Twins country."

"I really am convinced that *fan* is a more accurate word then *enthusiast*. How can you know all the pro athletes by name, how much they weigh, how tall they are, what position they play, what college they attended, and have trouble remembering the names of the Prophets or Apostles?" mused Bob.

He continued, "They must have symphonies and theaters in Minnesota. I understand the phrase *the play is the thing* didn't originate in a football huddle."

"We have an agreement we will preach at one another's first Mass," laughed Tom. "Would you mind if I chose a topic outlining sports from the time of the early Christians being thrown to the lions down to our own time, in which the Notre Dame Fighting Irish would tame the Penn State Nittany Lions?"

"Maybe if you teach me enough about sports, I might insist on it," quipped Bob. "By the way, you've made your point. Teach me. Is there a textbook? A definitive book on sports? A lesson plan? Let us begin lesson number one immediately."

Both laughed. They understood one another. Burns appreci-

59

ated visits to New York, Philadelphia, and Washington with tour guide Burke in charge. They visited historical places like Gettysburg, Harpers Ferry, and Mount Vernon. They were both enthusiastic about events of the War Between the States and were great admirers of Abraham Lincoln.

Bob was impressed with the farm near Janesville that was Tom's birthplace. He hadn't seen much dirt and was amazed that in southern Minnesota dirt was black.

Bob fell in love with things rural and was excited when Burns let him drive the tractor or handle any of the other machinery. The livestock intrigued Bob perhaps more than a herd of elephants would have surprised Tom in the heart of Kenya. Every day on the farm provided a new and wondrous experience for the doctor's son from the nation's capital. He was flabbergasted to find that Burns, by traveling an hour to the north from the farm, could hear the Minnesota Orchestra, attend a play at the Guthrie Theater, or hear a concert at the Ordway. It was unbelievable that right here in "Indian Country" was a civilization full of colleges and culture.

For the first time, the doctor's son, the superstudent, garnered knowledge that was not from books. He discovered that nature was more real than the printed page; that northern lights and sunsets were more magnificent than the mind can imagine or memory recall; that sports can be enjoyable for a spectator who understands the rules of the game; that book covers are not the parameters of life. With the less intelligent friend Tom as the teacher, Bob was beginning to have an ever-deepening appreciation of life, and he was happy with the relationship, which enriched them both.

Despite their growing interests in one another's world, the priesthood was always their main hope and ambition. Since Tom was much slower in every educational aspect, Bob found himself in the role of tutor. At first, it was difficult for them both. It was difficult for Tom to have such inadequacy and need for assistance. It was even worse for young Burke, who initially was unable to understand that anyone couldn't grasp and hold a concept with easy facility. Bob gradually became aware why "patience and long suffering" are truly gifts of the Spirit.

Both seminarians were from lower-middle-class situations. As a farmer's son, Burns understood what the phrase *There are two good years in farming: 1919 and next year* means. The average farmer is doomed to frustration and blessed with hope.

No doubt, if Bob's dad had not met an untimely death, young Burke would be from the upper class. As it was, his mother could scarcely meet expenses, which are so high in Washington.

Because of their financial circumstance, there was seldom any conversation about personal vestments and chalices, Both young men found consolation in the fact that most parishes were adequately supplied and one's ministry need not suffer, whether or not he had his own outward signs of their future sacrament.

At the end of third-year theology, when they were preparing for the order of subdiaconate, Tom received a happy epistle from his pastor, Fr. Robert Smith. It was with great elation that he handed the letter to Bob:

Dear Tom,

It gives me great satisfaction to inform you that one of our parishioners, James Moore, has indicated he wishes to present you with a chalice for your first Mass. He asked that I tell you this now. He will present it to you next Christmas so you will have it for your first Mass. He also requests that you study church-goods catalogs in order that the chalice may satisfy your own desire.

Congratulations on being called to the order of subdeacon. Congratulations, too, on the news from Mr. Moore on his offer to present you with a chalice of your choice.

Fraternally,
Fr. Robert Smith

Bob read, then responded, "That's wonderful. You must feel a temptation to choose one of solid gold enhanced with diamonds, sapphires, rubies, and emeralds."

"You know me better than that, Bob. I wouldn't feel comfortable with that. But I do have a reaction I want to share with you."

"Be my guest," Burke responded almost apologetically.

"Well, Bob," Tom began, "I know James Moore quite well. He is a daily communicant. His wife died last year. They have no children. I don't know how much money he has, but I suspect he wants to give the chalice in his wife's memory."

Tom's young friend was listening. "Proceed."

"It strikes me that perhaps Mr. Moore, instead of buying a chalice of gold and jewels in favor of his wife, might rather buy two more simple chalices. One could be in his wife's memory. The other could be in his folks' memory."

"Why do you need two chalices?" queried Burke.

"That is the point. I don't. I can talk with him this summer, and with your permission, I'll ask if he would like to donate a chalice for you."

"With my permission? Let me think about it a little."

"Take your time. You don't have to decide for a few weeks."

"I said let me think about it a little. A 'little' has gone by, and my response is: Amen." Tom's friend smiled.

"Agreed!" exalted Burns. "There aren't any guarantees, but it is worth a try. I think he'll consider it a privilege."

"Let him know I don't want to take advantage of him. Just his generosity," agreed Burke.

Robert Burke sat at his desk that night and wrote his priest friend in Washington the news of expectancy. As he penned the letter he thought of what Tom Burns's dad had said in reply to the question: "How much did you get for the hogs?" Mr. Burns had thought for just a moment before his eyes lit up and his mouth formed the words: "Not as much as I expected, but then I didn't expect to."

Chapter 8

Tom's dad's words were indeed prophetic in regard to the chalices. The would-be benefactor died before Tom's summer vacation began. Mr. Moore was a saint by everyone's estimation. In fact, it was generally agreed he would die in church, because that was where he spent most of his time. He had returned to his pew after Eucharist, offered his prayer of thanksgiving, sat back in his place, and died. No sound, no commotion, he just died. No one was sure exactly when. He was sitting there when everyone else left the church. For a moment he was alive with Christ, and suddenly, not for a moment but for eternity, he was with his Redeemer.

There was no hurry to tell Burke the news. It didn't make any difference. Nothing could be changed. There wasn't any mention of any chalice in Moore's will. His life savings went to the Propagation of the Faith and the Priests' Retirement Fund. It would be soon enough in September, at the beginning of their final year in the seminary, to tell Burke there would be no gift of a chalice from James Moore.

The deacon year was a strange contradiction. It seemed as though time was moving all too swiftly and, at the same time, the day of ordination would never come.

On a Thursday afternoon, after the final class of the day, Robert Burke was taking his books to his room before his visit to the chapel when he found the note pinned on his door:

Please call Fr. Jim O'Donnell at your earliest convenience.

Bob placed the books on his desk and hurried to the phone in the office. He placed the call.

"Father Jim left hurriedly about half an hour ago," the senior associate responded. "He is on the way to see you. Please wait for him. He says he must talk with you."

Burke was a deacon. This was his final semester before ordination. He was the best student in the class. What could be wrong? Why should Father Jim want to see him on such short notice? Had the bishop voiced some reservation about his vocation? What? What? What?

O'Donnell's face was grim. "Robert, I am not a bearer of glad tidings."

"I know. I know you wouldn't come like this unless it was something bad. What is wrong?" questioned the seminarian.

"Sit down, Bob. This is extremely difficult," choked the priest.

Robert sat on the edge of his bed, offering the chair with a hand gesture to his friend.

"I need to stand," suggested the priest.

"Sure. Sure. You've done enough sitting driving up here from Washington. What is the problem? There is a problem?" said Burke, not knowing for sure he wanted to hear.

"Robert, my friend, this is the most difficult thing I've ever had to do in my life. I would to God it weren't necessary," stammered Father O'Donnell, not certain where or how to begin. "It's your mother!"

"My mother?" questioned the young man. "She's alive, isn't she? She is alive."

"Yes. Yes, she is alive. I'm not sure if that is good or bad. . . . It isn't right. It isn't right."

"For heaven's sake, what isn't right? Is she sick? Is she hurt? Was she in an accident? Is she in the hospital? Is she home? Give it to me straight," pleaded the lad.

Father O'Donnell placed his hands on Robert's shoulders. Robert looked into the priest's face as though all the answers might be there without the futility of words. The clergyman turned his eyes as if all the answers were just outside the window.

He spoke huskily. "I hope in your priesthood you never have to endure what I'm suffering with you, Bob," and then as though the words weren't coming from him at all, "Your mother is a victim of AIDS."

"This is no time to jest about anything so serious," whispered the shocked seminarian.

"I wouldn't joke about it, but I wish I were," said Father Jim as he watched his young friend rise slowly to his feet and walk numbly to the window as if to acknowledge that there, indeed, were all the answers. The priest followed him and, when Robert turned around, embraced the young man's frail form.

"How long?" asked the stricken seminarian.

"We don't know. The symptoms became apparent about three months ago. She didn't want you to know, but I told her you must know. You are all she has. She is all you have. She knows I am here now."

"Is she at home?"

"Yes. She wants it that way."

"Is she suffering?"

"Yes."

"Is she on medication?"

"Just pain pills."

"God help us. Why didn't she want me to know?"

"I'm not sure," admitted the priest. "She claims she didn't want to interfere with your studies, since you are so close to ordination."

"Do you buy that, Father?"

"It doesn't make any difference what I buy or don't buy."

"Has she asked for me?"

"No, but that doesn't mean she wouldn't love to see you."

"I know she loves me. I know she would like to see me. Father, I think she is thinking of me instead of herself."

"What do you mean by that, Bob?"

"She doesn't want to embarrass me. She doesn't want people to know that her son, a seminarian, has a mother with AIDS. She is probably hoping, for my sake, that she will die before ordination. I've never been close to Mom, but I love her. I'll pack my bag and go home. Will you drive me, please?"

"What kind of a question is that? I'd do anything for you and for her," protested the priest.

"You've demonstrated that all my life, and I've always appreciated it. We are so indebted to you."

"I've told the rector you are leaving with me and won't be back until Monday morning," continued the priest, as he stood with his hand on the doorknob as though he were reassuring the young man that the exit would remain in place while he packed.

Nothing was said as they moved down the hall, but both men thought volumes. The rector had stationed himself at the front door. He spoke not a word but shook the seminarian's hand. The look in his eye, the compassion in his face, said it with quiet eloquence. "My prayers are with you in this terrible moment. May God accompany you on your journey, wherever it might take you and your mother."

Father O'Donnell unlocked the car door for Robert, and Burke crawled onto the seat. When the priest sat behind the wheel, he looked over at his friend sitting stoically beside him. Burke's shoulders convulsed briefly. He took a deep breath as though he were gasping for the last oxygen in the gas chamber and the breath would end the awful reality. He bent forward and sobbed.

They met cars in rapid succession as their own vehicle inched its way south. Father Jim cleared his throat and began huskily, "No one knows how. She is a nurse. No one knows when. AIDS has a way of not showing immediately. A nurse is constantly at risk. You remember when she needed a transfusion about five years ago. She lost so much blood in that kitchen accident. It may have been then."

Father O'Donnell continued, "Any speculation is a fruitless mental exercise. What you need to know now is that you will hardly recognize her. I'm not sure which has taken the greater toll, the AIDS or the terrible pain she endures. It is important that you are prepared. She stays by herself a bit, but most of the time her nurse friends are with her. I've been able to stop in nearly every day and bring her Eucharist."

Robert had sobbed his eyes dry. Any remaining liquid gathered in his nostrils. He alternately sniffed and blew his nose. Several times he summoned his voice to question his friend, but nothing audible escaped his lips.

Burke's heart sank into the depths as the priest's Pontiac entered the driveway. As he exited the car, his every urge was to run anyplace but to the house. His legs were rubber. He was transfixed to the spot until the priest half-led, half-carried, his friend to the door.

They entered without knocking. Once inside, Father Jim stepped aside and nodded toward the living room. The son walked bravely into the room. It was so quiet.

Becky Carpenter, Bob's dad's secretary from another life, stood to greet Bob. She embraced the seminarian as she had at the time of the doctor's funeral. She adjusted the pillow for Maria, invited the son to the chair beside his mother's bed, and moved into the kitchen to steep some tea.

He had decided, while riding in the car, that no matter how she looked, no matter how he might react to her sickness, he would immediately embrace and kiss his mother. He did so and then sat uneasily on the edge of the chair.

In the hope that much conversation could be avoided, he began, "Father Jim told me everything, Mom. I wish you had told me the minute you knew."

"Robert, you don't know how I prayed over it. At first, I couldn't believe it myself and wasn't sure if there really was a need at all. My denial was unbelievable." She forced a smile. "There was no deception, just uncertainty. If I've hurt you, I'm sorry. That is exactly what I wanted to avoid."

"Mom, does it hurt to talk? I don't want you to be uncomfortable." He bit his lip. Her whole demeanor indicated pain. Any conversation would cause additional physical hurt.

Father O'Donnell entered. "There must be room for me here for a bit. At least while the tea is served. You know, Bob, the old adage states that doctors and nurses are always the worst patients. Your mother sure makes a lie of that bromide."

"I'm lucky; that's why," responded Maria. "My best friends have spoiled me with constant attention. It's almost embarrassing. And, Father, you're the worst of all. I can't thank you enough for your visits and prayers. Is it true that you have prayer groups assaulting heaven for me?"

"That is beside the point. You have been a saint, and every parish needs saints. The problem is that saints often come with a terrible price. Mrs. Burke, you are in many people's prayers," answered Father Jim.

She spoke slowly and thoughtfully. "Heaven must be wonderful if one must go through this much hell on Earth. This is so total. It is physical, mental, and psychological. It's my entire being."

"The cost was established at Calvary, not by Judas and a mere thirty pieces of silver, but by Christ, who invites us to carry his cross. He knew what he was asking," rejoined the priest.

"Father, the Lord asks us to carry his cross willingly. If given the choice, my response would be in the negative." She spoke in a voice indicating a need for rest.

Becky's timing was excellent. She entered with teapot in hand. "Robert, will you help me with the cups and saucers?"

He was happy to move into the kitchen. He hadn't said much. He had listened attentively to every word. He carefully observed his mother's every movement. He asked himself, *How sick is she? How uncomfortable? Is there any hope? Has she surrendered to death?* His mind raced with unanswered questions.

Becky followed him to the kitchen to assist him with the creamer and sugar bowl. He wanted to ask her all those questions but was afraid she might answer them. He wasn't ready. Besides, this wasn't the time or the place.

She sensed his feelings. "Maybe we could have lunch tomorrow at the fast-food restaurant three blocks down the street."

He nodded assent and they returned to his mother's side. He rarely drank tea but was grateful for the interlude of silence it provided. Instinctively he knew that Father O'Donnell would leave as soon as his cup was empty. He would stand, excuse himself, turn and say some words of encouragement, and give his blessing to Maria. Bob wondered if he knew because he was psychic or because it was the priestly thing to do. Then he remembered how that ritual had been performed over him and his mother on the occasion of his dad's death.

The next morning, Father returned shortly before lunch. Becky had called him about the proposed luncheon.

"Why don't you go for a little walk, Bob? Grab yourself a sandwich before you return," volunteered the priest.

Robert hurried to the restaurant. He needed to talk to someone. He no longer needed answers and didn't expect Becky to have any. He appreciated the opportunity for the moral support that was much more important than any facts.

"Your mother's suffering is unbearable much of the time. At present, as you well know, there is no medical solution. All we are doing is trying to keep her comfortable. The doctors and nurses are in agreement. Her time may be short."

The young man was stunned. Less than twenty-four hours earlier his only care was the date the bishop had chosen for the ordination. Now, the whole world had buried him beneath an invincible cloud. He didn't know what to do, but one thing was certain: he would stay with his mother constantly until the end. Since starting kindergarten, he had been separated from her except for summer vacations. Even then, he had spent too much time at camps.

After lunch and a quick good-bye to Becky, he hurried home. A nurse and Father Jim were visiting. The son embraced his mother and kissed her. He introduced himself to the nurse. Father Jim was obviously embarrassed by his lack of etiquette in not offering introductions.

Robert nodded the priest outside, where he said, "Father, I've made up my mind. I plan to stay here with Mom."

"You mean not return to the seminary? You probably have a maximum of two months before ordination," said the priest.

"By then Mom might be gone."

"We can let you know if things get worse. Once you're ordained, you can be her priest. You can offer daily Mass for her right here at home."

"My mind is set. I stay here with Mom."

"What will the bishop think?"

"You talk to him, Father Jim. Explain the situation. If he wants, he can ordain me anytime. Today, if he wants."

"Okay, Bob, I will. In the meantime, what happens?"

"I know this is asking much of you, Father, but you know your way around. Will you go to the seminary and pick up my belongings? Tell Tom Burns to ask the fellows to pray for Mom and me," said Robert resolutely.

"Should I tell them your mother has AIDS?"

"Of course. They are my friends. They'll understand better than you can appreciate. They will only wonder why I didn't know earlier and, if I knew, why I didn't tell them right away. Make sure they know I wasn't hiding anything. There is nothing to hide.

"Also, if you will, when you talk to the rector, ask him if he will write a letter to the chancery office. He can explain that many of my classmates have left already for ordination. I'm as ready as any of them. He might remind the chancery that I have completed all the work for my Licentiate in Sacred Theology. His letter plus your talking with the bishop should cover all the bases." He chuckled. "I know what that means now that Burns has taught me all about sports."

He realized he hadn't chuckled for a long time, and even though it might not be proper, it felt wonderful. Even Mom had a better sense of humor than he.

Father O'Donnell responded to all the requests. When he returned with the seminarian's belongings there was included a letter from the chancery:

Dear Reverend Mr. Burke,

It gives me great pleasure to proclaim that you have been called to the priesthood of Jesus Christ. The ordination is scheduled for May 30 of this year.

Congratulations on your successful completion of seminary training. I am informed you are number one scholastically in your class. May your studies stand you in good stead in a holy and happy ministry.

The ordination will be in the Cathedral Church at 10:30 in the morning. Practice for the ceremonies will be at 8:00 the evening of the twenty-ninth. Please assess your vesting priest concerning this message.

With deep regard,
Msgr. R. F. Ryan
Chancellor

Robert read the letter and handed it to his priest friend without a word or any show of emotion. Father read it and offered enthusiastic congratulations.

"You haven't had a chance to talk with the bishop, have you? Maybe he will change his mind when he finds I have left the seminary without his consent. I think he would have granted permission, don't you?" worried Bob.

70

"I haven't had a minute to do so. I called this morning and have an appointment this afternoon with His Excellency the Bishop. I never try outguessing him. Only time will tell," responded Father Jim.

Father O'Donnell came by in the evening. "Well, I saw the bishop. He said he would be in touch with you."

"Did he seem upset?"

"More surprised."

"Did you explain Mom's situation?"

"Of course. Didn't you want me to?"

"Certainly. One needs a compelling reason to leave the seminary without even talking with the Ordinary. I sure hope the rector's letter arrives at the chancery before the bishop makes any final decision."

"Let me know when the bishop's letter comes. I want to know when I'm going to be assistant priest at your first Mass," said Father Jim. "I asked the bishop if he might move the date to an earlier time, due to your circumstances."

The priest returned to the living room for a quick visit with Bob's mother. Then to both, "We'll see you."

Three days later, another letter arrived from the chancery:

Dear Mr. Burke,

His Excellency the Bishop has instructed me to write this letter. Please accept our heartfelt sympathy for you and your mother. Be assured you are both in our prayers.

We appreciate the fact that you have saved the diocese deep embarrassment by asking for a delay of ordination due to the existing circumstances.

Please contact me after the funeral so a decision may be made at that time. At present, we have no organized programs in the diocese for AIDS ministry. You may find such an apostolate to your liking.

Yours truly,
Msgr. R. F. Ryan
Chancellor

Robert read it twice. He folded it neatly and replaced it in the envelope. He worried, *The first letter was addressed to Reverend Mr. Burke. This one is to Mr. Burke. Is this an oversight or is it a message?*

His musing was interrupted by Father O'Donnell's car pulling into the driveway. Burke was waiting. He handed the letter to the priest.

"What in God's name did you say to the bishop?"

Father read the letter, his face filled with puzzlement. "It doesn't make sense. I asked the bishop to ordain you without delay. He seemed in agreement until I mentioned AIDS. I presumed that was merely because it caught him off guard. Maybe all he heard was 'AIDS.' Now what?"

"Now what? Nothing!" steamed Bob. "The nicest response I can think of is that I need some time to think things over. He does mention the possibility of a special apostolate for me. He hasn't closed the door."

The priest shook his head in disbelief as they walked to the house. He opened the door and, in as cheerful a voice as he could muster, asked, "And how is the patient today?"

When Father O'Donnell returned to his rectory he, as was his custom, gave first attention to the day's mail. In the midst of the stack he noted familiar stationery, a letter from the chancery office:

Dear Father O'Donnell,

It has come to my attention that you are frequently visiting a patient outside the boundaries of your parish who is diagnosed as having AIDS. Let me commend your zeal.

You have been entrusted with the care of souls in one of our largest parishes. Please consider the risk at which you place them.

It is not my intention to legislate. I want you to enjoy freedom of choice in this matter, so I propose three possibilities:

First: Remain as pastor in your present parish, refraining from visiting the sick in another's fold.

Second: Ask for a small parish at some distance from the patient. That would allow you an excuse for not being able to visit and risk contracting the disease.

Third: Petition for a leave of absence, with pay, for medical reasons until the patient dies. Then, after a medical examination, you may ask for reassignment.

Sincerely yours in Christ,
E. B. Messick
Bishop

The priest looked into the infinity that space seldom allows. He didn't need another perusal of the letter. Then, slowly, as though the epistle were the epitome of all evil, he crushed it in his hands. He arose from his desk and walked out into the night hoping for some kind of purification.

He wandered into the early morning hours. As he reentered the rectory he discovered with a start that he was thoroughly drenched. He had been unaware of the nasty weather.

Mechanically, he sat at the desk, removed a sheet of paper, and began his response.

Your Excellency,

It is with deep regret that I ask for a leave of absence for medical reasons.

Your obedient servant,
J. P. O'Donnell

It didn't matter that it was still raining. He drove to the post office before he might change his mind. Then he returned to his desk to prepare his farewell sermon for the following Sunday.

Leave of absence, he pondered, *for medical reasons. What is more fitting, a smile or a frown? After all, there are some very important sick people who really are sick because they don't understand AIDS.*

The hour was late when he finally went to his bedroom. He felt cleansed by the rain, by his letter to the archbishop, by his thoughts, and he slept the sleep of the just and the justified.

No mention was made to Maria or Robert concerning the bishop's letter. The priest told them what he told the people of his parish in the farewell sermon. Medical reasons.

Reasons that involve Maria's physical condition and the preju-dicial sickness of His Excellency, he thought to himself.

The apartment Father Jim rented was but a few blocks from the Burkes'. He considered asking Maria's pastor for quarters at his rectory. However, because they were such good friends, he didn't want to compromise him.

On May 2, United Parcel Service delivered a package. As Bob signed for it, he noted it came from a church-goods store. It was in his mother's name. He placed the package on the bed beside her.

"What is it, Mom?" he queried.

"A wonderful surprise," she countered. "We won't open it until Father Jim comes. I want him to share the moment with us."

Bob's impatience was nothing compared to Maria's. Both kept alert to the sound of the priest's voice at the door. When he finally arrived, she asked that both men sit beside the bed. She had something to say.

"Remember, Robert, how excited you were when you read the life of Saint Pius the Tenth?" she asked.

"Sure, Mom, but that was at least three years ago."

"At least. As you read it you kept me appraised of its content. I thought what a model he, Pius the Tenth, must be for all people, but especially priests."

"Sure, Mom. I agree."

"His mother always called him Beppo. As a child, as a young man, as a priest, as a bishop, as the pope, to her he was Beppo. When he was consecrated bishop, he came to the home to show her his beautiful huge ring. She listened to her excited son with deep interest. When he finished she said to him, 'Beppo, if it weren't for this ring [indicating her wedding band], you wouldn't have that ring.'

"I really liked that story. Father Jim said you had hopes for a chalice. He indicated the possible donor died without making the presentation. That must have been a terrible disappointment.

"You must wonder why I'm using so much energy talking on like this. Well, I'm excited. When the doctor and nurses at the hospital asked if there was anything I wanted, anything they could do for me, I said, 'Yes. I want a chalice.'

"Father Jim showed me a catalog last year with the picture of the chalice you wanted. I had it ordered as soon as my friends donated the money. Open the box, Robert."

Tears streamed down everyone's face. Bob wanted to blurt out, "Mom, I may never be a priest," but he choked on the words.

The chalice was the same Bob had dreamed of the spring before. It was silver. On the base was a solid gold cross with a large diamond at the crossbar.

His mother beamed. "I've always been faithful to my wedding band. The cross is constructed of your dad's ring and mine. The diamond is from our engagement ring. I have prayed so much that you will be a good priest. I am so very proud of you. So very proud.

"Notice the inscription on the bottom. It reads: 'Please pray for your parents when you ascend the altar of God.' Be as faithful to your vocation as a priest as I have been to the sacrament of marriage.

"I know my time is short. My fervent prayer is that I can watch you say Mass. I know I can't go to the Cathedral for the ordination. The next day, God willing, you will say Mass here with me, please God."

Bob rose to his feet. He took the chalice, the cup of suffering, from his mother's hands. He studied the cross, kissed it, and wept.

Maria watched her son. "Robert, I have suffered much. It is evident to anyone who sees me that no part of my being has escaped. Will you both promise there will be no viewing of my body? Close the coffin. Let the symbol of my suffering be this chalice, purchased by my friends. They know I have not rejected the cup of suffering. At every Mass you offer, remember how I joined my pain to the saving cross of Christ. No homily. My life is the sermon."

He leaned over his mother and kissed her. "Thanks. Keep praying. I love you so much, so very much."

He walked to the door. "I need a whole box of Kleenex, Mom. Thanks."

Father Jim followed. "We never told her about the delay in the ordination. Now what do we do?"

Bob stared at his shoes. There was seemingly interminable silence. Then he spoke slowly through clenched teeth. "I can't believe what I'm going to say, Father. I can't believe it. But so help me God, I can't see her hurt more. I have just one terrible answer.

As of now, I pray that she dies soon, before May the thirtieth. I can't tell her the truth. You can't. It is better that she find out in heaven than here."

As though in answer to his prayers, Maria began to fail rapidly. Her time was short. No one knew how short. On the evening of May 27 Robert called Father O'Donnell. Together they decided the doctor should be called.

It was as the priest expected: pneumonia. The doctor wanted her hospitalized, but she asked to remain in her home. With Robert's assistance, Father Jim administered the sacraments for her for the last time. She thanked her friend, the priest.

She turned to her son with her final words. "Thanks for your loving presence these last few weeks. In a moment, we will both be free. I, from pain. You, from worry on my account. Use your freedom wisely and with love." She closed her eyes in peace.

The funeral was celebrated on May 30 at 10:30 A.M. Maybe it was fate. Maybe it was part of the subconscious. At any rate, it was the exact moment at which, a few weeks earlier, the bishop had invited Robert Burke to the sacrament of Holy Orders.

Father Jim was the celebrant. In accord with her wishes, there was no homily. The priest indicated it was at her request. However, he used the opportunity to make a point.

"Her final words were to her son: 'Use your freedom wisely and with love.' They are words by which we should all live. Just as important, the last word to cross her lips was *love*. Love is the Lord's great commandment."

The chalice rested on the coffin until the offertory. At that time, Robert brought it to the altar for the celebration. His mother's words filled every fiber of his body at the consecration. As Father O'Donnell raised the chalice, the words were visible to priest and deacon: "Please pray for your parents when you ascend the altar of God."

Chapter 9

In accordance with the instructions to notify the chancery office when his mother died, Robert Burke dutifully made the call. The chancellor made an appointment for him with the bishop.

"Should I have Father O'Donnell accompany me?"

"That is completely your choice."

"I'll ask him and he can decide."

Father Jim decided there would not be any advantage gained by his presence. But he would keep the time open in case Bob wanted him to come along. At the last moment Bob decided Father's presence might be good.

Nothing was said on the way to the chancery. After all, they had no idea what was on the bishop's mind. He was the one in control of the agenda.

"We are all very sorry to hear of your mother's death, Robert. If the time of the funeral hadn't been at the time of ordination, someone would have represented me from the chancery office," explained the bishop.

"Thank you very much, Your Excellency. I know you maintain a very busy schedule, and I'm appreciative of your concern. You mention ordination. That, of course, is the reason for this visit. Have you considered a time for my ordination?" asked Bob.

"It shouldn't surprise you that I have prayed much over that very subject. Needless to say, I was very disappointed that you left the seminary without permission," stated the bishop.

"My apologies for that, Your Excellency. Father O'Donnell was more than gracious in petitioning for me. Also, the rector said I had satisfied all seminary regulations and studies. He said he would write a letter to that effect," explained Robert.

"A person planning his ordination should be mature enough to plead his own case," snapped the bishop.

"Granted. I was under terrible duress due to my mother's condition. I am sorry if I acted incorrectly in this matter," pleaded Bob.

"Would you expect a priesthood in which there would be no duress? Would you throw protocol to the winds any time there was an emergency?"

"Is my whole future being decided based on one oversight?"

"The oversight, my dear young man, constitutes disobedience. In the priesthood, the virtue of obedience is paramount. Are you not aware of the Psalmist, who proclaims: 'Sacrifice or oblation you wished not, but ears open to obedience you gave me'?" quoted the bishop.

"Such obedience is demanded by the commandment: 'Honor your father and your mother.' Am I to be denied for keeping a commandment? Bishop, if you want to quote from Scripture, let me humbly remind you that religion pure and simple is caring for the widow and the orphan," Robert said calmly.

"Don't quote Scripture to me, young man!"

"Your Excellency, you introduced Scripture. I merely quoted in kind. My mother was a widow. I was her only son and her only relative."

"Your present attitude is one of disrespect and hostility. Am I to reward such an attitude by ordination? Are you questioning authority?" asked the bishop.

"On the contrary, I'm pleading with authority as one who wants to be a dutiful son. As I was dutiful to my mother, I want to be your dutiful son and priest," said the young man.

At this point, Father O'Donnell spoke out. "Your Excellency, I feel you are withholding ordination from Robert Burke because his mother died from AIDS."

"And why would you make that supposition?"

"Robert Burke had the best record of any seminarian in the over two hundred years of Saint Mary's Seminary in Baltimore.

Your invitation to ordination was placed before you were aware of his mother's sickness. I think Mr. Burke has defended himself adequately against your accusation of disobedience."

"What about your own disobedience, Father O'Donnell?"

"What do you mean?"

"You were asked not to visit Maria Burke!"

Bob looked incredulously first at the bishop and then at the priest.

"Not so," responded O'Donnell. "I was given three choices, and I selected number three. I've not been disobedient. Let us, however, get to the point. Your office asked that I not visit Maria because she had AIDS. Sure, it was couched in such a way that you could deny it. But that was the intent and purpose. And that is why you are denying ordination to Robert Burke."

"Are you calling my authority into question? It is my decision and mine alone as to who is ordained," shot the bishop.

"It should be an informed decision, not one based on prejudice," responded Father O'Donnell.

"The bishop's authority is based on the Lord's naming the Apostles as teachers, rulers, and sanctifiers. I am a successor of the Apostles," the bishop reminded them.

The priest shook his head and became silent.

"Your Excellency," began Bob, "even though Peter was the leader of the Apostles, the first pope, we must not lose sight of the fact that when Paul withstood him to his face, Peter changed his mind."

"What is your point?" questioned the bishop.

"I believe the church is both human and divine. That which is divine is not questioned. That which is human we must constantly question."

"For instance?"

"Very few question the good work provided by the Salvation Army. The Army exists because the human element in the churches failed. If Catholics, Lutherans, Methodists, and Baptists would have always taken care of the poor, the Salvation Army would never have been founded. People don't leave the Church because of her teachings. They leave because of some person: a priest, a neighbor, a bishop, whoever.

"The social ministry is important. At present, there isn't even an AIDS ministry in this diocese. I would be grateful if you would allow me to be chaplain for such a ministry for the rest of my life."

The bishop pondered, then set his jaw. "You will not be ordained. If Father O'Donnell wants to accept such a ministry, he may. If you are really interested, Mr. Burke, study; get a degree in sociology or psychiatry or whatever it might take. Then you can aid your friend O'Donnell, if you both agree.

"Mr. Burke, I will petition Rome for the necessary dispensations from orders. This conversation is ended."

"Thank you for your time, Bishop," said Bob.

"Yes, thanks much. I'm sure you have a busy schedule," added Father O'Donnell.

Not being sure whether the priest's words were born of sarcasm and hostility or genuine concern, the bishop merely smiled agreement, and Father O'Donnell and Robert Burke departed.

"I guess it has all been said," remarked the younger.

"I'm afraid you're right," answered the elder.

"Is there any possibility another bishop might want me?"

"There would be many, but ours will give you no recommendation."

They drove in silence toward Robert's home. "Let's stop for a hamburger and coffee," suggested the priest.

"I can't believe food can take my mind off what just happened, but let's give it a try."

While the two awaited attention at the restaurant, Bob turned to his friend. "Despite the fact that some would say I don't meet obligations, it strikes me that I have a very special obligation in Minnesota."

"Which is?"

"Tom Burns and I have an agreement that we will preach at one another's first Mass. He will be ordained the twentieth of this month in Winona, and his Mass will be the following Sunday. If it is all the same to you, since you are presently without a parish, maybe we could drive out together. On the way, you could explain what you meant by the three options and how you were told not to care for Mom."

"It won't take that long," countered the priest. "It may be good for both of us to get some fresh Midwestern air. How will you react to Tom's ordination and first Mass? Can you handle it?"

"I'd better be able to. I have to preach." Bob replied, smiling.

"Let's get started right away so the whole time can be the real vacation we both need," concluded the priest.

It proved to be a restless night for both priest and friend. When they finally met at the apartment for Mass, it was obvious that both lacked sleep and both wanted to talk.

"You go first," suggested Father Jim.

"Okay. Just one important question," began Burke.

"Be my guest."

"The bishop said you could be part of an AIDS program in the diocese," continued Bob. "Are you interested?"

"I'm not sure what that would mean," responded the priest.

"He didn't say. I believe he used the word *chaplain*. I don't think he knows what he meant. If you are interested, maybe we could outline a job description," offered Burke.

"Obviously, you've been thinking about this."

"All night long," said the younger man. "But there is no sense in venturing further unless you're interested."

"That isn't necessarily so. Give me your thoughts. Let me see how it sounds. Then maybe my decision will be easier."

"At least you haven't closed the door. First, forget the word *chaplain*. It doesn't ring with the sound of any authority. The word *director* is better. You want to be the director and establish a funded program."

"Funded by?"

"The diocese, of course."

"We have no idea how much the budget would be. Nor does anyone else," complained the priest.

"Not so. Other dioceses have programs. This is by no means a sailing of uncharted waters."

"So, how do we proceed?" asked the priest.

"First, we have to know if the bishop is serious."

"In his present mood, how do we approach him?"

"Hey, wait. He is the one who suggested it," chided Burke.

"You have a plan? You have a plan!"

"You are the director, Father, not I, but I'd be happy to make a suggestion."

"Let's hear what you've plotted."

"You fix breakfast, Father Jim, and while you are doing that maybe I can compose a letter to His Excellency."

"Does that mean a big breakfast or a small one?" laughed the priest as he started the meal.

Bob began to write:

Your Excellency,

In our discussion yesterday, you suggested the need for AIDS ministry in the diocese. I heartily concur.

You suggested also that I be the diocesan director. I ask your prayer in this endeavor. I have no idea what the budget would be and am fearful it may be prohibitive.

At your bidding, I would be most pleased to study the many aspects required for establishing the ministry.

Would Your Excellency kindly write the necessary letter of appointment for me as diocesan director of AIDS ministry? That could serve as a letter of introduction for me to investigate dioceses that have successful programs in process. From facts collected from such sources, we could move on to such decisions as staff, budget, office, and other concerns of which we may be presently unaware.

Such an investigation on my part would require some funding, which I would make every effort to keep minimal.

Your obedient servant,
Fr. James O'Donnell

While they ate, the priest digested the letter as well as the food. "Do you think he'll go for this?"

"Only one way to find out. If you're in agreement, let's get over to the Priest Personnel Office and test the gears," rejoined Burke. "He can present the bishop with the letter right away."

"You are really in a hurry, aren't you?" quizzed Father Jim.

"Yes. We can stop at every diocesan AIDS ministry office between here and Minnesota and back, if we move," insisted Bob.

"You are a mover and a plotter, aren't you, Burke?"

"The way I figure it, we can sleep and have breakfast in rectories both ways. All we need is money for lunch and dinner. Tell that to Personnel, but you may have better results if you don't mention my name. Agreed?"

"Agreed," replied Father O'Donnell enthusiastically. "I'm on my way."

The priest wasn't surprised that Personnel was unaware of the bishop's meeting the day before. The personnel director, Father Sam Wood, listened attentively and with Father Jim's urging agreed to talk with the bishop before noon. Indeed, he already had an appointment for ten-thirty, followed by lunch together. Father O'Donnell jokingly promised to pay for the meal if the results were right. He reminded Sam that it would be much appreciated if the letter of appointment could be forthcoming shortly. He needed the letter as an introduction.

The director was kind enough to allow O'Donnell to help him in framing the letter of request so all the bishop would need do was have his secretary type it and prepare it for his signature.

"In fact, the letter could be in the afternoon mail. With many appointments, the line forms to the right and to the left. For this ministry, Jim, you are the line. I think it is important. More important than anything else I have to discuss with His Excellency."

Shortly after one o'clock, Father Jim's phone rang. It was Sam.

"Good news, if you haven't changed your mind, Jim."

"You mean the bishop agreed?"

"He agreed. The letter of appointment is in my hand. Do you want me to mail it or do you want to pick it up?"

"I'll pick it up as soon as I can drive over."

Father Jim was on his way. Burke decided he would get a few winks, since he hadn't slept the night before.

Father Wood was waiting. "Here's the appointment. Can we talk?"

"Sure. I owe you that much, and for the lunch."

"Forget it. My pleasure," said Sam. "Tell me, how is Bob Burke doing?"

"Much better than I would be under the circumstances. To lose your mother and then within a week be told you aren't fit for ordination is too much. He is as qualified as anyone could be," said Father Jim, his face growing red.

"I didn't know about it until the bishop told me this morning.

In fact, that is why he asked me over. My office wasn't consulted. I don't think he consulted anyone. I tried to change his mind, but the door is shut. In fact, he is adamant," continued Sam.

"In such a mood, I'm surprised he didn't throw you out concerning my letter of appointment to the AIDS ministry."

"I sincerely believe it gives him an out to appoint you. This way he doesn't have to admit to anyone he won't ordain Burke because Bob's mother died from AIDS. Now, he can say he is interested in the whole AIDS picture and may be able to convince himself that he refused the ordination because of disobedience," Sam continued.

"I'm telling you these things not to save my face in the whole situation. I'm saying these things because you are Burke's best friend."

"Best friend? Right now I'm like his only friend. I'm his family. I'm everything to him. That all may help him, but it doesn't help me. I won't repeat anything you've said, not because he can't take it, but because I couldn't take telling him. This isn't fair to you, Sam. I'm ranting and raving to you and you're the only one who has been understanding. I mean anyone who is official. I'm being hard on you when I should just say, 'Thanks for the letter,' and leave."

Jim took the letter from Sam, shook his hand, and began to leave.

"Just one more thing, O'Donnell. The bishop wants you to keep a record of expenditures, and he will reimburse you. Meanwhile, note a check for $3,000 for seed money. Congratulations and good luck."

The priest returned to his apartment with the news.

"This is the first good news I've had since finding out about Mom's sickness," Burke said quietly. "We'd better get started right away."

"Get started?" questioned the priest.

"Yes." Bob seemed impatient. "We don't have much time. You run over to the Chancery Office and borrow a copy of the *Catholic Directory*. Let us get the name and address of every diocesan AIDS ministry between here and Minnesota. Now that we are funded, there is no reason to wait."

"I'm on my way." Father Jim suddenly was cognizant of the

84

fact that what was happening had a certain therapeutic value for his young friend.

"This trip can be for both business and pleasure. I'm anxious to get away from Washington, to get on the road, to begin a mission." Then Burke stopped. "Am I presuming too much? You want my help, don't you? I need you to need me."

"Yes, I need you. Now be quiet so I can get the *Directory*."

Two days later they headed west. They had a series of questions ready for every director of AIDS ministry, but most of all they were prepared to listen.

Much of what they heard had to be translated into the situation they might encounter in their own diocese. Gradually, their file increased to overwhelming proportions. They knew they would have to discard what was beyond their capacities. They knew, too, that their final proposal should not be so cumbersome as to frighten anyone with the magnitude of the task.

They journeyed to New York City, then up the Hudson to Albany. Cities along the Great Lakes offered scenery of the lakes themselves. Michigan's Upper Peninsula was gorgeous. They spent a day hiking in the Porcupine Mountains.

Because they wanted to see the Northshore Drive along Lake Superior in northern Minnesota, they chose to travel in Canada from Michigan to Minnesota.

They were on schedule for Tom Burns's ordination in Winona, but Bob became nervous and aggravated.

"You'd rather not make the ordination?" guessed the priest.

"It doesn't make sense. Up to now, I've managed, but I don't think I can handle it," confessed Burke.

"No problem, Bob. We can spend some time in the Voyager's National Park instead. The Porcupines almost did me in, but let's give it our best."

"I guess we'd better get in touch with Tom so he won't be nervous about the preacher showing for the first Mass," responded Burke.

"If that is going to be too rough for you, maybe I can pinch-hit," offered Father Jim.

"*Pinch-hit!* Now there is a word I wouldn't know the meaning of if it weren't for Burns. I'll think about your offer. Fact is, I've labored on the sermon for several weeks and I may have at least a double, if not a home run, in the works," assured the younger man.

He continued, "We should be in Janesville on Saturday afternoon. We are expected to stay with the pastor overnight. He is a holy, humble man whom you'll really like."

"Great. We can close the book on our project as soon as we've stopped in Saint Paul. We won't discuss the AIDS ministry from then until after the first Mass," concluded Father Jim.

Chapter 10

Father O'Donnell and Robert Burke arrived in Janesville shortly after noon. Since Bob had visited Tom on two different occasions, he knew where the rectory was. It was Burke's privilege to introduce his friend Father Jim to Tom's pastor, Fr. Robert Smith.

Father Smith proudly announced that the women of Saint Anne's were hosting a social and dinner in the parish hall starting at five-thirty. O'Donnell and Burke were expected as guests.

Home cooking was something Burke had enjoyed only twice in his memory. Both times he was visiting the Burnses in Janesville. Father Jim had not eaten such since he had resigned from his parish. The two thoroughly enjoyed the people, food, and short program by which strangers became friends and friends became closer.

Anyone who wanted to say a few words was given the opportunity. Father O'Donnell merely introduced himself and avowed that he was present in the role of spectator. Bob allowed that even though his chance to speak was really supposed to be at the Mass, he nonetheless had something to say.

He excused himself for a moment, went into the cloakroom, and came forth with a black box. He unlocked the container and brought forth a beautiful silver chalice.

His voice was uneven as he told the story of the cup. Friends of his mother had purchased it for him. The cross at its base was formed by his parents' wedding bands. The diamond in the cross center was from his mother's engagement ring.

Tears streamed down his face. He had totally lost his voice.

He motioned for Father O'Donnell, who came forward. Burke pointed to the words. The priest knew what Burke wanted and read the inscription under the chalice: " 'Please pray for your parents when you ascend the Altar of God.' "

For a moment Bob found a whisper willing to escape his throat. "Tom, will you please use my chalice at your Mass tomorrow?"

Tom took the chalice and placed it on the table. Then his muscular arms embraced the thin body of his friend. They separated and shook hands. "Believe me, it will be my privilege."

In the name of Tom Burns and his family, Father Smith thanked the ladies for their generosity, thanked the invited guests for sharing the night, and invited all the guests to depart for rest that would prove quite necessary for tomorrow.

Father Jim walked to the rectory beside Bob. "Are you going to be able to make it tomorrow? That was sure tough on you just now. Just say the word and I'll take over for you."

"Thanks. That was more difficult tonight than anything could be tomorrow. You pray and I'll do the rest," Bob reassured the priest.

The next morning's sunshine harbingered a day of beauty and grace. Father Smith bubbled with joy at breakfast. His seminarian was about to have his first Mass; his parish was to witness a lifetime experience.

It is normal that a lawyer exult when his or her son or daughter passes the bar. It is natural that a doctor be pleased when his or her offspring can add "M.D." to his or her signature. It borders on the supernatural when a pastor rejoices because a young man from his parish becomes a priest. This young man had always called him Father.

The Immaculate Heart of Mary Seminary provided its choir. This was an insurance policy that the music would be beautiful and correct. Most important, it allowed seminarians to witness the fact that ordinations and first Masses were part of their lives that they could more easily visualize as well as anticipate.

Also, as Father Smith was to repeat often during the day, it gave his young people the opportunity of seeing that seminarians are human just as they are human. Who knows who may be inspired to follow Father Tom's example?

An hour before Mass began, the choir provided inspiration for those who for various reasons were already present. Some came from a distance and wanted to be on time. Some wanted a choice spot in the church (places never coveted for an "ordinary" Sunday Mass). Some were told to get out of the house because of "relative crowding." Some youngsters were sent to church, where it was less likely they would prematurely soil their clothes, and so on.

The Burns family was popular in Janesville, so Saint Anne's had standing room only both inside and outside the church. The moment had the feeling of a state basketball championship rally, with a deep religious reverence to add inspiration to all present.

Those who shed tears of sorrow were unable to explain their emotion any better than those whose eyes were moist with joy. The tears of young people are embarrassing because there isn't always an explanation. The tears of the old are not embarrassing because they know no explanation is needed.

The parents, the brothers, and the sister had always been proud of Tom. Now, their feelings went beyond pride to a humble gratitude as they sat in the reserved front pew awaiting the beginning of that wonderful moment called the First Mass.

Tom was not merely pleased to have Bob as deacon. He was totally comfortable. Burke was always the best on ceremonies, so it was more than friendship involved. Bob provided assurance and insurance that all would go well, and Tom was grateful and relaxed.

The pastor was the subdeacon. Burns always had had a deep respect and reverence for Father Smith. Such reverence was not always shared by all the parishioners. Some had once actually formed a committee to make an official complaint against the pastor to the bishop. After an investigation of the charge that the father was not spending enough time visiting parishioners it was determined that the opposite was the case. The priest was spending "too much time visiting the Hispanics of the parish," who weren't accepted by a faction of the community.

In Fr. Tom Burns's eyes, his pastor was always a model priest. Tom had happily accepted his mentor's advice to study Spanish in high school and college. Tom was encouraged to befriend the Hispanics to better develop conversational skills. He learned to love them, and they loved him.

Tom was pleased with the number of Hispanics at the Mass. He also noted that the members of the "committee" to the bishop were present for the festivity.

Father Burns had a deep, pleasant speaking voice. While he had little time for music in his life, he nonetheless had a melodious singing voice that was always on pitch. As the Mass proceeded these facts were self-evident to all.

Since Bob was preaching, the celebrant had left the selection of Scription to his deacon. Burns worked on his sermon first and then sought readings appropriate to the theme.

The first selection, read by Tom's brother Matt, was from the opening lines of the prophet Jeremiah:

" 'The word of the Lord came to me thus:
Before I formed you in the womb, I knew you.
Before you were born, I dedicated you.
A prophet to the nations, I appointed you.
"Ah, Lord God," I said.
"I know not how to speak; I am too young."
The Lord answered me,
"Say not, I am too young.
To whomever I send you, you shall go.
Whatever I command you, you shall speak.
Have no fear before them because I am with you
to deliver you," says the Lord.
                    The Word of the Lord.' "

Matt's voice was as pleasant as Father Tom's, but he was out of his element. His embarrassment was earned by his rather inept reading. Now, he paused. He became more composed and proceeded to the responsorial from Psalm 40.

" 'Here am I Lord; I come to do your will.
        I have waited, waited for the Lord,
            and He stooped toward me and heard my cry.

He put a new song in my mouth,
a hymn to our God.
Here am I Lord; I come to do your will.
Sacrifice or oblation you wished not,
but ears open to obedience you gave me.
Holocausts or sin-offerings you sought not;
then said I, "Behold I come."
Here am I Lord; I come to do your will.
In the written scroll it is prescribed for me,
to do your will, O my God, is my delight,
and your law is within my heart.
Here am I Lord; I come to do your will.
I announced your justice in the vast assembly;
I did not restrain my lips, as You, O Lord, know.
Here am I Lord; I come to do your will.' "

Tom's other brother, Jim, came to the podium for the second reading. He began with greater ease than his brother could attain. Matt's sudden composure was continued in Jim: "This reading is from the First Letter of Paul to the Corinthians, chapter 11, verses 17 to 29."

" 'But in giving this charge, I do not commend you in that you meet not for the better but for the worse. For first of all, I hear that when you meet in church there are divisions among you, and in part, I believe it. There must be factions, so that those who are approved may be made manifest among you.

" 'So then when you meet together it is no longer possible to eat the Lord's Supper. For at the meal, each one takes first one's own supper, and one is hungry and another drinks overmuch.

" 'Have you not houses for your eating and drinking? Or do you despise the church of God and put to shame the needy? What am I to say to you? Am I to commend you? In this I do not commend you.

" 'For I myself have received from the Lord, what I also delivered to you, that the Lord Jesus, on the night in which He was betrayed, took bread and giving thanks, broke it and said, "This is my body which shall be given up for you; do this in remembrance of me."

" 'In like manner, after He had supped saying, "This cup is the new covenant in my blood; do this as often as you drink it, in remembrance of me. For as often as you shall eat this bread and drink the cup, you proclaim the death of the Lord, until he comes."

" 'Therefore, whoever eats this bread or drinks the cup of the Lord unworthily, will be guilty of the body and blood of the Lord.

" 'But let each prove oneself, and so let each eat of that bread and drink of the cup; for one who eats and drinks unworthily, without distinguishing the body, eats and drinks judgment to oneself.

" 'The Word of the Lord.' "

After a short pause, Bob picked up the Holy Book, asked Tom for a blessing, and proceeded to the podium.

"The Lord be with you."

The people responded, "And also with you."

He had never really thought of it before, but now suddenly he heard their words and prayed fervently, *Please be with me, Lord.*

"This is the holy Gospel according to John." He sealed his mind, his lips, and his heart with the cross of Christ and read:

" 'I am the bread of life. Your fathers ate the manna in the desert and have died. This is the bread that comes down from heaven, so that if anyone eat of it he will not die.

" 'I am the living bread that has come down from heaven. If anyone eats of this bread, he shall live forever; and the bread that I will give is my flesh for the life of the world.

" 'The Jews on that account argued with one another saying, "How can this man give us his flesh to eat?"

" 'Jesus responded, "Amen, Amen, I say to you, unless you eat the flesh of the Son of Man and drink his blood, you shall not have life in you. Who eats my flesh and drinks my blood has life everlasting and I will raise him up on the last day.

" ' "For my flesh is food indeed, and my blood is drink indeed. Who eats my flesh and drinks my blood, abides in me and I in him. As the living Father has sent me, and as I live because of the Father, so one who eats me shall live because of me.

" ' "This is the bread that has come down from heaven; not as your fathers ate the manna, and died. Who eats this bread shall live forever."

" 'The Gospel of the Lord.' " Burke kissed the Holy Word and made a very slow and deliberate sign of the cross. "In the name of the Father and of the Son and of the Holy Spirit. Amen." He studied the crowd with eyes that were filled with "Welcome"; he didn't need acknowledgment by words. He looked across the sanctuary to his friend Father Burns, the pastor, and finally his friend Father O'Donnell. The latter had a serious smile, which when translated by Burke said: "You will do great because you are great, and you are great because God is with you."

Robert Burke began in a subdued and gentle manner. "Dear friends of Fr. Thomas Burns, it is a distinct honor to be chosen to preach for the chosen. At such a moment as this we reflect on the words: 'You have not chosen me. I have chosen you.'

"Moses did not want to lead the people. He protested he was no leader. He had a speech problem. God persisted and promised Moses his younger brother, Aaron, would be his spokesman.

"Jeremiah pleaded with God, claiming not only his unwillingness but also his inadequacies. God merely promised Jeremiah any necessary assistance. Jeremiah rued the day he was born, but again, God persisted.

"God demanded Hosea marry the harlot Gomer. He insisted that Hosea take her back even after she bore two sons in adultery. God chose these men despite their refusals.

"Isaiah was happy to be God's prophet. He was prepared for the role. Samuel, too, from his beginning was dedicated to the Lord. In the middle of the night, Samuel, three times, responded to the Lord by awakening Eli with the words, 'Here am I Lord, I come to do your will.' Then Eli, needing his sleep, told the young Samuel to remain in his own room and await the message of God. God did the choosing.

"On different occasions in the life of Jesus, when he had cured the sick, those healed began to give glory to the Lord. And Jesus silenced them. They were not his messengers.

"Nicodemus came in the middle of the night to listen to the teacher. He desired the wisdom Jesus offered. The Lord left Nicodemus confused and bewildered when he told him, 'You must be born again.' He did not choose Nicodemus.

"From a human point of view, why would Christ choose Apostles who, for the most part, could neither read nor write? We know that John and Matthew could do so. Of the rest we don't know. And

Matthew was a hated tax collector. From the human point of view, he should never have been chosen. But God's ways are not man's ways, and Christ chose the Apostles.

"Saul was the most notorious enemy of the Church in the first century. It was he whom Christ chose to be the great Apostle to the Gentiles. Such an Apostle was he that Aquinas, in referring to Paul, calls him 'the Apostle.'"

Bob's face presented a smile as he continued. "I strongly suspect that many of you have recently heard the words, indeed perhaps spoken the words: 'I knew all the time that Tom Burns would one day be a priest.'"

Now Burke became very deliberate. "Who becomes a priest? This was the question asked by vocation directors at a meeting held for them in 1950. They decided to construct a questionnaire to make their task much easier.

"The list of questions was long and, to the best of their abilities, all-inclusive. Do vocations come from large families or small? Do vocations spring from parochial schools or public schools? Do vocations come from the rich, the middle class, the poor? Do vocations come from the oldest, the youngest, or the middle child? Do vocations come from families in which there are uncles or great-uncles who are priests? Do the first thoughts of vocation begin in grade school, junior high, high school, college years?" The questions went on and on and on.

"The questionnaires were sent to every priest and seminarian in the United States. The results were carefully scrutinized and categorized. After months of interpretation by the experts, one conclusion was evident. There are no common denominators. God chooses whom He will!

"Each one of us has a personality. Each has a character. Personality is who we are; character is what we are. Our newly ordained is Tom Burns. That is who he is. What is he? He is a priest.

"Who is the Lord? He is Jesus Christ, true God and true Man. What is Jesus? He is 'the' priest. There is one priest. The rest of us share in the priesthood of Jesus Christ."

Now Bob became very pedantic. "In the Sixth Chapter of Romans, Paul writes: 'Do you not know that all we who have been baptized into Christ Jesus have been baptized into his death?' On reading Paul we recognize that Christ exercised his priesthood of sacrifice and love on the cross. So, in Baptism, you and I receive the character of Christ the priest. The church refers to that as the priesthood of the laity. Confirmation is an even greater sharing in the character of Christ."

Burke was now relaxed. "Today we honor one who has been blessed with ordination. His has a greater sharing in the priesthood. The Apostles and their successors alone share the total character of Christ, who is the Priest.

"The role of priest is to offer sacrifice and forgive sins. The Old Testament is replete with sacrifices from the time of Cain and Abel to the Books of the Maccabees.

"The Book of Hebrews attests to the old and the new in 3:13: 'Now in saying a new covenant, he had made obsolete the former one; and that which is obsolete has grown old and is near its end.' And again in Hebrews 10:9–10: 'Behold, I come to do your will, O God,' he annuls the first covenant in order to establish the second. It is in this 'will' that we have been sanctified through the offering of the body of Jesus Christ once for all.

"The new covenant is Jesus Christ's sacrifice on the cross. The Lord's Supper, Calvary, and the Holy Sacrifice of the Mass are one and the same. Calvary is the bloody sacrifice. The other two sacrifices, however, are unbloody. Malachi, the prophet, anticipates the perfect sacrifice when he speaks in 1:11: 'For from the rising of the sun, even to its setting, my name is great among the nations and everywhere they bring sacrifice to my name and a pure offering, for great is my name among the nations, says the Lord of hosts.'

"Three of the four evangelists write concerning the Lord's Supper. John, in filling in what was missing, apparently considered the subject adequately covered. John, rather, speaks of the promise of the Eucharist in chapter 6. Paul, in his First Letter to the Corinthians, does speak of it, however.

"Matthew, in quoting Jesus' words, speaks of the covenant in the present tense. He writes: 'Take and eat. This is my body,' and: 'For this is the blood of the new covenant which is being shed'!

"Mark also writes in the present tense. 'Take, this is my body,' and: 'This is my blood of the new covenant which is being shed for many.' Again the emphasis is on 'is being shed.'

"Luke speaks in the present concerning the body. He speaks in the future concerning the blood. Does that future refer to Calvary, future Masses, or both? Concerning the body, he speaks of a command that could mean only the Mass.

"Listen to Luke: 'This is my body which is being given for you. Do this in commemoration of me.' And: 'This cup is the new covenant in my blood, which shall be shed for you.'

"Paul takes us a step further: 'This is my body which shall be given up for you. Do this in commemoration of me,' and: 'This cup is the new covenant in my blood; do this, as often as you drink it in remembrance of me.'

"When one takes all four authors together one finds the use of the present, the future, and a continuing future mentioned at the Last Supper. The present is the meal. The future is Calvary. The continuing future is the Mass."

Burke saw the attentiveness of the people and was encouraged. "In the sixth chapter of John's Gospel one finds the promise of the Eucharist. Christ explains it is a mystery of faith: 'Amen, Amen, I say to you, unless you eat the flesh of the Son of Man and drink his blood, you shall not have life in you. He who eats my flesh and drinks my blood has life ever lasting and I will raise him up on the last day. For my flesh is food indeed and my blood is drink indeed. He who eats my flesh and drinks my blood abides in me and I in him. As the living Father has sent me and as I live because of the Father, so he who eats me shall live because of me.'

"The thousands who had searched for Christ throughout the night then left him. Only the twelve remained with the Lord. They alone possessed faith in Jesus and his message.

"In the Old Testament the people had a custom in which they would place hands over a goat and recite their sins. Then they would destroy the animal. Even today we have the term *scapegoat* derived from that practice. We are told that the sacrifice of sheep and goats is no longer adequate. Now Christ is our sacrifice. Indeed, the name Jesus Christ means 'anointed savior.'

"In the twentieth chapter of John's Gospel, Jesus comes from the dead to address the disciples: 'Peace be with you.' When he had said this, he showed them his hands and his side. He said to them again, 'Peace be with you! As the Father has sent me, I also send you.' He breathed upon them and said, 'Receive the Holy Spirit; whose sins you shall forgive, they are forgiven them; and whose sins you shall retain, they are retained.'

"Christ was present. He could forgive sins, but he gave the power to his disciples. Was this a power that was to last only as long as they lasted? If the power was needed then, is it not needed today as well?

"We all appreciate the need of faith. Faith is beyond reason. Otherwise, of what value is faith? It takes faith to believe that the Lord leaves us his actual body and blood in the Eucharist at Mass. It takes faith to believe that the Lord leaves his power of forgiveness to the church.

"Peace be with you, Fr. Thomas Burns. Peace be with you! Peace be with the people you serve at the Mass and in Reconciliation.

"To you, Father Tom, I repeat the words of Christ: 'The Advocate, the Holy Spirit, whom the Father will send in my name, he will teach you all things and bring to your mind whatever I have said to you.

" 'Peace, I leave with you, my peace I give you; not as the world gives peace do I give it to you. Do not let your heart be troubled or be afraid.

" 'You have not chosen me. I have chosen you.' "

Robert Burke made the sign of the cross and returned to the chair on the celebrant's right. He heaved a deep sigh as the petitions were introduced.

After the collection of gifts, Tom's parents and their three grandchildren brought the gifts. One of the grandchildren, Thomas, carried Father Tom's high school athletic sweater, heavy with medals and designs. Lori carried a tray. On the tray were small containers filled with various seeds from the farm and some 4-H ribbons from county and state fairs. Mike carried the bread prepared for the Mass.

The priest's father carried the wine and water cruets. His mother brought forth the chalice. Father Tom accepted the wine and water. Father Smith took the bread. Robert Burke took the beautiful chalice with trembling hands and placed it on the altar.

The Offertory was followed quickly by the Consecration, the

words spoken by Christ at the Lord's Supper. Once more, the body and blood of Jesus were present in the chalice and on the altar.

Many gathered for the celebration understood better than ever before the mystery of faith taking place in the presence of all.

At the Lord's Prayer, the people were asked to hold hands as a sign of unity with all present and those absent.

"Forgive us our trespasses as we forgive those who trespass against us." Everyone said the words loudly and with fervor.

Robert Burke said the words as he thought to himself, *I haven't forgiven the bishop for his insensitivity, for his failure to understand, for his refusing Holy Orders. Will I ever forgive him? Can I?*

How can I forgive that which is ongoing? How can I forgive when there is no repentance? It would be easy if he knew not what he was doing. He knows. He has to know he has taken eight years of my life.

Father Tom nudged him. "Bob, introduce the sign of peace."

Burke responded, "Peace I give you; my peace I leave with you. Not as the world gives peace, says the Lord. Let us offer a sign of Christ's peace to one another."

The people embraced, some kissed, and some merely shook hands. The whole church stirred to demonstrate the love Christ had for them all, and which they held for one another.

Robert Burke continued his thoughts. *Would I feel comfortable giving the bishop a sign of peace? Could it be sincere? He did all he could to make me feel uncomfortable. His words were not kind. His final words: "Mr. Burke, I will petition Rome for the necessary dispensation from orders. This conversation is ended." My God in heaven. I may not even be a deacon anymore. I had no right to give the sermon. No right to be at Tom's right hand.*

It was Communion time. Father Burns handed Burke the particle of the Host: "Lord, I am not worthy to receive you. Say but the word and my soul shall be healed." After Tom, he held the chalice, the essence of his mother's last wishes, the blood that is the will of Christ for all. He drank and handed the cup to Father Smith.

Father Tom distributed from the central station, where his immediate family and relatives were. Father Smith distributed on Burns's left, Bob on the right.

Almost as though they knew the story of his life and were rejecting him, even as the bishop had, the people passed Burke by to receive from the newly ordained. A few acted as though they knew nothing of his past, knowing it was the Body of Christ regardless. Some even smiled at him as though it didn't matter when they responded, "Amen," to the Body of Christ.

The only course he hadn't liked in the seminary was Canon Law. It wasn't that he rejected it; he just didn't care about it. Now his mind went to Canon Law. At least, since he didn't know the answer, that was where it must be.

Bob's mind raced. *Is one dispensed from orders when Rome gives the ruling? Is one dispensed when the word is received at the chancery? Is one dispensed only when one is informed?*

Father Tom gave the blessing and once more nudged his deacon. Burke momentarily hesitated, then blurted out, "The Mass is ended. Go in peace and love to serve the Lord."

The choir began to sing "Joyful, Joyful, We Adore Thee" as the celebrants kissed the altar and descended the steps to the main aisle and the main entrance. Burke found himself singing along to a hymn he had always liked.

" 'Joyful, joyful, we adore thee,
God of Glory, Lord of Love;
Hearts unfold like flowers before thee,
Opening to the sun above.
Melt the clouds of sin and sadness;
Drive the dark of doubt away;
Giver of immortal gladness,
Fill us with the light of day!' "

Everyone else proceeded singing the next three verses. Robert Burke hummed along, repeating the first verse each time: " 'Melt the clouds of sin and sadness;/drive the dark of doubt away;/Giver of immortal gladness,/Fill us with the light of day.' "

This was Father Tom's day. A day of celebration. At least for now, put away sadness and doubt and appreciate the gladness of the day like the hymn says, thought Robert Burke.

Many people spoke at the banquet that evening. Few took much time. The parents expressed gratitude to God that a wonderful son had become a priest. They promised to continue praying for him as a Father as they had during his seminary years.

Tom's high school coach opined that the new priest had all the natural abilities of an athlete but always worked hard at every sport and never violated training rules. He knew Father Burns would work even harder for the Lord.

Three of the cheerleaders during Tom's senior year gave a yell for his success. During the ensuing eight years they had lost their cheering abilities while gaining weight. One of them admitted that at least for the occasion they should have worked harder on the cheer and some of the pounds may have been eliminated.

The real star was the pastor, Fr. Robert Smith. He spoke with deep emotion: "This is certainly one of the happiest moments of my life. Nothing is a greater vindication of one's priestly ministry than to have a lad from the parish become a priest.

"Father Tom was an exemplary child. He willingly set all else aside to serve Mass, to assist in the Stations of the Cross or whatever the church asked of him.

"You have already heard what a tremendous athlete he was in high school. He also excelled in college. What hasn't been mentioned is the fact that before every athletic event he would stop in at the church for a moment with the Lord.

"On the day of my first Mass, over thirty years ago, my pastor said something I shall never forget. He remarked that God gives us memories so we can have roses in December. Today, I better understand what he meant.

"I can go back in my memory to days that were difficult. Sometimes difficult because I was misunderstood. Sometimes difficult because I didn't understand someone else. Many times difficult because no one seemed to love me. There were dark nights of the soul when it seemed that even Christ had abandoned me.

"But I hasten to say that just when someone who was a friend failed the relationship, someone who I thought was the enemy became the champion.

"I have been fortunate in every appointment ever given. One cannot expect 100 percent cooperation ever. All one can do is promise, to the best of one's ability, to give 100 percent.

"We live in a world in which prayer is seen as superstition, in which faith is considered unreasonable, in which love is something merely physical and relationships are merely used for personal gain and discarded when the burden seems greater than the reward.

"Today is a moment of faith for the community of Janesville. The pastor, the people, the bishop, have faith that Father Tom will be a man of faith. That faith is a gift, but it is a gift nurtured by prayer. We know love is physical and spiritual. We cannot deny our emotions, but there are times when it may be good to control them. Control is the ultimate realization that emotions are real.

"The sermon today by Father Tom's friend Bob Burke was a masterpiece in content and delivery. Very few have the ability to speak of such lofty realities without talking down to the listeners. Today, the listeners heard and learned. Reverend Mr. Burke, I congratulate you and pray your future in the priesthood will be happy and fruitful.

"Father Tom, know that wherever the bishop sends you, there is the assistance of the Holy Spirit. Always be a person of prayer, with the Eucharist as the center of your life.

"As you have provided a bountiful bouquet of roses for me this day, may your own life be such that one day, the heaviest of crosses and the most glorious of crowns will equally provide you with good memories. Father Burns, I salute you. Ad multos annos!"

The final speaker was Father Tom. He thanked everyone who had brought him to this special moment: his priest, his parents, his family, teachers, professors and all. He admitted, to no one's surprise, that he was not a scholar. If it hadn't been for the preacher of the day he would never have made it through the seminary.

"But," he added, "except for me, the future Father Burke would know nothing about sports. Consequently, we are both responsible for the completion of the other person."

He asked for continuing prayer and promised he would never forget his roots. All in all, he did a commendable job before a group of people with whom he could do nothing wrong.

Father Tom asked Father O'Donnell to close the festivities with a prayer. He obliged. Then everyone came forward to shake the newly ordained priest's hand and let him know he was a hero. Then, by the carload, people left the hall knowing they had been part of a very special day they would never forget.

There had been no alcoholic refreshments at the banquet, so it was very natural that Father Smith would atone as soon as

Fathers Burns and O'Donnell and Robert Burke returned to the rectory for the night. The priests accepted the hospitality, but Burke asked to be excused for the moment. Father Jim looked at him with a worried countenance, but Bob assured him it really would be but a moment.

He went to his bedroom, took a piece of paper from the desk, and wrote:

My dear friend Tom,

I have not been able to discuss what I'm about to write now. My bishop has refused me ordination on the grounds that I was disobedient in leaving the seminary early. My suspicion is that he doesn't want a priest in his diocese whose mother died from AIDS. At present, I have no plans except to stay close to Father Jim, who shares my sorrow. Since I have no need for this chalice. I want you to have it. There is just one condition: remember my parents as well as yours when you are at the altar of God. Since Mom rented a furnished apartment, the chalice is my only possession. I would not part with it for any amount of money but am pleased to give it to you.

I cannot tell you how I am emotionally. The best explanation would be to describe me as totally numb.

If, in any way, my present mood caused me to give anything less than a good sermon or to cause any problems at your Mass, I am most sorry and humbly ask your forgiveness.

Please pray for me.

Your devoted friend,
Bob Burke

Having concluded the note, Bob went down the steps to the living room and asked for a double martini.

"Are you serious?" queried Father O'Donnell.

"Can you celebrate that much?" asked Tom.

"The poison you order is the poison you get," laughed Father Smith.

The double martini lasted long after O'Donnell's vodka and tonic as well as Burns's glass of wine. After all, they had a head start. As their glasses emptied they excused themselves to seek blessed sleep.

Father Smith, as Bob had guessed, was the perfect host. He remained with his double-martini guest.

"Father, I have a favor I need from you," said Bob.

"Certainly. Whatever I can do."

"I understand that you are taking the week off and Tom will cover the parish in your absence."

"Right," responded the priest.

"When you return from your minivacation, you will find a box and a note on the dresser in my bedroom. At that time, and no sooner, will you give them to Tom?" asked Burke.

"Certainly."

"Thanks, Father. By the way, I never could handle a double martini. Especially as tired as I am now. It was an excuse to have this conversation alone with you. Please don't be insulted if I pour it down the drain.

"Good night, Father. And thanks."

Chapter 11

To take a step back in time, Tom Burns had been raised on a farm near Janesville, Minnesota. His parents were John Burns and the former Hannah O'Brien. John was no more than an average farmer whose main boast was the fact that he had survived many devastating years in regard to weather and farm product prices.

Hannah was the salvation of the family. She had a ready and constant wit, which at times was the only thing that could raise her husband's spirits. Both were hard workers and had the respect of the entire community.

All four of Tom's grandparents were born in Ireland. From them he inherited their every gift except the thick Irish brogue. Both John's and Hannah's parents came from the old sod as teenagers. John's parents had met and married in Janesville. Hannah's had married in Boston and moved to the Janesville area shortly thereafter.

Tom was the oldest of four. Following him in order of age were Jim, Matt, and Bridget. Because Tom was oldest, much of the work fell on his shoulders as soon as he was capable. He loved the farm, and it was generally acknowledged the farm would one day be his. It was the Irish custom for the eldest to inherit the farm and be responsible for siblings.

The eldest Burns was a superior athlete in every sport. Time spent in athletics didn't hamper his educational progress at the secondary level, but at the college level it forced him to work extra hard just being an average student.

Tom's handsome face, his full head of hair, his physique, and, above all, his ever-present sense of humor helped much throughout the educational years. His ready wit allowed him to seem absolutely brilliant at times. His sandy hair gave him an appearance of being well-groomed without being fastidious. His alert, almost piercing gray eyes indicated an intensity in human relations that was often lacking in other areas. His school aptitude tests gave him average scores in all areas save one. The tests indicated he would excel in salesmanship.

Tom's sense of humor and ready laugh gave others the impression of an intellect he didn't possess. His ready smile and general handsome appearance often allowed him marks undeserved by his scholastic ability. If popularity were the sole measure of success he would have been capable of anything.

Jim, the second child, was the apple of his father's eye. He lacked the flair of his older brother, but he was a straight A student. He was not the athlete Tom was, but if it weren't for Tom's presence, one would have to admit he was far from clumsy.

Jim was a self-starter. He had a problem-solving mind and was often able to perform tasks with little effort that his older brother would work on overtime. Jim was in an excellent position to make fun of his older brother, but size and intelligence dictated otherwise.

Matt was the soul of kindness. Opportunities to help others literally consumed him. He was smarter than Tom and more athletic than Jim. While Jim was generally serious like his dad, Matt had a sense of humor that matched his mother's. However, where Tom would laugh intensely, Matt merely chuckled.

The attributes of the boys were not shared by Bridget. She might have had the mental capacity to be street-smart, but there weren't many streets in Janesville and none on the farm.

Bridget's humor was so lacking she failed to know it. When people laughed, for any reason, she wasn't sure whether they were laughing at her or not. She knew they weren't laughing with her because she never laughed. If a sense of humor had any place in life, she wasn't aware of it.

Tom could make it through school by athletics and personality. Jim could make it because he was a brilliant student. Matt could make it because in helping others, he first had to know things himself. Bridget made it through because John Burns, her dad, was on the school board.

When Tom graduated from high school he knew he wanted to attend college. He also knew his scholastic ability didn't warrant any scholarships.

He stopped at the rectory one evening to talk to Fr. Robert Smith, his pastor. The logical question was: "What do you want to be?" Tom had thought of his answer often but never discussed it with anyone.

Before he could respond, Father Smith provided a possible solution. "Don't you suppose that with three boys one of you ought to be a priest? Have you ever considered it?"

Tom reacted as though the thought had been plucked from his own brain. "I've thought of it all my life and often. You know the problem, Father. I don't think I have the smarts for the seminary. My aptitude tests indicate only that I'd be a good salesman."

"How will you ever know if you don't try?" questioned the priest. "Besides, the best product to sell is Jesus Christ."

"Wouldn't it require more money than I have?"

"It certainly would. The diocese would pick up the difference if you show promise. Let me scout around to see if I can find a patron, Tom. Could your dad spare you a day while you and I go to Winona to see the bishop?" continued Father Smith.

"I think so. Most of the planting is completed."

"Fine. How about tomorrow?"

Tom had wanted some advice from his pastor, something he could mull over for a while. Things were moving too fast. *I've never talked to anyone about being a seminarian, much less a priest. I'm not sure of anyone's reaction, not even the family's.*

The silence was taken as assent.

"Great, I'll be out to pick you up tomorrow morning right after Mass. Better still, you come to Mass. We'll have breakfast in Rochester. Let me check the bishop's schedule in the *Courier*.... Hmmmm. Nothing official. I'll call his office right now."

Father Smith dialed, talked, and then replaced the phone in its cradle. "He has Mass at the seminary at eleven tomorrow. He asks that we have lunch with him there. How are your table manners?"

"No one ever complained."

"The question is not whether anyone complained. The question is whether anyone taught you!" The priest smiled. Then he continued, "We'll cover that on the way to Winona."

Tom's dad's reaction was as Tom had anticipated. "I'm not sure if you can make it. You and books have never been good friends. The only way you can make it is by spending the next eight years in the study hall. Right now, you can't sit still for an hour."

"You've expressed one of my two fears, Dad."

"What's the other one?"

"Tuition."

"Well," said his mother thoughtfully, "if you aren't smart enough and you can't afford it, the deck seems stacked against you."

Tom and his mother laughed heartily as the lad went on. "I think the grace of God is going to be pushed to its ultimate."

"Now that might be the problem," said John Burns very seriously. "You know my cousin Mary Ellen. Well, she lives in a beautiful condominium on Washington Avenue in Minneapolis. She uses the skyway to get to work and back. She uses the skyway when she goes shopping. The only time she leaves the skyway is to cross the street from the bank to Saint Olaf's Church.

"Like everyone else, she has a thermostat in her car. Her problem is simple, yet dangerous. She has forgotten that God is responsible for the weather.

"Now here on the farm, even though we have a thermostat in the house, in the barn, on the tractor, and in the car, we know that hail can ruin the beans, that heat can ruin the corn, that lightning can kill a cow.

"It is only on the farm and on the golf course that one really knows there is a God. You're welcome back here anytime for your soul's sake. Otherwise, don't spend all your time studying. Get out and play some golf for your faith and eternal salvation."

"Don't suppose you two will ever make sense. I hope someday you'll have common sense," chuckled Hannah Burns. "That's about the funniest thing you've ever said."

"Wasn't intended," he responded, not certain whether he was being flattered or ridiculed.

"One more thing, Mom and Dad: could we keep this our secret

for a while? It would be embarrassing if the bishop wouldn't accept me or if I flunked out the first semester. After that, maybe I could handle it better," implored the son.

The next morning, all went according to plan. After Mass, they drove to Rochester for breakfast. From there they proceeded to the seminary in Winona. En route the pastor taught manners for table and proper decorum with the bishop.

Tom towered over the bishop. He immediately recognized that the man had a wonderful sense of humor and felt totally comfortable. The meal was rather frugal. The bishop offered him first helping, and he politely deferred.

On the return to Janesville, Father Smith complimented his parishioner for being such a good student of manners. "If you can learn that fast with the books, you'll have no problem. Or am I a good instructor?"

"The fact is," admitted Tom, "I watched the bishop and imitated him as well as I could."

"Imitation is the highest compliment. Don't I get any credit?"

"Yes, you really had me scared with everything I had to remember."

Tom filled in the application when it arrived from the chancery office. For the present, it looked like finances would be a major problem. The bishop had stated that the diocese would help only after the second year of college, so Burns was worried. His concern evaporated when the pastor informed him that an angel had come to the rescue.

Twice during the summer, the bishop had stopped at the farm. The first time he wanted to meet the family and learn more about farming. He was born and raised in Chicago and was interested in every aspect of rural life. The second time he was pleased when Tom accepted the challenge of a round of golf.

The night before classes began, the first-year seminarians were assembled in the conference room. The rector led them in prayer. Then he officially welcomed them to Immaculate Heart of Mary Seminary on the campus of Saint Mary's University of Minnesota.

"All of you are here because you have been accepted and sent by your bishops. It is a vote of confidence from them for us as well as it is for you.

"Please know that we are just as anxious to prove that their confidence has not been misplaced as you are. At any time, as the year progresses, feel comfortable coming to me or any of the staff with compliments or grievances, with joy or with sorrow, with helps or needs. May we never disappoint you.

"Saint Mary's University has a high standard of excellence. Students, seminarians or otherwise, are here to attain the best education possible. The faculty wants you to succeed.

"Don't put off your daily assignments. It is much easier to maintain your day-to-day work than it is to catch up. Time is your friend if you keep the pace. If you fall behind, time is your greatest enemy.

"It is enjoyable when you love a course. It can be hell if you don't. Loving a course or a teacher is contagious. When you need help, find someone who loves the work. Study with that person that you may be inspired also. Teach one another. Jesus established the Church to teach, rule, and sanctify. Teaching is part of your role.

"So, if you fall behind, seek help immediately from your professor or a classmate. A professor wants you to learn. This is his main purpose here. The classmate must know the subject well before having the capacity of sharing it with you.

"Are there any questions? . . . Good.

"Your schedules were placed on the desks in your rooms. Please be prompt for all exercises and classes. If there is any confusion, talk with me or an upperclassman.

"By the way, you are new here. You are prime targets for practical jokes. These should not be present among us. Indeed, the 'old-timers' have been warned against them. Now you are also warned.

"Please know that getting even or one-upmanship is never as desirable as a good sense of humor. In fact, a sense of humor in the seminary may be second only to the state of grace.

"There are refreshments on the tables in the back of the room. Use this as an opportunity to get acquainted. Good luck and God bless."

At the conclusion of the first day of class, when everyone was assembled for the evening meal, Tom tapped his water glass for attention. Once he had attained it he asked the question: "Is there anyone here who loves college algebra? I mean really loves it? Boy, do I need you."

Everyone laughed. *Here,* they thought, *is a fellow who is honest and has a monumental sense of humor.* By the end of the meal he had three volunteers who remarked, "Take your choice; we are all willing to help."

Tom thought for a moment before he responded, "I think this may be like learning bridge. I'll be the fourth while you all try helping me."

Tom Burns had always succeeded because of athletics and his sense of humor. Since there was no football at Saint Mary's and because his grade-point average made it obvious he was no genius, he decided to forgo basketball and baseball as well.

In his sophomore year he earned a letter in the winter and spring sports. In his junior and senior years he was team captain in both sports. He was still far from genius but he had developed excellent study habits.

At the conclusion of four years of study in Winona he was pleased when his Ordinary sent him to Saint Mary's Seminary at Roland Park in Baltimore. What the rector had said at Immaculate Heart of Mary Seminary now proved the case. He liked theology much more than undergraduate courses, and consequently, theology was easier.

More important, he found a friend, Robert Burke, who was a genius. Burke helped Burns in all his studies except Canon Law. Both had an equal distaste for the subject.

For the first time, Tom met a person who had absolutely no love or knowledge of sports. Burke's sense of humor was much more subtle, so at times Burns wasn't sure of its existence.

Despite their differences, they became close friends. When Tom brought Robert to the home farm, the entire family chuckled over Burke's excitement and ignorance concerning things rural. Tom found the same excitement when shown the historical places and cities in the East that were well known to his friend.

Burns also decided that no one should be ignorant of the sports world. It became his mission to develop a knowledge and love for athletics in Burke even as Robert was helping Tom have a deeper love for theology, travel, and opera.

But back to our story. After Father Burns's first Mass, his pastor took a short vacation. Father Tom was happy to cover for him. On the pastor's return, he handed Burns the letter concerning Burke's rejection by the bishop of Washington.

Upon reading Bob's note, Father Burns called the chancery immediately to make an appointment with his bishop. The bishop was at a meeting for the bishops from the province and would not return until the following Monday. Tom's request for an appointment immediately on his return was acceptable: ten o'clock Monday morning.

The bishop was, as usual, in good spirits. After listening to Burns, he quickly dictated a letter, in Tom's presence, to the bishop of Washington:

My Dear Brother Bishop in Christ,

It has come to my attention that a certain young man, Robert Burke, of your diocese, is desirous of being ordained to the priesthood.

There must be adequate reason for your denying his request. Perhaps given a change in geography, Reverend Mr. Burke may find happiness as a priest in the diocese of Winona.

If you would be willing to release him, I would welcome the opportunity to invite him here to see if he would fit into our environment. If so, we would incardinate him here with your permission.

> Fraternally in Christ,
> John G. Brezina,
> Bishop of Winona.

By return mail from Washington:

Your Excellency,

Your suggestion regarding Robert Burke is most welcome and would solve any problem we have with him. You have my blessing and permission to incardinate Mr. Burke.

> Gratefully,
> E. B. Messick
> Bishop of Washington

The bishop of Winona called Tom immediately. "Can we get together?"

"Yes."

"When?"

"Immediately."

"I'll be at the office all day. Come today."

Burns couldn't believe it. The bishop was beaming as Tom entered. "Thanks for coming on such short notice."

"You must have heard from Washington," said Tom.

"Indeed, and all is go." The bishop smiled. "What good fortune to get the best in the middle of such a priest shortage."

"What now, Your Excellency?" asked Tom.

"I have had this letter written:

"'Reverend Mr. Burke, your friend and classmate Fr. Tom Burns has informed me that you are desirous of ordination and have satisfied all the requirements except an accepting bishop.

"'The Bishop of Washington has freed you of any obligations to that see. Consequently, if our hopes can be the same, I extend an invitation to be incardinated by the diocese of Winona.

"'Please let me know your willingness by return mail. Sincerely, John G. Brezina, Bishop of Winona.

"Is that sufficient, Father Tom?"

"I think so."

"Is the address you gave me accurate?"

"I hope so."

"Then it is in the mail."

Four days later the letter was returned to the chancery office in Winona. In red ink: "Addressee has moved. No forwarding address."

A phone call to the chancery office in Washington received this reply: "We have forwarded all information concerning Robert Burke to the diocese of Winona. His file is closed."

The bishop of Winona relayed the message to Father Burns: "Any suggestions?"

"If it isn't too much, ask the office in Washington for the phone number of Fr. James O'Donnell. He would know where Bob is," responded Burns.

The bishop called and received the answer: "Father O'Donnell is in the process of establishing an office for AIDS ministry. At present we don't have any address or phone number for him."

For two people to drop from the face of the Earth didn't seem possible. Tom considered a quick flight to Washington to find Bob, but his first appointment precluded the possibility. Besides, the bishop had already spent much time on the situation and Burns wasn't sure what was precedent.

His appointment was to Saint John the Baptist in Mankato. He also taught religion classes five days a week at Loyola High School. The bishop asked him to serve as temporary athletic director and coach the B teams. Burns laughed at the latter as he recalled his conversation in the seminary with Burke. He now had the very assignment Robert Burke had considered a nightmare.

Janesville had played against Loyola when Tom was the best in the area in every sport. Now the students from both schools considered that unimportant ancient history if they were told about it. Even he recognized that past glories are quickly passed. Now it was important that Loyola defeat Janesville.

One of the best aspects of the assignment was the proximity to his parents. He loved visiting them. He also enjoyed relaxing in faded jeans as he worked with his dad in the fields and in the barn.

With each home visit, Tom became more aware of his younger sister and her situation. She was as unattractive as he was handsome. She stood less than five feet tall, even with heels. Her large facial features seemed to beg a more generous head. Thick glasses were a necessity and seemed to be the justification for her huge nose.

Bridget was void of style. Her inquisitiveness sought everything except moderation. Her dull life searched for any avenue of relief, even though it meant unlimited gossip at anyone's expense.

She remained trim despite her voracious appetite. It was almost as though her body, working overtime to digest all the food, kept her thin.

Her social graces were excellent when compared to her physical style. Her dress draped dismally down from her shoulders to her calves. Not even her belt was capable of putting a single curve in the garment. She quit wearing heels and settled for sneakers while still in high school.

A woman's crowning glory with her seemed totally unmanageable until she began combing and brushing it straight back and gathering it in a huge bun that rested on her collar. Any balance she may have had seemed totally at risk because of the tightly managed mane.

Any attraction she may have possessed for the opposite sex was never overwhelming. Bridget's want of social and physical grace seemed necessary to her as a reason for not having any romantic moments, even in her own imagination.

The three brothers accepted her for what she was. They knew it wasn't a matter of choice for them. She made it evident she was not about to change. A good sense of humor may have been her saving quality, but Father Tom had her share as well as his.

Bridget's parents recognized that fate had dealt her a poor hand and she was content, in her own way, to stand pat without so much as an ace in the hole. In John and Hannah was her salvation and condemnation.

They praised her with such eloquence that one wasn't certain whether or not they were daily kissing the famous stone of Blarney Castle. "Sure'n we don't know what we would do without you," and, "Why should you go bothering your pretty head about the future out there when you're so needed right here?"

These and like thoughts were totally devoid of reality. Their one and only daughter was absolutely helpless in the home. She couldn't bake or cook; she couldn't mend or clean; she couldn't wash or iron clothes; she couldn't make a bed or set the table. People wondered what would become of her and her parents when John and Hannah would have to face judgment day with their dissimulations and she would be an orphan.

During the one quarter she was enrolled at Mankato State University she felt herself to be totally out of her element and incapable of maintaining either a social or intellectual comfort.

She was spared similar taunts and problems when Mr. and Mrs. John Burns withdrew her from the university because it didn't seem to meet her needs.

Father Tom's second assignment was temporary. The bishop explained the situation in person: "This is an excellent appointment. When Father Connor was pastor, he was outstanding at fund raising and refurbishing the entire parish plant. He worked miracles in every way with the people.

"It is only logical that to follow him is a mighty difficulty task. The present pastor, Father Jones, pleads overwork and burnout. He is on leave of absence. You are assigned as the pastor of Saint Felix until he returns.

"Physically and financially, you are to do nothing. Father Connor left everything right.

"Good luck; God bless. Stay in touch if any problems arise."

In the seminary, Father Tom had developed a deep spiritual life. The hustle and bustle of teaching at Loyola and coaching sports as well as having parish duties gave him little time to develop the prayer life he desired.

He remembered the words of the spiritual director at Immaculate Heart of Mary Seminary in Winona counseling that if you are too busy to pray, you are too busy!

At times, in Mankato, he felt too busy. Now, in Wabasha, he was able to fashion his own schedule. Unless an emergency arose, he always made time for meditation before and after Mass. Even on his first appointment he was faithful to the Hours of the Office, which he dearly loved.

Father Tom loved Wabasha. He loved the rivers and the bluffs. His love for them had begun at Saint Mary's in Winona. He became an avid fisherman. One of the parishioners had a sailboat at Lake Pepin. He was taught sailing and was given access to the boat. The hiking and biking trails were numerous in number and gorgeous in beauty.

Most of all, he loved the people of Wabasha. They in turn loved him. Father Burns gave wonderful, appreciated sermons. He was enjoying that honeymoon time in the life of a newly ordained priest when one can do nothing wrong. Gradually, the era ended.

He continually showed improvement to the point where the parishioners took his virtues for granted and began to search for vices.

He was much chagrined, yet pleased, when he heard a youngster speak: "There is Father Burns. All he has to do is put on that dress and he can really talk." The priest appreciated the help the Holy Spirit provided much more than the parishioners appreciated the long hours he spent preparing his sermons.

The elderly used to say to Father Burns, "I sure do want you to preach at my funeral." Tom never understood that. *The funeral sermon isn't as important as the wedding sermon, or any other, for that matter,* he mused.

The days at Saint Felix ended abruptly when the bishop learned the "real" pastor had entered the monastery at New Mellerey near Dubuque, Iowa. It was time for Tom to move again.

Father Burns's appointment was to Boomer. The bishop, again, wanted to talk with him, to talk about things that really couldn't be covered adequately in a letter.

"The old church needs replacement. I think you are just the person to raise the money and build the new one. The rectory is almost as good as the day it was built, despite various pastors' improvements!"

Father Tom accepted with a heavy heart. What a change from Saint Felix. The only thing appealing was the challenge. He ignored the odds. Immediately he began a parish census to learn what he had inherited.

The Amish were everywhere. Their farms encircled the community for miles in every direction except to the south. Most of Assumption Parish consisted of widows whose husbands had long ago sold their farms to the Amish. The occasional infant heard in the church on Sunday morning was usually a grandchild whose parents had come home to visit Grandma.

The few young couples in the parish had found Boomer a cheap place to live. Taxes were low on houses that found little market when a widow's estate was settled. Groceries were expensive in the gas and food establishments, but that mattered little, since the young worked in one of the neighboring communities where prices were kept reasonable by competition.

At each Catholic home, the priest would obtain the desired information: address, phone number, names of all family members, ages, sacraments received, and faithfulness to the sacraments, and would ask: "Are you registered," and "Do you use your envelopes?"

The last question was a natural introduction to the bishop's interest in the new edifice for prayer. As a youngster, he had heard too many money sermons and had vowed he would never give one. Now, he thought, it would be much easier to talk about money with the pulpit protecting the priest from the people.

During his teaching at Loyola, he had come to the conclusion that he had excellent class attention when he had done his homework and the lesson was well prepared. On the rare occasions when he had failed to prepare and he lost the class's attention, there was one quick solution.

"All right," he would say. "If you won't pay attention, we will find out how much you know. Take paper and pencil and we will have a quiz!"

He often thought a money sermon was similar. When the priest didn't take the necessary time in preparation of the homily, he need only attack the people for their unwillingness to share burdens financially. With that concept in mind, Father Burns always prepared the sermon.

It hurt him that parishioners weren't responding to his visits. Some would say with sarcasm, "This parish is the Assumption. Everything was okay until Father Burns came. Now it is 'get some money; get some money!' We should be called Gethsemane!"

The income increased when he quit discussing monetary problems. He was much better accepted and appreciated when his home visits were strictly spiritual and friendly. In his own mind, he resolved to talk with the bishop. This parish has no future except in its history.

In the second month of Father's pastorate at Assumption of Mary in Boomer his mother had a fatal heart attack. Father Tom was the celebrant at her funeral. Father Smith gave the homily. The crowd of mourners was nearly as great as the crowd of rejoicers had been at the First Mass. She was respected and loved. Because of the number of priests who attended and the number of other mourners, it really was a happy funeral.

But for Burns, the heart and soul of the family was gone. The memory of her grand sense of humor hung like a pall over all of them. It wasn't quite so bad at first for Father Tom. He was able to return to business as usual.

The two brothers were married with children of their own. The concept of family was not lost for them. For the widower, life was suddenly a living hell. He wasn't able to take care of himself, and the added burden of Bridget made his existence untenable.

Out of sheer desperation, John Burns allowed Jim to take

over the farm. Then, presuming that the daughter would remain on the acreage, John retreated to a small house in Janesville. Bridget chose to move with her father.

Now there was just one avenue of escape for the man. Within three months of Hannah's death, Father Tom was celebrant at the wedding of John Burns and Mary Herron.

The new Mrs. Burns was a superior woman. She was beautiful and talented, possessed a remarkable personality, and had a character above reproach. Her husband had passed away when their youngest of six was a child of three. Insurance had paid the indebtedness on the house and allowed her a fair amount of capital and a modest monthly income. Her youngest was recently a college graduate.

By nature, Mary was an idealist. From experience, she was a realist. She understood Bridget was a problem early on. So when the honeymoon was over and the new Mr. and Mrs. John Burns returned to a disaster never before known by the house (due to Bridget's ineptness), the new wife determined it couldn't be a home as long as the stepdaughter remained.

Bridget told her dad she understood and didn't want to cause any problems. She would take some time visiting each of her brothers until Mary came to her senses. It seemed logical to her to start with Father Tom. He needed her most since he had no housekeeper!

She explained, to the flabbergasted priest, it would only be temporary. "It's understood that this is the best possible solution," she announced.

He agreed it was understood. Like most things understood, he didn't understand.

"After all," she observed, "the rectory is large and you'll hardly know I'm here." She continued, "You need a housekeeper."

He was aware of both situations and knew she wasn't necessary. However, since it was only temporary, he agreed. After a few months he mused unhappily to himself, *My entire life is temporary, praise God!*

Bridget couldn't manage herself or the rectory. Every inadequacy of her being became more pronounced under parishioners' scrutiny. Novenas were offered regularly to Saint Jude on behalf of the pastor. It seemed dreadfully apparent that saints, even

Jude, in the midst of eternity had forgotten what temporary was. The priest was under the control of his sister, "Mighty Mite."

There seemed no escape. No amount of prayer would produce a suitor for his sister. No matter how much faith he might have, he knew God would never take away a man's reason.

Often Father Tom thought of a story he considered very humorous when he heard it as a newly ordained. He wanted to tell it to Bridget, but she had no sense of humor. Also, now the story didn't seem funny to him either.

It was in an Irish setting. In the story, the bishop had called all his pastors to a special conference. The agenda concerned itself with many irrelevant matters until the Ordinary began discussing the issue of "housekeepers."

"Now," said the bishop, "I'm hearing stories that too many housekeepers are running the parishes. From now on, the priest is to answer the phone, the priest will answer the doorbell, the priest will count the collections, and he will decide the time for the Masses. You, the priest, the pastor, are henceforth in charge of the parish. And that includes the rectory."

Father O'Toole listened attentively and nodded his head in total agreement. After the meeting he walked slowly across town to his rectory. Once he arrived, he decided he needed some more time to strengthen his resolve. For some time he paced the sidewalk back and forth in front of the church.

Suddenly he set his jaw. He resolutely walked through a huge mud puddle on the playground, entered the rectory, and began tracking across the living room carpet.

The housekeeper cleared her throat in a most menacing way as she put her fists at her hips. "Have you taken leave of your senses?" she demanded.

Then Father O'Toole repeated the bishop's message: "From now on, I'm the pastor. I'll count the collection. I'll answer the phone and the doorbell. From now on I'm in charge!"

Molly placed her arms across her chest. "And what gives you these high and mighty ideas?"

The pastor responded with his trump card. "The bishop himself orders it!"

Molly turned heel and with finality commanded, "I forbid you to ever see that man again!"

119

Then it finally happened for Father Tom and Bridget. Temporary had ended. With unfamiliar logic she finished it. "No house should have two women in it. Dad and your brothers are married. You aren't. I've decided you need me here, and I won't abandon you."

Father Burns's bishop knew the situation, even though he pretended an unbelievable ignorance. Before Bridget, the bishop would often stop by to visit, eat, play golf, or maybe stay overnight. The bishop appreciated the needed solitude Boomer offered. He often wrote his pastoral communications in the rectory's peace and quiet.

Now, it was different. The bishop came just once to the rectory at the time of Confirmation. He endured the evening meal, slept in an unkempt bed, rose early in the morning, skipped breakfast, and slipped out.

Since that memorable occasion, Confirmation was always scheduled at two in the afternoon. Father Tom brought all the official books to the sacristy for the bishop's signature. Bridget controlled Tom 365 days of the year. She controlled the bishop one day of the year.

So it was with all Tom's priest friends. One Ash Wednesday and one Good Friday was enough. Any visiting was done on their grounds, not his. More accurately, not on her grounds. So the Boomer rectory became known as "the hermitage."

Father Tom knew he would never have a two-priest parish. There was no way a sane bishop would ever assign him an associate as long as Bridget was ensconced in "her" domicile.

Parishioners referred to her as the moat. There was no crossing her, and she protected the castle from intrusion, friendly or unfriendly.

With her arrival, the pastor stopped his home visitations that were social. Bridget had a sentence that was a real sentence for her brother: "My sources tell me . . . " Even the most innocent situations were somehow tainted with immorality, in fact or intention.

Mary Murphy was sick unto death and Father Tom was faithfully and regularly preparing her for passing on. Of that situation the housekeeper gave these words of knowledge, warning, and destruction to Father: "My sources tell me that Mary Murphy's daughter, Monica, is a very beautiful woman. My sources also tell me she is with her mother a great deal since you've begun your calls."

It sounded vicious when Bridget said things like that. It would have sounded vicious no matter who would speak that way. It sounded vicious because it was vicious.

Gradually, Father Tom's sense of humor dissipated. He became all the more amazed his mother had maintained hers. He secretly wondered if she had died trying to protect it. In any case, she should be canonized a saint.

The priest began to look over his shoulder for his sister's sources. Somehow, to his dismay, everything he said or did was presented to her by the sources, sometimes accurately, sometimes inaccurately, but always presented.

How could a woman who never left the rectory, had no friends or confidants, never had any mail, have any sources? He seriously considered stopping the phone service.

He would think to himself that if he could stand the thought of alcoholic beverages she would drive him to drink. But he hated the taste and the smell of anything alcoholic. He sometimes wished he had a hankering for it so he could tell his friends he was forgoing the pleasure as a sacrifice.

In the seminary he had to overcome his adverse reaction before he could be recommended for ordination. It wouldn't look good to the people if he had a disdainful expression on his countenance whenever he offered the Holy Sacrifice of the Mass.

The options for the future were shrinking for him. He considered the foreign missions but was not a great linguist. He thought about chaplaincy in the military but theologically was a conscientious objector. Thoughts of hospital or jail chaplain were stifled by the fact that those institutions within the diocese already had full-time chaplains or didn't have one at all.

The poor priest went on a retreat at the New Mellerey monastery. The atmosphere was a vast improvement. The bread, water, and cheese were a welcome and palatable change in diet. At first, the silence was welcome, but by the end of the week he was anxious for any voice save the one with the sources.

After much prayerful deliberation he made the decision. Henceforth he would have his office at Carolan's. He discussed the possibility with Sean. He and his wife, Colleen, were delighted at the prospect of the priest coming to their establishment every day. Just to show his appreciation, Sean said he would be happy to install a private phone in booth number one for the pastor.

So it was made official in the next Sunday bulletin without Bridget's consultation:

Beginning tomorrow, immediately after the 7:30 Mass, Father Burns will have toast and coffee in booth number one at Carolan's. Anyone wishing to make an appointment, please call 1-800-FOR HELP. Father's office hours will be kept there daily (except Wednesdays) from 8:30 in the morning until 5:30 in the evening. Anyone willing to invite your pastor for dinner in your home or in a restaurant will be honored by his presence.

Chapter 12

The pastor of Assumption Church finished his luncheon sandwich, which Colleen had made from leftovers. As he was perusing his appointment book a man came bounding into the establishment.

"Nothing to eat, nothing to drink, if I could just use your phone for a long-distance call." His face was flushed, not so much from recent activity as much as a lifetime of inactivity. "The pay phone at the highway is out of order. Please, may I use yours?"

Sean looked at the man. "For a long-distance call? We never do that." He thought, *This fellow doesn't look like he could afford a quarter for a local call.* Then he spoke on, "You're right, that phone hasn't worked in months. To make things worse, ours has caught the malady and is out of order also." Then he nodded toward booth number one. "Check with Father Burns; maybe you can use his phone."

The man turned toward the priest and looked quizzically at Father Tom. "You are a priest?"

"Yes," came the reply.

"You have a phone here?" the stranger queried further, not knowing whether the emphasis should have been on *you, phone,* or *here*.

"This is your office?" questioned the man in utter amazement. "Did the rectory burn down?"

"No, would that were the reason," meditatively responded the priest. He was burned up, but the rectory hadn't burned down.

"No matter," spoke the stranger incredulously. "My name is Dominic O. Crotty the fifth and I'm in desperate need of a phone."

123

Father looked at the man. He was quite bald on the top; his sideburns were graying. The long mane flowing down over his collar more than made up for the hair missing on top.

What can this man want with the phone? he thought. His faded jeans, denim shirt, and buttonless vest indicated a need to check with his parole officer. The scuffed boots repeated the same message.

"Dominic O. Crotty the fifth. I've been called DOC since I was an infant. The initials, you know."

"And to what purpose would you be using my phone?" asked the priest.

"To call my stockbroker," responded DOC. "I don't mean to sound impertinent, but my man expects me to call each weekday at one o'clock and it is already one-twenty."

"Stockbroker?" said the priest. It was now his turn to be incredulous. He wanted to ask more questions yet decided they would best be answered by handing DOC the phone. He had heard him mention long-distance and he couldn't afford such calls, but his curiosity allowed him to forget all but the pleading man before him.

"Sit down," said Father Tom, pointing to the opposite seat in the booth. "You're welcome to the phone." He pushed the phone in his direction.

Quickly the stranger took the phone and dialed the number. It rang several times. Finally, "Hello, Jim; DOC." Pause. "I know I'm late and I apologize. Is there anything that looks promising? Anything I should unload?" Long pause. "How's your health? The wife? The youngsters? The weather? Thanks now. I'll be on time tomorrow." He hung up.

Throughout the conversation Father Tom studied the man. He was clean-shaven. His hands were smooth and nails well manicured. His teeth were perfect and very white. Glasses covered his steel gray eyes. He seemed unaware of the fact that he was quite handsome. He was, except for the moments before the call, extremely relaxed and confident. The priest concluded that DOC was not overweight, not because of exercise, but because his eating habits suffered. The question of contradiction was evident. How could this man who seems so unaware of himself and surroundings be so intent on the stock market? The pastor was

124

intrigued. No more so, however, than DOC was intrigued by a priest who had an office in the number one booth of a saloon.

"Where you from?" asked Father Tom.

"New Jersey," responded DOC.

"What part?" continued the interrogator.

"South Jersey," he answered, knowing it was an answer both revealing and concealing.

"Near Atlantic City?" asked the priest, wondering if he had any connection to the casinos.

"Not too far," came the reply. He was answering everything in a matter-of-fact manner, but he wasn't answering at all. Then the priest realized that the questions and answers were inconsequential to DOC and were a waste of time for them both. If there was nothing important about his geographical past, perhaps the future might hold more.

"Where are you headed?" he asked.

"I have no idea," DOC responded. "I don't even know where I am."

"You're in Boomer, Minnesota. You came here from somewhere to make an urgent telephone call that could have been made anyplace—even South Jersey," the priest informed him. "What determines where you go from here?"

"The winds of whim. I'm a free spirit except for those winds. I enjoy life but don't understand it. I study it, but I don't understand the winds of whim. Isn't it insane to be driven and controlled by that of which one is ignorant?" said DOC.

Intrigued, the priest made a gesture to a small brown sack that rested between them. "Here's half a sandwich, which I couldn't finish. You're welcome to it. I'll order you some coffee."

He had suspected DOC was on drugs, but the pupils of his eyes weren't dilated and no other signs were evident. He presumed this unreal person was for real.

"Father," DOC said, "I don't know your name. Could I have an introduction?"

"Sure. I'm Fr. Tom Burns, pastor of Assumption Parish right here in Boomer, Minnesota. Any other questions?"

"As a matter of fact, yes. How long have you had your office in this saloon?" He had been told never to ask why.

"Nearly three months. This really isn't a saloon; it's Carolan's.

This is sort of the unofficial meeting place in town for everyone. It isn't that it satisfies any requirement. It is just that there isn't any other place," said Father.

"Is this a good place for people to bring their problems? Aren't they embarrassed to talk with you in public?" queried DOC.

"People don't come to me only when they have problems. I have many conversations that have nothing to do with the sacrament of reconciliation.

"Initially, though, it wasn't easy for them. They were willing to say hello and speak pious platitudes or joke about the weather. In fact, they all talked real loud so all the town would know it was just a friendly visit.

"Once they started talking with the same decibels as those in other booths, things changed dramatically. Now anyone can spend a few moments or hours without difficulty. For the most part, I'm here to listen, not talk.

"Even more important, I talk with people whom I wouldn't otherwise meet or know. Everyone comes in here and everyone says at least, 'Hi, Father.' Often the conversation starts casual and next thing one knows, a person can be in the midst of some pretty heavy counseling or spiritual direction. The difference is simple. In counseling, I listen. In spiritual direction, I talk.

"This is a fine place for an office. The best. There isn't any rent and no heat or light bills. At first Carolan's paid for the phone. Now, all I pay for is the telephone . . . which by the way . . . "

DOC dipped his hand into his pocket and took out a small roll of bills. He peeled a ten-dollar bill off and put it in front of the priest.

"Yes, DOC, my expenses are minimal here. Once in a while I have to buy a cup of coffee, but most of the time the customer pays. No, no," Father protested as DOC reached back into his pocket, "the ten will cover the call and the coffee, thank you."

"Okay, Father Tom, so this isn't a saloon. Even though that being the case, isn't it, shall we say, a bit compromising for you to be here at all?"

The priest laughed. "People in Boomer know I never imbibe spirits. Amen. Parents know their offspring won't hear vulgar and offensive language when I'm here or may come in unannounced and unexpected. Even the walls in the facilities are kept lily white.

At least in the men's room. Every establishment such as this should have a full-time member of the clergy as a constant guest."

Almost as though to check the veracity of the priest, DOC slid out of the booth and went to the room marked GENTS. Regardless of his reason, he came forth eventually looking satisfied. He studied the place thoroughly but quickly, stopped for a brief moment at booth number one, looked gratefully at the priest, thanked him, and left.

As DOC departed, Father shouted after him, "May we meet again! God bless you!"

"It all depends on the whim of the winds. Bye now," said DOC.

The priest reopened his appointment book and saw nothing, so he opened his Office to read the Psalms.

The next day at almost the exact same time, DOC returned. "I made my one o'clock call on my own phone, Father."

"You did?" asked the priest. "And where is your own phone?"

"At the house, the house I rented after I left here yesterday. I checked at the bank to see if it had rental property and am extremely fortunate. The house on the northeast corner of Elm and Main was available, so I moved right in. Had the phone connected by four o'clock. No furniture yet except appliances. Want to go somewhere to select a bed, table, and easy chair?" DOC rambled on.

"Thanks all the same," said the priest as he shook his head, partly from amazement and partly because of schedule. "I have an appointment for marriage counseling in about ten minutes."

"Where would you recommend I go?" asked DOC.

"Well, Rochester, LaCrosse, Winona, and Decorah are all less than an hour away. Fountain and LeRoy have fine furniture stores also. Where did you sleep last night?" asked the priest.

"In my van. It is set up for sleeping. Father, if I wait until tomorrow, would you want to accompany me?"

"Well," responded the priest, "I'm free at four. Would you want to wait until then?"

"Sure thing." DOC smiled. "Meanwhile I can get set up here."

DOC went outside to his van and returned shortly with some books under his arm. Without hesitation, he moved like a homing pigeon to booth number three. He shouted past booth number two to the pastor, "I noticed this heart on the tabletop in this booth! I

127

need to study it for a while! Do you know whether or not it has a history?"

"No, I don't, DOC. I've asked about it and no one seems to know. Isn't it interesting that all the other tables are filled with initials and symbols, yet that one has just the heart and the letters saying: 'J.C. loves?' Everyone treats that booth with respect," offered the priest.

The people of Boomer wondered about DOC. He seemed to know everything. He seemed to have been everywhere. But to all the questions he would merely respond, "I like to discuss ideas first, places second, and people last. And I find myself a very dull person."

At first they didn't know how to react to that. Everyone knew everything about everyone in the community. They knew the good and the bad. They accepted and were accepted.

The old people stayed distant because there was too much unknown. The youngsters felt close to him for the same reason. He in turn had a total respect for everyone. He welcomed everyone to booth number three even as Father accepted anyone in booth number one. The smaller the town, the greater percentage of characters. DOC was obviously a character.

DOC had nothing to hide. He was an only child. His mother was overprotective; his dad was extremely rich. No matter what one's name, to add the fourth needs no further explanation. He was certain his son, Dominic O. Crotty V, would also make an imprint on society.

Young Dominic would ask his dad, "What is the O for? Or is O'Crotty one name?"

The father would respond, "The O stands by itself. It is as much a name as Dominic. Crotty doesn't need an O. Besides, people will call you DOC as they have called me and three generations of Dominic O. Crottys in the past."

Because his dad wanted the best for young DOC, he had a butler who spoke only French to the boy and a maid who spoke Spanish and German. Consequently, languages came easily for the lad. He attended the best private schools, first in Baltimore and then in Boston. He graduated from Yale at the age of twenty with a double major in English and history.

The father was anxious that DOC the fifth would join him in

business. He had been disappointed when the son refused to major in business but knew his stubbornness as well as precociousness was an honest inheritance.

He loved school. He studied for his master's degree in English at Villanova. He received his master's degree in history from Boston College. Then he went to Harvard for his doctorate in both. In his Harvard time, DOC's mother passed away. He didn't know his mother well but knew she protected him from his father's wrath.

Up to this point an exasperated parent pretended understanding and even appreciated his son's intellectual prowess. Now he asked his son to enter the business world with him.

DOC wasn't interested in the real world. He wanted to understand it, not from a historical point of view and certainly not from a business point of view. He wanted to understand the very being of the real world. Against his father's judgment he began the study of philosophy at the Sorbonne in Paris. Within three years, the perpetual student had his doctor's degree in philosophy. He returned to the States and threw his energies into psychology at Princeton.

At the beginning of his second year at Princeton his father ceased funding his idiocy. "Enough is enough and this had been more than enough. It is time to quit hiding behind books and get on with life."

DOC could understand his dad's frustration but knew the frustration would be heightened if he tried to put this square peg in the round hole his father had fashioned.

For the rest of the term, DOC began to accept money for tutoring his classmates who were in need. He had been tutoring others since his sophomore year at Yale, so the only difference now was the remuneration.

In a conference with his adviser over his dad's actions, DOC was informed that the university was looking for a temporary professor to replace Dr. Sharpe, who was recuperating from a nervous breakdown. The class was titled The Philosophical Origins of Atheistic Communism. DOC had studied Hegel and Feuerbach and understood their influence on Karl Marx. He applied for the position.

The new professor loved teaching. He had a thorough knowledge of the material and loved young people. Each class provided an exhilarating experience. He spent hours in Dr. Sharpe's office helping students.

There appeared just one insurmountable obstacle to his professional career: grading! He had no difficulty presenting exams; his problem was in grading them.

DOC was certain that every student deserved an A. If they didn't, it was a reflection on him, not them. If anyone were to get less than an A, it meant DOC either didn't know the subject or was incapable of teaching it.

He was satisfied that an A was deserved by all, as were the students, but Princeton frowned on the probability of an all-perfect class with a perfect professor. The perfect philosophy professor humbly left the position.

During DOC's short career in the teaching field, his father was killed in a plane accident. It happened when his company's Lear jet went down on a business trip to the Kenai Peninsula in Alaska during the salmon run.

DOC inherited the business, the money, the homes, everything. He called a hasty meeting of the board to explain his absolute inadequacy. His woeful explanations left no doubt in their minds.

He suggested that the seven of them would elect a vice president in absentia. Every four years a new vice president would be chosen. Further, he gave each of them equal shares in 49 percent of the company's assets. He maintained 51 percent so that they couldn't sell the business without his permission. Each day at one in the afternoon, he would call his vice president–broker for a report. Unless, of course, he was climbing Mount Everest or engaged in some other like enterprise.

After the "business" meeting, DOC finished his career as a student and became a world traveler. The day he stopped in Boomer was all happenstance. He was in the midst of his latest whim of exploring caves of the world and was on the way to Niagara Cave near Harmony.

Dominic O. Crotty found a pastor with an office in a booth of a saloon much more intriguing than any cave. He never needed an excuse for anything he had ever done, but this was close to one. Then, too, he could return to his caves whenever the whim struck.

He had asked Sean if the priest in booth number one was good for business. The immediate response was: "Indeed, indeed. During the daytime hours, very few came. Now there are always people here. This has become a social place in the morning and afternoon. Every card club in town meets here. The women especially appreciate not having to clean house or even remember whose turn it is to hostess. Sometimes they bring their own refreshments; sometimes I provide. Oh, yes sir! He is good for business."

DOC had good lighting installed in booth three. He had the permission on the condition that he would cover the cost. Atop the table, next to the wall, he placed his books neatly between two simple bookends. Then he began to read.

Father never played cards, so it was convenient that DOC was present whenever a fourth failed to show for bridge, five hundred, or pinochle. The priest began to take lessons in the "sport." He never resented DOC's presence but sometimes had negative thoughts about his popularity. Gradually everyone was taking to the professor.

One day the priest asked DOC about sports. DOC professed he knew nothing of sports and was totally disinterested.

Father Tom didn't know whether to feel sorry for Dominic or secretly gloat over the fact that there was an area in which he was totally superior. He also didn't know that the resident in booth number three was 51 percent owner of the Phillies baseball team and of the new pro football team in Baltimore. To DOC it was of no consequence.

One area in which both were ardent advocates was education. In no way was Father Tom the scholar that Dominic was, but he was no less interested.

The curiosity of youth began paying handsome dividends at Carolan's. As the young became better acquainted with DOC they soon found he was a veritable encyclopedia anxious to share his wealth of knowledge.

As he had tutored classmates at the university, he began helping any youngster who came in search of knowledge. Booth number three became a study hall, classroom, and workshop.

The high school teachers were initially amazed at their students' keen interest in classwork and the completion of homework.

131

DOC challenged the students and they found it unbelievably exciting.

Often when he had read a book, he would give it to a student for perusal. When the student completed the book, the youngster and DOC would discuss it at great length. DOC never kept a book he had read, except in his head. The youngsters of Boomer were all proud owners of ever-growing libraries.

Sometimes DOC would invite Father Tom into a discussion that pertained to religion. The professor had great knowledge about religions of antiquity but seemed to know little of current theology and began having a lively interest.

On one occasion the pastor had commented, "I never see you at Assumption. Can I presume you attend the Presbyterian services?"

"No," said DOC, "I've never gone to church. Dad never had any religion as far as I know. Until recently, I never had much thought concerning church. In college I found out that generally a person was more acceptable if he had some religious affiliation. One of my profs said he became a Universalist because only larger cities had places of worship. Since talking to him I've always claimed to be a Universalist. The prof never told me what the denomination holds as doctrine, and I've never investigated."

Father Tom didn't pursue it further. He was satisfied the professor wasn't an avowed atheist. At the same time, with all the influence DOC had on Boomer's youth, the priest wished DOC were a dedicated Christian.

DOC never had the courage to tell his priest friend the only course he ever taught was Atheistic Communism. That might be too much for Father. Indeed, DOC hadn't told anyone anything about his past. He was lavishing himself with the present joys.

One evening a large group had assembled in booth number three. It exploded into booths number two and four, and extra chairs were drawn up to the edge of the table.

DOC called over to the priest, "Father, I think we need you!" All the students looked over to booth number one, where the pastor was working on the Sunday homily.

He stood up and walked through the assemblage. "Hank," shouted DOC to one of the boys, "bring that chair over here for Father!"

Hank obliged. "Okay, DOC."

"Repeat your question, Angie," DOC encouraged one of the girls.

She blushed. "How can I have free will if God knows everything I am about to do?"

The priest smiled. "That question has triggered some of the great heresies in the church. I think the problems comes from the fact that your question is a question of the will and it needs to be translated into time and eternity."

He continued, "Humans basically have three time references. We have the past, the present, and the future. We are capable of placing ourselves in any one of these times in our own minds."

"Some people don't like to recall the past and are successful in blotting it out. Some are afraid of the future and make no plans beyond dinner. Healthy people are content with the present. They are happy where they are."

He looked about to see if his words were registering and then moved ahead. "For instance, Angie, suppose that you had a wonderful time at the school dance last night. You don't want that moment to die; you want it to live. So you ask your memory to let you relive last night now. You can close your eyes and hear the music, appreciate the dance steps, and enjoy. Now, in the present, you enjoy it once more."

Father glanced at DOC, who was listening attentively. "The same with the future. Angie, suppose you have a date for next Friday night. You've dated this fellow before and had a great time. The date is in the future, but now instead of memory, which brings the past to the present, you use your imagination to bring the future to the present. Again you can imagine your date at the door talking with your dad, awaiting your entrance. You can, by your imagination, make next Friday night now. It is like the old, old song, 'I Can Dream, Can't I?' "

Everyone chuckled as Father continued, "Again, then, humans can bring everything to the present by memory or imagination. We are finite creatures of time. God, on the other hand, is infinite. He exists in eternity. Notice, I didn't say existed or will exist. He exists. He is."

"When Moses spoke to God in Exodus 3:14, he asked Him, 'Whom shall I say sent me?' God's response was: 'I Am sent you.'

"God, in the Bible, calls himself I Am Who Am or I am existence in the present tense, eternally.

"The Greek word *kronos* means time. It refers to time as known to people. From it we derive our word *chronology*, which refers to things placed in a time sequence. The Greeks also had the work *kairos*, which refers to God's time or fullness of time, eternity. The Bible used both words referring to Christ: 'He is God and Man.'

"The Judeo-Christian tradition says that 'God knows all things.' We don't say God knew or will know. He knows. He exists in the present tense.

"So," continued the priest, with DOC's and everyone's undivided interest, "God knows what we are doing now. He knows, not knew, what we did yesterday. He knows, not will know, what we do tomorrow. He also knows that what we do today, did yesterday, or will do tomorrow is of our own free will or it is not a human act."

"But," interrupted Angie, "sometimes people are forced to do things they don't want to by others."

"That's right," responded Father Tom. "That is why we make the distinction between a human act and an act of man. A human act is that which a person does freely. An act of man is anything that a person does, whether freely or not. If I intentionally break a window, it is a human act. If I am frightened by lightning and instinctively jump through the window, it is an act of man.

"Ignorance is a destroyer of freedom. Christ said he was 'the way, the truth and the light.' He also says, 'The truth will make you free.' That is the reason we are so fortunate in Boomer to have DOC with us. He comes as a teacher. He comes to overcome any ignorance, and consequently prejudice, within our community.

"Are there any more questions?" asked the priest. Hearing none, he turned toward DOC. "Thanks for asking me over."

DOC answered in all honesty, "Thank *you*, Father Tom. That was most interesting and informative for all of us." He was amazed at his new admiration for the priest.

Father returned to his booth. He wasn't sure what had happened. Did DOC ask him over to ask what would be an embarrassing question? Was DOC offering him a pulpit in booth number three? Did DOC need help? DOC could have made light of Angie's question and moved on to another matter. He could have silenced her by saying, "Why don't you ask Father or your minister sometime?" as if it was unimportant because it was about God. Did DOC consider him a good theologian? DOC certainly knew Father wasn't sharp in philosophy.

One thing that had happened was obvious to everyone. Father considered it with mixed emotion. He had stated openly that DOC was a welcome teacher in the community and had his respect.

What he had said he said with conviction, but all the same he wished DOC would go to church, any church. He could teach so much by his example, so much in the one area in which he never ventured.

From that time on, any time DOC was presented a question on religion, either from the people or from reading, he always invited the priest's knowledge and wisdom.

Sometimes Father wished DOC would say to the questioner, "I never thought about that before. Let's think about it. Meanwhile, I'll talk with Father and we will all discuss it tomorrow night." But DOC always stayed totally within his own parameters and never discussed religion, positively or negatively. The priest thought, *The silence is negative.*

Regardless of what anyone else thought about the activities in booths number one and three, Sean Carolan was absolutely pleased. "Things couldn't be better," he said to himself.

But they got even better. DOC had talked to a dealer in Decorah, and all at once Carolan's had air-conditioning from "Anonymous." "Gosh," said Sean in an unusual show of humor, "I thought all 'Anonymous' ever did was write poetry."

DOC never told how wealthy he was. Perhaps he didn't know. He knew he didn't want anyone approaching him for anything but learning. He loved filling open minds.

Because of this, on one occasion he entered booth number one to keep a half-hour appointment he had made with the priest. "Father," he said, "in my travels I've met people from time to time who have substantial wealth. I stay in touch with some of them. One of them is willing to offer college scholarships for the deserving and the needy. Could we be a committee of two to help this fellow decide who is deserving and needy in Boomer?"

The pastor of Assumption Church was enthusiastic. "That is the best news ever in Boomer. Can this be the first meeting of our committee?"

"On two conditions," answered DOC. "First, you are the chairperson. Second, you tell the student, not I, that the person is to be a recipient."

"Agreed."

"Don't you think our committee should help decide what college is best for the student? I know the school counselor has had input and she is good. Let the student approach her first and then return to us . . . I mean you," DOC suggested.

"Between the two of us, we should be able to help pick the right place for further education. I have friends who seem to know a plethora of colleges," DOC concluded.

The two nodded in happy agreement and DOC picked up his book from the table and ambled back to booth number three for further perusal.

Chapter 13

Moving back in time again, early one Monday morning, Father O'Donnell and Robert Burke had begun the journey from Minnesota back to Washington. They made stops in Milwaukee, Chicago, Kalamazoo, Fort Wayne, and Scranton to complete their investigation of diocesan programs in the AIDS ministry. They discussed Bob's future each day. He asked the question, "Do you think our bishop's successor might ordain me?"

"There is no way to know. The present personnel members would request it."

"How old is the bishop? When is mandatory retirement for bishops?"

"I don't know how old he is. I think they retire at age seventy."

"You know, Father Jim, I'm getting angrier each day over his refusal to ordain me. I don't know what I would do without your friendship. It looks like the bishop's tenure is not short," said Burke.

"The real question we have to face, Bob, is what about the meantime?" said the priest as though he was thinking aloud.

"Do you have anything in mind?"

"My education hasn't prepared me for a great number of things. We both know that. I'm really interested in helping you create the AIDS ministry in the diocese. If I could fit in, would there be a salary?" asked Burke.

"So far, every such ministry in each diocese has a paid staff of at least three. The salary isn't much, as you know, but it has never been less than fifteen thousand a year," was the partial answer.

Bob presumed that the discussion on salary precluded the question that he would be hired. "Living costs are high in Washington."

Bob continued, "Where will you have the office? What are the plans?"

Father Jim spoke thoughtfully and slowly. "Once upon a time, Saint Veronica's was one of the richest parishes in the city. It had a good school. The convent housed sixty-four sisters. When everyone began the migration to the suburbs the parish was decimated. Most people who live in the area now are not Catholics. The parish has been closed for nearly five years. It's for sale but hasn't been sold. What do you think?"

"I think, *Great!*" Burke spoke with exhilaration. "We could live in the rectory. Initially, the convent could be used as the infirmary. The school could be used to instruct people about AIDS. The parish hall could be the exercise area. In fact, we could use the school as a youth center for the area. The people who are there now have nothing. I think Christ might bless such a situation."

"It is amazing how much we think alike," responded Father Jim. "This could really be a magnificent opportunity."

"Do you think the bishop will allow it to sail?" questioned Burke.

"It depends on how it is approached. Concerning AIDS, he has demonstrated an ignorance. Ignorance has led him to fear, and fear so easily introduces hysteria. Nothing less than hysteria would be the cause for his refusal to ordain you. Saint Veronica's provides the perfect setting. It is a distance from the chancery office. That is good. We will give him regular reports. That is good. He can remain aloof and responsible at the same time.

"Meanwhile, we do what is necessary for our ministry's success. We pray. We pray. We pray."

"Where the bishop is concerned, I think the pronoun should be first person singular, *I*, referring to you. Where God is concerned we can use the first person plural; *we* should be used. You will see and report to the bishop. We shall pray," rejoined Burke.

Father Jim agreed. "In fact, I won't even mention your name as a member of the staff. It would serve no purpose."

The following day, as the pair was leaving Chicago, Bob introduced a whole new subject. "Could we speak more of my future?"

138

"Of course," invited the priest.

"I've been thinking. If there is no possibility I will ever be ordained, perhaps I should consider being a doctor."

"Bob, you would be in your thirties before you'd get your shingle."

"I know. But if I don't, I'll be thirty just as quickly," responded Burke. "I could work with you. I'd have to for tuition. In fact, the salary probably wouldn't cover tuition."

"Where would you want to study?" asked Father Jim.

"Georgetown," came the answer.

"That's a lot of money," Father O'Donnell replied.

"That's a lot of education. Your dad is a doctor. Is there some fund he is aware of that could be tapped?" persisted Bob.

"As a matter of fact, Dad is on at least two Georgetown scholarship committees. Let's check with him," Father Jim said joyfully.

Good news suddenly became the order of the day. The bishop was pleased with the report and the requests. Saint Veronica's Church became the headquarters for the diocesan AIDS ministry.

Bob contacted the doctors and nurses who had been such caring friends of his mother. He explained the situation of the new ministry. Volunteers from their number and from their friends not only helped organize the program but ensured its success with their donated help.

The diocesan newspaper carried a series of articles authored by Robert Burke under the pen name of Father O'Donnell. The secular press featured the venture at its inception and regularly carried updates on its progress.

The other good news was the scholarship to Georgetown arranged through the work of Father Jim's dad. Bob immediately registered in premed. The school reviewed his scholastic ability and told him if he were to attend the summer sessions he would finish premed in a year's time. He was elated.

Burke's favorite classes were in qualitative and quantitative analysis. Chemistry was his interest. He was determined to become a doctor, a doctor who would spend whatever time necessary in an experimental laboratory.

The results would be fame and maybe fortune, but that was to be the result, not the purpose, of his work. His ambition was totally singular. He would discover the cure for AIDS. He could do it. He would do it.

Once he was successful, no one would ever again have to suffer as his mother had suffered. All his talents, his energies, his time, his money had one purpose. He would satisfy a world's need.

His daily labors of love at Saint Veronica's found him ever watchful, ever alert. Each person might provide an answer. Time spent with volunteer nurses and doctors was relished by the premed student. Each moment might provide an invaluable observation for his future need.

He was always aware that learning from the classroom and from Saint Veronica's was one and the same. He read; he listened; he observed and somehow knew that one day it would all come together as the answer he sought.

As it had been in the seminary, he was at the head of the class in premed at Georgetown. Long hours at Saint Veronica's seemed to add to his enthusiasm and endurance rather than detract from his formal education.

Conversations, especially with the doctors at Saint Veronica's, indicated that the University of Minnesota Medical School was a leader in AIDS research. Consequently, he was determined to obtain his degree from that school.

Again the problem of finances became a paramount concern for Burke. He applied for several scholarships, but none seemed available to him. Georgetown gave him glowing recommendations. Father O'Donnell, as head of the AIDS ministry, was lavish with praise in his letter to the Minnesota school.

Then, an idea came to Burke. *Why not?* he thought. *I've nothing to lose.* He called the bishop for an appointment and received an affirmative answer. As he sat across the desk he first listened to the man.

"Well, Mr. Burke, my apology for not keeping in touch with you. I owe you my thanks, which I've never expressed. I was worried that your friends and family might come to the Cathedral on ordination day and I would have been embarrassed to explain the situation to them.

"I sincerely appreciated it when you had your mother's funeral on that day, so those people were with you and not at the Cathedral.

"By the way, some bishop out west tried to get in touch with you. I didn't have your address or phone number, so I couldn't help him. I don't remember which bishop.

"Now, Mr. Burke, what can I do for you?"

Robert had never seen the bishop in such a pleasant mood. *Maybe my luck is on the good side,* he thought. He leaned forward in the chair in the direction of the bishop.

"Your Excellency, to bring you up-to-date . . . I have just completed my premed courses at Georgetown. The field in which I am interested is most emphasized at the University of Minnesota in Minneapolis."

The bishop interrupted, "And what field is that?"

Bob hesitated, then stated very deliberately, "AIDS research, Bishop."

The bishop flushed briefly, then cleared his throat, but said nothing.

Burke continued, "In the eight years I studied for the priesthood for the diocese I was funded entirely by my mother. Her illness dissipated whatever funds she had. I was able to obtain a full scholarship for Georgetown.

"At present, no moneys are available for Minnesota. I have come to petition you, Bishop, for financial help so I may pursue studies leading to my becoming a doctor."

Bob knew the answer from the bishop's expression without any vocal proof. His Excellency was searching diligently for the right words.

"My dear son, would that the diocese had such a fund for every deserving candidate who wants to be a teacher, a lawyer, a doctor, or whatever. The fact is, we don't have such a fund.

"However, I want to help you as your bishop. Please send me an itemized statement of costs for your textbooks, and I will reimburse you. Thanks, again, for being considerate of the diocese and me at the time of ordinations and your mother's funeral. Let me know if there is ever a time when I can be of assistance. God bless, you my son. I'm sure you'll find a way to solve your financial problems."

"Your Excellency," protested Burke, asking for more time by his tone, "I need to say something. The English used to say, 'Britannia rules the waves.' The Irish, in response, would exclaim,

'Britannia waives the rules!' I think you speak as the Englishman and I speak as the Irishman.

"I believe the church is both human and divine. It is obvious she is divine because she was instituted by the Son of God. She is human because he gave authority to the Apostles. Sometimes the greatest proof of the church's being divine is that it survives the human element in every century.

"Both the human and the divine are capable of love. We expect it of God. God expects it of us. Sometimes we blame God for the cruelty in the world. He can always blame us.

"A definition for *liturgy* is 'celebrating where the people are.' That should be a definition of the church, a constant celebration where the people are. A pastor must celebrate with his flock where they are, not where he wants them. A successful orchestra doesn't play fox-trots for people who know only how to waltz.

"My mother would have thought she had gone to heaven without dying if you had visited her just once. Her pain would have been much less for that one moment. But you decided you were above visiting anyone with AIDS. Any celebration was impossible for you and for her.

"I appreciate the money the diocese is now spending on the AIDS ministry. I feel, as far as the guests are concerned, the funds could as well come from any number of sources. You haven't taken ownership of the program, and I have a feeling that is your way of helping without dirtying your hands.

"Your Excellency, your schedule of rules and regulations may keep you overworked, but let me tell you this: if you were to come to Saint Veronica's one hour a week, talk with the people, and bless them, it would be putting yourself where your money is."

The bishop stood to full stature at his side of the desk. "Robert Burke, you may leave. I never want to hear from you again. Never!"

"And you won't!" rejoined Burke. "I guarantee you, you will never hear from me again. But mark my words, you may one day hear about me in spite of you. Good day. And again I say in parting, it would be 'meet and just' to visit the sick."

It had been a long time since the air in Washington, D.C., had ever seemed so clean to Bob. He walked around the block a few times to breathe as much as possible before returning to his normal self and then to Saint Veronica's and his one true friend, Father O'Donnell.

"Well, what happened?" asked Father Jim.

"Three guesses," responded Bob.

"I suspect I only need one: no deal! I'd have to say this, however: in the midst of denial, you sure look happy."

"The better word would be *satisfied*. In fact, I'm more happy than if he had given the affirmative to my request," said the priest's young friend.

"You want to tell me about it?"

"Yes. For beginners, I wouldn't have said the things I did if I were a priest. In essence, I told him it was all right for bishops to have and display heart. I let him know that all the diocesan funds aren't as important as one visit he could make to Saint Veronica's. Once a week, that is. I let him know I was bitter because he had never visited my mother. Almost as bitter as she would have been happy had he done so."

"Do you think it did any good?" queried the anxious Father O'Donnell.

"I'm not sure if it did him any good at all, but it sure did me a lot of good," asserted Bob.

"Well, if you are in a better mood over the incident, we should talk about your future," continued the priest.

"I'm ready for anything but really would prefer good news."

"This may be the best. You may not know it, but two of our volunteers, Dr. Schultz and Dr. Scheidel, are partners in Dad's clinic. Dad mentioned to them, a few months ago, that you were interested in the University of Minnesota Medical School, their alma mater. He explained your financial need but, more important, your intention of dedicating your life to AIDS research. They have both written letters of recommendation, as have I and three others interested in AIDS, to the university.

"But the best news is yet to come. You certainly remember Becky Carpenter, your mother's friend and nurse. Which reminds me, you aren't staying in touch with her very well. Anyway, she and three of your mother's other friends remember you more than you remember them."

143

"How is that?" asked Bob.

"They have kept in touch with me concerning your progress. They are concerned about your physical, mental, and spiritual welfare.

"All four confess to one shortcoming in their lives. God knows they can afford a dollar each for the lottery. They consider it extra money for the government."

"What does that have to do with me?" queried Burke.

"Well," continued the priest, "last week they picked the winner. Forty-two million dollars! That is ten million, five hundred each.

"Becky told the others she was going to pay for your education. Since none of the four have any children, it was decided each would pay an equal share. They are interested in finding the solution for AIDS.

"What do you think . . . ? Are you still interested in spending the rest of your life in AIDS research? If so, you're in." The priest beamed.

Robert Burke couldn't believe the message. He had heard and understood the words, but the message was beyond his comprehension. He sat down. After a few moments he responded, "Mom must be watching over me, and she sure has found me some wonderful guardian angels. I promise you, Father Jim, and you can promise the powers that be, I will never disappoint them. I put my hand to the plow on our trip from Minnesota, and I'll never look back." He paused for a moment. "That is almost a play on words. I said 'from Minnesota, and I'll never look back.' The truth is, I'm going back to Minnesota."

Everything he owned fit into two suitcases and a handbag. He had no one to whom he needed to say farewell except the people of Saint Veronica's, the doctors, the nurses, the guests, his "guardian angels," and, of course, Father O'Donnell. Robert Burke boarded the first plane scheduled for Minneapolis after the following Sunday Mass.

Burke had always been a dedicated scholar. He continued to excel in medical school. His professors recognized his innate intelligence and his zeal to succeed. They appreciated his thirst for knowledge and satiated it to the best of their abilities.

Those about him could complain of cold winter days or a "dog day" of summer. They could speak of the short days of December or the length of a day in June. For Bob Burke, however, there seemed no season, no temperature change, no moment of equinox. Every moment was simply time that brought him ever closer to the final solution, the discovery of the medicine to cure AIDS.

Only twice did his direction and energy flag. Both times he had been sent to another department of experimentation, the department of sports medicine. He protested that it was not according to his contract with the university, which specified that he was to work strictly in AIDS research.

The university's response was clear: "This has been ordered by the National Collegiate Athletic Association. What is sought is a medication which will provide any desirous athlete with the ability to run one hundred meters in seven seconds."

"I don't know much about sports, but I know what distance one hundred meters is and how quickly seven seconds pass. It can't be done," protested Burke.

The doctor looked at Bob. "Some say there will never be a cure for AIDS."

The argument angered Burke. He knew the cure wouldn't be found if the NCAA kept interfering. He began to resent the fact that a friend in the seminary, Tom Burns, had interested him in sports.

Almost as though to add to Burke's discomfort, Dr. O'Toole, a sports enthusiast, was his coworker in working for the miracle to speed up a small portion of the human race.

By some quirk of fate and lucky gambles, the pair resolved the impossible problem within three months. It amounted to special exercises combined with special dietary combinations. Dr. O'Toole was thrilled. The NCAA was elated. Bob was chagrined over the ridiculous waste of time spent on the project.

In the middle of Bob's fourth year at the university, the head of the department of sports medicine again requested his presence. Beside him was Dr. O'Toole.

"Okay, what does the NCAA want this time? And the answer is 'no,'" said Bob.

The department head gave no heed to the protest. "This time it is not only the NCAA. The NBA is financing this project."

Burke thought, *Let's see now; what did Burns say the NBA was? Oh, yes, the National Basketball Association.* Then aloud: "And what do the giants want this time? And the answer is 'no'!"

"They are interested in research that would allow anyone wanting to have the ability to reach a mark twelve feet high, from a standing jump, to do so," said Dr. O'Toole.

"This is a joke?"

"It may be, but the desired result is worth eighteen million dollars to the university if we succeed. Three million if we fail. We have twelve months to complete the study," gloated O'Toole.

"In that time, how many people will die of AIDS? The answer is 'no'!"

"This has been cleared by Dr. Conley, the AIDS research chairperson. Please don't forget, you are still a student." Dr. O'Toole reminded him.

Burke grudgingly complied. One month before graduation from medical school he completed his project for the NBA. Again success. He warned those who congratulated him, "Remind the athlete it isn't automatic. They must train right and eat right."

Robert Burke received the Doctor of Medicine in June. He feared remaining at the university because of the two intrusions by the NCAA. He was very grateful, however, that through those intrusions he became convinced of the medicinal benefits of diet.

Some of his classmates were leaving for the Mayo Clinic in Rochester to complete their internships. He had the deepest respect for Mayo and applied there with the hope that he could continue his labors in research. Fortunately, the clinic had recently received a large grant for AIDS research. He was highly recommended for the Mayo project by the University of Minnesota. To make certain what was expected of him, he agreed to come on the condition that his time and energy would be spent solely in AIDS investigation.

Mayo was delighted. The majority of doctors had a great interest in the field but preferred not to work on the research thereof, as there was always some fear of contagion.

Dr. Robert Burke was allowed to work as the spirit moved

him. His long hours of dedication allowed his request for several assistants to be granted. His mental attitude was catching, but his energies were beyond others' limitations. All of his colleagues shared his ambitious desire to discover the cure for the feared malady.

As he grew closer to others in the program, he gained their total respect and admiration. They began to call him Dr. Bob. All were aware of his intensity and devotion. At the university, his research had become more important than an active participation in religion. His faith was totally abandoned.

The medical world was making monumental strides. One after another, the world's diseases were becoming history. Even the common cold was not only uncommon, but nonexistent.

The most celebrated discovery was the cure for cancer. Because of such universal success in medical research, the labors of Dr. Robert Burke took not only front and center stage, but all the stage. He was searching for the final solution in the annals of medical science.

As his notoriety grew, it was natural that he would be in demand as a lecturer. At first, he resisted because it would remove him from the laboratory. Then he was notified that continued funding would depend on his availability for talks. His affirmative answer was given on the condition that all his personal appearances would be limited to Rochester. He had no objection to his lectures being televised.

He noted that among all the people who attended was a very attractive black-haired nurse with beautiful blue eyes. Despite her ever-present attentiveness, her countenance always bore a radiant smile. Often she would remain for the question-and-answer session.

On one occasion, while she was waiting for a nurse friend at the exit, he paused to ask if she was alone. She explained that she was waiting for a companion, but the caretaker's locking the doors seemed adequate proof that her friend had departed.

"I'm rather tired from the lecture tonight," Dr. Burke said. "Would you be kind enough to accompany me for a late night snack?"

"I can't think of anything I'd rather do," she answered honestly. "In fact, after I attended so many of your presentations, you must think I'm stalking you."

Dr. Bob laughed. "Do you have any favorite place?"

"You invited me, which means you should pay, which means you choose!"

It wasn't until they had settled in the booth and placed their orders that he asked her name. "I'm at a disadvantage. You know the name of tonight's speaker, but the speaker doesn't know your name."

"I'm Elliota Burton," she responded.

"So you are Elliota Burton!" he exclaimed like a great mystery had been solved.

"I didn't know I was notorious," she ventured.

"Notorious? You are the subject of more coffee breaks than all the rest of the nurses put together," he answered.

"Do I get any explanation for that remark?"

"Of course. You are a wall, not a door," he explained.

"Yes?" Her eyes and voice searched for an explanation.

"You must know what I mean."

"I'm totally at a loss." She was completely baffled.

"To more than one date you responded to his overtures with words from the Song of Songs. You said, 'Do not arouse, do not stir up love before its time.' That is a quote from chapter 3, verse 5, and chapter 8, verse 4."

"I knew it was from the Song of Songs, but what is this I'm a wall and not a door?" she asked.

"From the same book of the Bible, chapter 8, verse 9. A wall refers to a woman who has high moral values, a chaste and pure woman, as the king wants his bride to be. A door refers to a woman with easy or no morals," he explained.

"So the coffee breaks project me as a prude?"

"Indeed they do! I don't agree. I would say you are prudent. Whenever I hear the conversation, I thought, *She must be a wonderful woman. I'd like to meet her.* And now, quite by chance, I have." He smiled.

"It must be by chance," agreed Elliota. "I understand you work morning, noon, and night and have no time for a social life."

"That's true," he said. "It has always been true, now that I think about it."

"You must have had a social life sometime," stated Elliota.

"I guess it depends on one's definition of social life," he responded.

"Can we go back a few comments?" asked the woman.

"Sure, nothing to hide," answered Bob.

"You seem to know your Scripture very well. Are you a born-again Christian?" she queried.

"That depends on definition also. I was born again as an infant, not as an adult. I've always been a Catholic."

"So am I, but I have a feeling you know Scripture better than I do."

"I'm sure I do. I've read it. I've studied it. And it helps to have a photographic memory," explained Dr. Burke.

"I never see you in church. What parish do you attend?" she pursued.

"I used to go to daily Mass. Once I was at the U. of M. and became so busy, I lost track of months and days. I had a fellow call me half an hour before each class so I wouldn't miss," he explained.

"Would you want me to call you half an hour before Sunday Mass each week?" she asked.

"I'd appreciate that. In fact, we'd better get to confession, too. It has been a long time for me," continued Burke.

"Great! It's a deal. Now, can we get back to your past social life, which hasn't been defined?" she asked with great interest.

"I went to all-male private schools from kindergarten through high school. My social life there was the same as anyone else's, except I never went to school dances. I have never learned to dance," he explained.

"Not even in college?" she asked in dismay.

During his talk, she had watched him more carefully than she had listened. She had judged him as one very quiet, yet with so much to say. But more than anything else, the word that captured his person was *gentle*.

Now, she began to change the word from *gentle* to *timid*. Was he afraid of women? Had he no interest in women? She studied him to the point of mutual embarrassment.

"College?" he responded. "I never really went to college."

She looked at him with total incredulity. "No one becomes a doctor without college."

Dr. Burke suddenly wanted two things. He wanted to terminate the conversation, and he wanted to continue. He had never considered himself secretive. At the same time, he didn't feel comfortable talking about himself. He wasn't certain what her reactions would be to his past. Somehow, for the first time in his life, how someone else felt about him seemed to matter.

"It wasn't exactly college. It was the same as college. I went to the seminary right after high school. Dancing wasn't part of the curriculum," he stammered.

"You were in the seminary?" She wasn't sure if that was a statement or a question. She was positive it evidenced surprise.

Burke was no less certain. At least she wasn't shocked. Somehow, though, he knew the questions about dancing had all been answered. He knew, too, that he was in an unaccustomed place . . . front and center stage.

"This may surprise you. It surprises me. For some reason, I've told you more about myself in half an hour than I've told anyone else in my life."

"Does it make you uncomfortable? If it does, I'm truly sorry. I didn't mean to intrude," she said.

They were the words he needed to hear. He suddenly wanted to tell her everything about himself, then realized something more. He needed to talk about himself. In fact, it had been so long since he had talked of his personal life that he had quite forgotten who he was.

"Shouldn't we be talking about you a bit?" he asked.

She laughed. "I am nosy, and it's unintentional. I wouldn't appreciate it if you told me to mind my own business, but I'd understand."

"I would never tell anyone to 'mind your own business,' least of all you. The fact is, I can't believe I'm talking about myself and actually feeling good about it." He smiled appreciatively. "In doctors' jargon, I think it is actually therapeutic."

"Let me know if and when the therapy is ineffective. Believe me, I'll never say, 'Doctor, heal thyself.' Not if I can be helpful," said Ellie in an encouraging tone.

"All right. We have me in the seminary. I really liked the atmosphere. It was given to peace and solitude, prayer and study. I felt comfortable. But . . . " and his voice trailed off.

"But what?" she asked earnestly.

"The tuition was keeping my mother strapped." He spoke as though with guilt. His eyes were downcast, studying his thumbs as they protruded above his clenched hands, which rested stiffly on the table.

"Your mother? What about your dad?"

"He was killed when I was five."

"How?"

"By a burglar he surprised in the house. It is theorized that the intruder may have come to kidnap me."

"Theorized?"

"Yes. He was never apprehended."

"Did they suspect kidnapping because your dad was wealthy?"

"If so, that wasn't the case. Dad was a young doctor connected with a prestigious clinic in Washington. Our home, in a wealthy neighborhood, could have fooled the burglar. Because it looked as though Dad had a brilliant future, he was allowed to assume a huge mortgage with a small down payment. The wealth was all in the future," continued Bob.

"Why did you want to be a priest?"

"A young priest, Fr. Jim O'Donnell, was tremendous to Mom at the time of Dad's death. His dad was a doctor also. Father Jim became the father figure in my life. I thought it normal for a doctor's son to be a priest."

Ellie studied the doctor's pain-filled face. She comprehended the hurt in his life. She hesitated, not knowing whether to ask more questions.

His eyes rose to hers for the time needed to encourage her. They seemed to beg, *Ask any question you want. The answers may be difficult, but unknown and undetermined wounds are not easily healed.*

"What did your mother do?"

"She was a nurse. She went back to school for recertification. Dad had little insurance, so the house was history. I was already in a preschool program, so living in an apartment wasn't such a big deal for either of us."

He continued, "Somehow Mom managed to send me to the best private schools. She made certain my education was second to none. She must have been on a tight budget. She paid for the seminary expenses because she didn't want herself or me in debt to anyone."

"Did she ever remarry?"

"No. She must have had opportunities. She was a beautiful woman. I'm not sure whether it was out of loyalty to Dad or dedication to my education that she remained single."

"You and your mother must have been awfully close."

"Yes and no. She had to work and I was always at some boarding school. Even on the rare occasions we were together she was undemonstrative in regard to her love. It was as though Dad's death had robbed her of any possibility of emotion."

Instinctively Ellie placed her hands around his. He started to pull away but remained in place when he looked into her face covered with tears of compassion. She sensed his momentary attempt at withdrawal. She felt the tenseness leave his hands.

He wanted to cry also but had seldom shed tears. The occasion for tears had been present, but he seemed to have shed them all on the fateful drive home from the seminary with Father Jim.

She spoke the words as though she were not the source. If was as though she wasn't certain whether she was being used by a ventriloquist or mouthing a question inspired by the Holy Spirit. "Has a woman ever held your hands before?"

"I hear your words," he responded, "but am uncertain about the meaning. This is the closest I've been to what might be called a date.

"My early years, from the time of Dad's death, I thought if I were to be a priest dating might be an obex to the priesthood. Since I left the seminary, I have been totally dedicated to healing the world's wounds . . . to finding the final solution to human suffering.

"I left the seminary because of my mother's sickness. The nurse at Mom's bedside, Becky Carpenter, met me for lunch to talk about my mother's possibility of recovery. She and I sat as we are sitting now. She held my hands that day. I needed it then, and I need it now."

"And your mother died?"

"Those last all too short, yet horrible, days, we became so close. I hugged and kissed her so much. Except for the last few weeks of my mom's life, I never displayed affection, before or since."

Ellie squeezed his hands firmly yet gently. "What was your mother's illness?"

"AIDS."

For an instant Ellie's hands went limp. Then she quickly reached out to regain his hands. They were gone. For the first time in his life he was holding someone's hands. For the second time he was crying.

"Thanks for telling me all this."

"Thanks for listening."

Her mind was strangely troubled but also at peace. Now she knew him, but who was she? Was she his mother? His sister? Was she acting in the role of wife? What was she?

He caught her puzzlement. "Would you be my friend?"

"I'd like that very much." She smiled.

Dr. Burke suddenly became aware of the world about him. He and Ellie were the only patrons in the restaurant. Most of the lights were shut off. The hostess was walking toward them. He pushed up his coat sleeve to check his watch. He was astounded at the time.

"I think we are being thrown out. I'll drive you home, if I may."

The drive was short. Bob had a good station on the radio that made any conversation superfluous. He walked her to the door.

"Thanks for the evening, friend," he said.

"Yes, my friend! I will call you at nine on Sunday morning so you will have plenty of time to meet me here before we go to eleven o'clock Mass. After Mass, if you want more of *This is Your Life,* you can be my guest for breakfast at a restaurant of your choice," she offered.

"It's, dare we say, a date?" he responded.

Both laughed and he departed.

153

Chapter 14

Dr. Robert Burke's phone rang promptly at nine o'clock Sunday morning. He answered quickly, "Dr. Burke," and waited for Ellie's voice.

"I hope I didn't awaken you. In any case, my friend, this is your wake-up call for Sunday Mass," she said cheerily.

"Awaken me? I haven't slept a wink all night. I've had friends before, but they never cost me sleep. You must be either a special friend or more than a friend," he chuckled.

"We'll see you in an hour. We can talk about it after church. Right now, you'd better get ready. By the way, you said I could pick the restaurant for breakfast or brunch. I have. Dress casually, okay?" And she hung up the phone.

Within the hour, he was at her door. She was ready. "It is such a beautiful day," she said. "Let's walk to Mass."

"Funny you mention wanting to walk. When I said good night to you, I wanted to walk all night," he responded.

"What do you mean?" she asked.

"First, I wanted to whistle. No special tune, just whistle. I suddenly realized I didn't know how to whistle. I'll bet most fellows learn to whistle before they start to school. Anyway, I can't whistle. So, I wanted to dance. But I don't know how to dance either. Anyway, David danced all by himself, much to his wife's chagrin. He danced because he was happy.

"So I danced all the way to the car. Then I danced round and round the car, over and over again. Thank heaven it was dark or I swear I might have been arrested. Finally, I unlocked the door and fell exhausted behind the steering wheel. And then I laughed like I've never laughed before," he exulted.

"You're crazy, unlike the Dr. Burke I know," she laughed.

"The fact is, I'm young for the first time in my life. I lost my dad before I started kindergarten. I was told I was the man of the house. I didn't want to go to any of the schools I attended because by doing so I was neglecting my mother.

"By the time I was six, I was already studying for the priesthood. That was a very adult and serious decision. I should have been trying to whistle, but that wasn't part of the program. I was the man of the house." He spoke half-seriously, half-jokingly.

After Mass, they walked back to her apartment. Much to his surprise, she unlocked the door and invited him in. "You said wherever, so this is wherever. The table is all set; have a chair. It isn't much, just coffee, toast, juice, and cereal. So, you see, this is both wherever and whatever." She smiled.

"Great. Sunday morning breakfast is so often hurried and harried in restaurants. Here we can talk without interruption. I like the plan," he agreed.

"But we will be interrupting ourselves," she continued. "Early this morning, I packed a picnic basket. If it is all right with you, we can hang up the DOCTOR IS OUT sign and enjoy the afternoon with Mother Nature."

"I've never been on a picnic in my life. I've seen them at the movies. I'm excited. It seems like my association with Mother Nature in recent years has been through a microscope or in a test tube. I really appreciate what you are doing for me," he said honestly.

"In no way, shape, or form am I being altruistic. I spend too much time indoors. Also, friend, I'm enjoying your excitement as much as you are." Ellie smiled.

She carried the blanket and tablecloth, and he carried the picnic basket. As she spread the tablecloth on the table, she motioned him back to the car. "Would you go back and bring the cooler with the refreshments?"

He hurried on his errand, grabbed the cooler, and began his return. Suddenly he began to twist and turn like a whirling dervish. Ellie watched him anxiously. She thought, *Is the man pos-*

sessed? Is he all right? What in heaven's name? Do I ignore what he's doing?

All at once his antics ceased and he came straight to Ellie. She studied him. "What, in the name of all that is good or evil, was that all about?"

An enthusiastic grin spread across his face. "I was just thinking how wonderful I feel. Then I noticed the whirlwind running across the parking lot. I tried to stay in its center, dancing with its every capricious movement. So, I've danced twice now, both times for the same reason; I'm the luckiest man alive since I met you."

They sat across from one another at the picnic table. He began, "I guess you know my life is dedicated more to success than to happiness. I've nothing against happiness. It's just that I never really experienced it. The wonderful taste of it that you present is much appreciated.

"Until I talked with you, I somehow was looking at my life through the wrong end of a telescope., Everything seemed clear enough, but oh, so distant. In our talks, I've been able to turn the telescope around. You present a broader picture. One that demands happiness. It is all so new and strange and, I think, wonderful."

Both felt a wonderful attraction to the other person. He told her, in all honesty, "You are the only woman in whom I'm interested, to whom I'm attracted."

"That must be your fault. Any woman would be flattered by an opportunity to know you better," she responded.

"It isn't that I have no interest. My involvement in studies has been too hectic and all-consuming," he admitted.

She understood he had been too busy to have a woman in his life. She, in a sense, knew the importance of his work, not only for himself, but the whole world.

"If you want, we could set aside a minimum of time for getting together. We don't have to think of it as dating. If you want, we could come together as friends to have an occasional meal and relaxed conversation," she offered.

"Our age difference may make being more than friends out of the question. I don't even know your age, but you look at least ten years younger then I," he guessed.

"You just told me you never felt younger in your whole life. Also, my old friend, I wouldn't attempt trying to dance within a whirlwind. Sometimes, when you talk to me, I feel more like a mother figure than a friend . . . a very young mother," she chuckled.

He picked up on the conversation. "How lucky can one man be? I had a beautiful nurse mother as a boy. Now as an adult I have a gorgeous nurse mother."

"Thanks for the compliment, Doctor. Since the sunset, I think the chill has been having an effect on your brain," she suggested.

"I agree, but by the same token, your personality has done much to warm my heart. God knows I've used my head more than my heart from the beginning. When one loses mother, father, and all one's friends, it is easy to lose heart and escape to the mind. It has been my experience that one can deceive the head much easier than the heart. I know what I feel better than what I think," he said half-joking.

"And what do you feel?" she asked.

"Never having been in love, I can't be sure. I would, however, conjecture that if this isn't love, it is a very satisfactory substitute. Does the nurse have any corroborating evidence in this case?"

"I've had puppy love many times but easily became convinced such love would lead to a dog's life. Sometimes we in the medical profession diagnose whatever the patient wants to hear. Sometimes we diagnose what we want to hear. And sometimes we diagnose the facts. . . . "

"And what have you diagnosed? Which of the three?" he asked.

"Doctor, I feel in your case all three point to the same conclusion. The patient is in love." She smiled.

"Is the nurse satisfied with her conclusions? If so, what does she prescribe?" he taunted.

"I prescribe this medication be administered immediately," she said as she stood up and walked to his side of the table. She threw her arms over his shoulders and kissed him on the lips.

Catching his breath and her spirit, Dr. Burke asked Ellie, "And what prescription would follow the initial medication?"

"If the medication works, it should be administered at the will of the patient and the pleasure of the nurse," she taunted.

Bob rose to his feet and held out his arms. She moved forward to share a warm embrace. "Thanks, Nurse," he said quite simply.

"Thank you, Doctor. A willing patient certainly makes the nurse's task much easier," she said with pretended discipline. "I think you've had a full day and might need some time to yourself for meditation and rest."

On the ride back to her apartment, the conversation was basically weather talk. "Wasn't this a beautiful day?" and, "Another week and it should be a full moon," and, "What a nice place for a picnic," and, "The picnic idea was great."

At her door, they embraced for the second time and joined the embrace with their second kiss. "Thanks for a most wonderful day, Ellie. I've never been so happy in my life."

"In all honesty, I feel the same way." She smiled.

"When can we get together again?" he asked.

"My schedule isn't as busy as yours," she offered.

"But I determine my own schedule. I work whenever I want."

"The week ahead is busy for this nurse. I'm free from Wednesday at two in the afternoon until Thursday at the same hour. Would you like to schedule time for play instead of work?" she asked impishly.

"What a novel idea. I never would have thought such an idea remotely possible. However, I do see some merit to your question. Or is it a suggestion?" He smiled.

"Does that mean Wednesday at three? You'll pick me up here?"

"Indeed it does. Let us seal our pact." For the third time they embraced and kissed. For the second time in his life, he wished he knew how to whistle.

Wednesday's meeting was filled with accusations and recriminations. "My dear woman," spouted the doctor, "I told you on Sunday you had affected my heart. Now, my dear, I find you are also a total distraction for my mind. I have thought of nothing but you since we were together. This whole experience is delightfully disconcerting, and novice that I am, I know not what to do or where to turn for an honest, unprejudiced solution."

Ellie studied her friend's face. "I wish I could help you in your daily dilemma, but I cannot. Any opinion I would have would be totally prejudicial. However, if I may be as objective as possible, there seem to be two possibilities present for consideration. First, you might decide, without my approval, to walk away and never see me again. That might take time and even effort, but I believe that given your tenacity, it might accomplish your purpose."

"And second?" he asked.

"Second, you might decide, with my approval, to propose marriage as a happy, somewhat effortless solution," she teased.

"Methinks the fair young maiden doth propose marriage."

"Methinks this fair young maiden is wise beyond her years." Her eyes sparkled.

"Unaccustomed as I am to being the recipient of a proposal, I must say my heart doth beat with joy," joined Burke.

"I suspect you haven't even considered the time or the place." Ellie smiled.

"You are free to make all those decisions, Nurse. I place my present and my future completely in your hands," submitted Burke.

"Bob, you know I want a Catholic wedding and that any children will be raised in the church."

"No problem, Ellie."

"I don't know any priests very well. One of my nurse friends says the priest in her parish, Saint Felix in Wabasha, is loved by his parishioners. She goes home every weekend possible so she can hear his sermons."

"Ah, yes," said Dr. Bob with a sudden moment of recollection. "Chief Wabasha was the father of the beautiful maiden Winona. Would you believe I learned that in the seminary?"

"What class?"

"Outside of class in a friendly discussion with a native Minnesotan. A Fr. Thomas Burns. I gave the sermon at his first Mass. Strange as it may seem, I haven't seen nor heard from him since."

"I never heard of him. Let me check with my friend about the priest in Wabasha. Okay?"

"Sure. Whatever you do is fine."

The next afternoon Ellie approached her friend. "The priest you like so much . . . could I make an appointment with him in the near future?"

"He was moved from Saint Felix two weeks ago. If you want to see an unhappy congregation, it is in Wabasha. We all really loved him. We knew it was too good to last."

"Where is he now?"

"A real small town named Boomer."

"You're kidding! That's my hometown. What is his name?"

"We just called him Father Tom. His last name is Burns."

"This is unbelievable!" exclaimed Ellie. "Fr. Tom Burns?"

"That's right. You'll really love him. If you don't, just send him back."

Ellie called her parents that night. "Mom, I need to talk with you. So much has happened these past few days."

"I hope it's good news, honey," encouraged her mother.

"I hope so, too, Mom. I'm engaged to a wonderful doctor. You've never met him and it is all terribly sudden, but I'm positive he is Dr. Right for me. I am really happy like you wouldn't believe."

"Dear, I hope you aren't making a mistake. Your dad will be hard to convince. He doesn't think anyone could be good enough for you, and I agree. He'll say you are rushing into this too fast. How long have you know this fellow?" questioned the concerned mother.

"Just a week tonight."

"You'd better have an arsenal of good reasons for Dad. He'll have a barrage of questions for you."

"Mom, I have only one good argument for you and Dad. You'll meet him in person and understand everything," assured Ellie.

"When and where will we meet Dr. Right? And when and where is the proposed nuptial to take place?"

"We don't know yet. I only proposed last night. Will you be a sweetheart and see if you can get an appointment with the new pastor for us?" asked the daughter.

"He really is a fine priest. Everyone loves him already. I'll call right away to see if I can get an appointment. Call back in an hour and I'll give you the report."

In an hour, the call was made. "Good news," said the mother. "He'd like to see you in the rectory after Mass on Saturday evening. Would you, your friend, and Father like to have a late dinner after your meeting? It's all right with Father if it's all right with you."

"Mom, you're terrific. Every answer these days is in the positive. I am so happy and excited. Really put on the dog, Mom."

"Sure thing, Honey. Dad can't be quite so hostile if the priest is present. Warn your man about Dad."

Dr. Robert Burke was pleased with all the arrangements. He wanted to meet Ellie's parents. He wanted to see her hometown. He wanted to meet the priest and begin the premarriage instructions.

When warned about Dad by Ellie, Burke was extremely pleased. "I feel much more comfortable if he is convinced I'm not good enough for you. It means your father and I start on the same foot. I don't think I'm good enough for you either.

"If I had any feeling that he might want you to marry me, I would be disturbed. No matter how much he might like yours truly, we all know you could do better. No one could love you more than I, but there must be persons worthier than I."

So it was that the future Dr. and Mrs. Robert Burke drove to Boomer on the following Saturday afternoon. The first stop was at Ellie's home so Dr. Bob could meet her parents.

The four proceeded together to Mass. Promptly at six-thirty, the procession from the back of the church to the altar began. Robert Burke thought his eyes were playing tricks on him. It couldn't be!

The priest genuflected, approached the altar, and kissed it. Instead of immediately starting the ceremony, he asked everyone's indulgence for an introduction.

"This is my second weekend as your pastor. For you who went elsewhere last week, I take this opportunity to introduce myself. I am Fr. Thomas Burns. You may call me Father Tom. Any appreciation you can show me will remove any possibility I might have of being a 'doubting Thomas.' I pray we will get along. In the name of the Father and of the Son and of the Holy Spirit." And Mass was begun.

"My God in heaven. This can't be. He's your pastor. My best friend in the seminary. My God in heaven!" whispered Burke to himself.

Not knowing the circumstance, Ellie's dad pondered what manner of man it was who talked to himself in church and thought he was good enough for Ellie.

Dr. Burke was overjoyed to see the chalice on the altar. He

161

wanted to run forward and embrace the man of God at the altar.

He thought better of that, since he knew he didn't want to cross over his future father-in-law to gain access to the aisle. He casually removed his sunglasses from their case and placed them over his eyes. If Tom Burns recognized his old friend at communion time, he might just drop the ciborium with all the precious hosts.

All the wonderful memories of seminary days flowed into the doctor's mind. All the joys and sorrows provided total distraction throughout the entire service. After the sermon, Ellie observed, "Wasn't that a fine talk!" Even though he hadn't heard a word of it, or her question, he nodded his assent.

After Mass, the four proceeded to the rectory. Ellie's parents entered first and introduced themselves to Father Tom. "Father, I am James Burton and this is my wife, Jeanne. We are the people who will host you for dinner tonight. This is our daughter, Ellie. With your permission, we will run along and work on the meal. We live only four blocks from here. If you want to walk, Ellie can be your guide. If you want to drive, these two can be your passengers."

As her parents exited, Elliota moved forward toward the priest. Directly behind her, still wearing the dark glasses, was the doctor.

"Yes, Father, I am Elliota Burton, Ellie for short. This is my fiancé, Dr. Robert Burke."

With the introduction and a beaming smile, Bob Burke removed his sunglasses. He extended his hand in friendship.

For an awful instant, the priest stood frozen as though hit on the head with a sledgehammer. He recognized his best friend from seminary days and hugged him as an athlete would hug a teammate on winning the final game of the NCAA championship. Dr. Burke felt himself being raised off his feet and put down again, over and over.

"What a sight you are for sore eyes, Bob. I've read about your work. But you are a Minnesota graduate. I can't believe you are the one and only Dr. Robert Burke whom I have read about."

"I am he. After that pummeling, I suggest there is a very lucky woman someplace who, thank God, is not your wife. You haven't lost any of your strength, have you!" responded Dr. Bob.

"This is great. I have a thousand questions, but nothing comes to my tongue that makes any sense to me. How can it make sense to you? If it is all right with you, let us be about our business of picking a time and day for the wedding. Then let us go to the Burtons' for dinner.

"I know this is a lot to ask, but why don't you stay overnight with me? Then you and Ellie can go back to Rochester in the morning," suggested Tom.

Dr. Bob looked at Ellie for permission. She nodded her head in agreement, and they made the initial arrangements for the wedding.

Jeanne Burton prepared a five-course dinner; she spared nothing to make an impression on the guests. Except for Ellie's attention to the fare, her mother's talents were totally wasted. Father Tom and Dr. Bob were elated with their restored acquaintance. They rambled and babbled and laughed. Their laugher caused much of the conversation to be somewhat incoherent at times as they discussed "the good old days" at the seminary in Baltimore.

At regular intervals, the priest would turn to Ellie with a well-intended apology: "We should be discussing your wedding instead of ancient history," and immediately return to the field of memories.

The Burtons understood that the doctor and the priest were old friends. They rejoiced with them to the point that James Burton was at least impressed that his future son-in-law had a priest as his best friend. That was good.

Elliota was pleased to hear the conversation. It filled her in on some missing years from her fiancé's past, but much more important, she could observe that Dr. Robert Burke was capable of being a deep and loyal friend. That was great.

After the meal, the two friends returned to the rectory. They remained excited, but the wonderful events of the day left them both exhausted. They slept soundly.

Ellie picked the doctor up early the next morning. Both men were awake and continuing on as they had the night before.

"I feel foolish advising the man who was the head of the class on what must be done. We will fill in the marriage papers next time. You need to make sure you have papers indicating you are no longer a deacon.

"By the way, getting to that, did you know our bishop wanted you to be a priest for this diocese? It was all right with your bishop, but no one could locate you.

"Guess that makes no difference now. When can we get together for the marriage instructions?" asked Father Tom.

"The instructions, if it's all the same to you, need to be on Wednesday evenings. We are both free then. I suspect your Sundays are full enough," suggested the doctor.

"Any time you say is fine, Bob. We'll see you on Wednesday at seven," responded Father Tom. "Do you remember my sister, Bridget? She is going to come for a short visit next week. Since Dad remarried, everyone is finding it difficult to care for her, so I want to do my share."

The doctor and Ellie walked hand in hand to the car while Father Tom hurried to the church for the early morning Mass. The last few hours had been a wonderful awakening to his spirit. *Boomer isn't all bad,* he thought to himself.

Ellie and her fiancé enjoyed breakfast at her parents' and began to make serious plans for the wedding. It was a foregone conclusion that James Burton would give his daughter away in marriage. The parents wanted a big wedding. Ellie and Robert wanted a small and informal wedding.

The doctor had no relatives and very few friends. Ellie's high school friends were numerous but were scattered to the four winds.

Dr. Burke said little concerning the preparation for the wedding. Only two things really mattered outside of the fact that his bride would be Ellie. "First, I want my friend Father Tom to witness the ceremony. Second," and then he paused for a moment, "did you folks see Father Tom's chalice? My mother gave me that chalice as an ordination gift. When it was decided that Holy Orders were not to be for me, I gave the chalice to Tom. So the second thing is that we share the Precious Blood from that chalice at our wedding Mass."

So the decisions were all made. It would be a small, intimate wedding. Indeed, no guests would be invited at all. Tom would be the priest. Jeanne Burton would be the attendant. James Burton would walk his daughter down the aisle and be the best man.

There would be no groom's dinner as such, rather a meal served immediately after the wedding practice. There would be no wedding reception.

"For obvious reasons, no dance. I'm afraid there isn't time to teach the doctor how to be adequate as a dancer," explained Ellie.

Dr. and Mrs. Robert Burke were happily united in connubial bliss. For the honeymoon, they journeyed to the nation's capital, where, once again, Robert was the expert guide. Ellie enjoyed the nostalgic mood in which her husband explained his childhood and his city.

They visited his parents' graves and prayed for them both, first aloud and then in silence. Almost as though his mother needed some kind of assurance, Bob spoke to her softly. "Mom, this is my wife, Ellie. I'm happier than I have ever been. At our wedding, Mom, we drank out of your chalice. God bless you, Mom. God bless you, Dad. Thanks for so very, very much."

On the return to Rochester, their discussion at one point found suffering as the focus. He explained that at present the only major unsolved sickness was AIDS. He dreamed of the day physical suffering could be erased from the earth.

"It seems to me," said Ellie pensively, "that suffering has an important place in life; it seems that every sense we have is essential.

"To be able to see, to smell, to hear, to touch, are all things that are good. If one abuses any sense, there is the pain that shouts, 'Stop!'

"We use sunglasses to protect the eyes, plugs to protect the eardrums; we move quickly off a tack or we are forced to forgo basketball, momentarily at least, when the blisters say, 'Enough.' Pain is important."

"I agree," he joined in, "but it is the duty of the medical field to alleviate as much pain as possible."

"Sacrifice is an important element in human existence. We prove the value of life and love through sacrifice," she countered. "Sacrifice is the willingness to endure hardship, even pain, for another."

Both enjoyed the many challenges their conversation often produced. In fact, they enjoyed one another more than either could explain.

Dr. Burke's salary was good, but not sufficient to allow his wife to rest from her nursing profession. Her job helped financially, but because both worked, they were unable to spend as much time together as they wanted.

She never asked about his progress in research. He never spoke of time spent without desired results.

Ellie knew he was doing all that was humanly possible in his search for the medical solution for AIDS. At most, she would express concern about the lengthy hours he spent in the laboratory and about his health.

Before marriage, they had dated on Sundays and Wednesdays. Now, they reserved those evening for dining out. Meanwhile, Ellie, who had given up her apartment to share his, was becoming an outstanding homemaker.

He often told her that going out might save her sanity, but he much preferred her cooking to restaurant fare. She noted, however, that there were times, especially at Michael's, when he would suggest she ask for a recipe they traditionally made available to the clientele.

Three months into the marriage, Ellie called her parents with the good news: "We are pregnant." When they informed Father Tom, he proclaimed that it would be a happy privilege to perform the baptism.

In her seventh month of pregnancy, Ellie quit her hospital commitment for maternity leave. The apartment was adequate for a nursery, and she anxiously began preparing the room.

Everyone was pleased that the fortunate baby girl, even as an infant, was a new edition of her mother. The name chosen was Elliota Marie.

The priest chuckled, "I think this is wonderful. She is just like a little Elliota. Remember, Dr. Bob, from the Greek, the *iota* is the ninth and smallest letter of their alphabet. One of the meanings is 'a very small quantity.' We will baptize her Elliota Marie. Her mother is called Ellie and the child will be called Iota, pronounced 'Eeota.'"

The dad laughed. "If she continues not varying one iota from her mother, I will always be a happy, happy father."

Ellie chuckled contentedly. "Father Tom, this is wonderful. We have celebrated two happy events with you in the month of May. Last May our wedding, this May our baby's baptism. I really appreciate how close you are to the three of us."

"That's a fact," the proud father joined in. "I'm not sure where or what I would be without Ellie and you, Tom. My mother's funeral was in May also. We buried her on the day the bishop had scheduled my ordination."

There was a long moment of silence in which the priest and wife knew they should say something. Finally, Father Tom broke the silence. "I can't imagine what a terrible day that must have been for you, Bob. I think I would have been a very hurt and bitter person."

"My mother's death was a blessed relief. I remember her last words so vividly. It's as though it were yesterday: 'In a bit we will both be free. I from my pain, you from your concern on my account. Use your freedom wisely and with love.' She suffered so much but had such a beautiful death."

He went on, "I was bitter about the bishop's lack of understanding about AIDS. He wasn't very diplomatic. He could have just written 'because you left the seminary without notification or permission, I must assess again your concept of obedience,' but he didn't, so I had to keep second-guessing him.

"That May 30 was really a day of mixed emotions such as I never knew before nor have known since," concluded the doctor in a manner that closed the conversation and served as a request for a new subject for discussion.

As though she wanted to hear more, though it be at another time, Ellie spoke in a way that kept the book open. "One thing for sure: you are heeding your mother's admonition to use your freedom wisely and with love. You are the love of my life, an excellent parent, and you are working for the betterment of the human race."

"Right," responded the priest. "We are here to celebrate the present and the future for Iota. Ellie, pour the champagne for you, Bob, and your parents. The baby and I will settle for milk."

The doctor popped the cork and filled the glasses. Ellie filled Father's glass with milk. She thought to herself, *I don't know why it is this way. Just when I think I know all about Bob, I hear a conversation between him and Father Tom and learn so much more about them both.*

In the middle of September, Dr. Burke suddenly became moody and easily irritated. "Is there something you want to discuss?" asked his wife.

"No," he lied, not knowing where to begin.

She knew from experience that he kept no secrets from her. She also knew when he wanted to talk but couldn't. She was patient.

"You know," she ventured, suspecting financial problems, "I'm absolutely delighted staying home with Iota. There doesn't seem to be a money pinch. But would you like me to go back to work?"

"Honey, I'm uncertain about many things at present. Everything is in turmoil. Would you mind remaining at home with the baby for the time being?" he questioned.

She answered honestly, "No dear, I'm happy either way. How real is the turmoil?" She searched his face.

"Very real. The clinic is pushing for results, and I can't do any more than I am doing. I can't push any harder. Under ordinary circumstances, anyone in research should have not only an M.D., but also a Ph.C. I lack the latter.

"They accepted me at great risk. The grant, which was set up for the work here at Mayo, was with the provision that I would be the researcher. The clinic stuck its neck out to afford me the opportunity."

Ellie understood the situation concerning the clinic's position. She was puzzled that any grant money would be so specific as to demand a particular person.

"I just found out today. Remember the nurse we visited in Washington on our honeymoon?" he asked.

"Why, certainly. She was your mother's best friend."

"Right. She and two nurse friends won a large lottery at the time I was looking for a scholarship to attend medical school at the University of Minnesota. They shared my interest in AIDS research, so they paid all my expenses," he explained.

"Either it was a huge lottery or they are special friends."

"Both. I was aware of their help while I was at the university. What I didn't learn until this morning is the fact that the grant money was provided by them. The clinic in no way wants to compromise its standards. As of Friday, they must release me," explained Bob.

"Do you have any plans, any ideas?" asked Ellie.

"The clinic will release me. I will be able to keep the results of the research to date. They are convinced my whole approach will come to naught. I am just as convinced I'm right on track toward the final solution to AIDS."

"What will we do for money? We have to be realistic about finances," she said, trying to hide her distress.

"I don't know. I only know I can't compromise. Maybe I could start a family practice somewhere," he conjectured.

"Would that leave any time for experiments?" Her voice was edged with a little hope and much despair.

"It would if my practice was small. It means it would have to be a small town for the needed time, but even more for the privacy," he said almost inaudibly.

"Obviously, you've done some thinking. Do you have any town in mind?" asked his wife.

Dr. Burke had a definite town in mind. He knew Ellie's parents had moved from Boomer to Minneapolis. He knew the family home, once the Stage Coach Inn, was empty. That was on the plus side of the ledger.

He also knew his wife had counted the day of her departure from Boomer as one of the happiest moments of her life. Now that her folks lived in Minneapolis, there wasn't one single reason she would want to return to the scene of her childhood.

"I'm sure we can come up with the right place. Something we can afford. Something somewhat isolated." He spoke as if in a trance.

"Such a place sounds horrible," she said and was immediately sorry. She at least had friends in Rochester.

"I'd need to set up the lab in the house. Except for house calls, I'd be home twenty-four hours a day," he offered.

"Behind closed doors," she countered, thinking of the advantages there would be. "One good thing about a small town is it's a good place to raise children."

"It would need to be a fairly good-sized house for us, for the office and the lab. The rent or taxes could be monumental," he added. "Father Tom might know a good town. He knows this area of Minnesota quite well, I would think."

Suddenly Ellie felt frantic. She was trapped but knew there were few alternatives. She looked away and offered with as little emotion as possible, "I suppose the folks might be happy to have us in their house. No house should stand empty."

"Would that be all right? Would it be a terrible disappointment for you?" he asked.

"It isn't as though it is a life sentence. I have confidence that you will attain the final solution shortly. You've worked so hard. Then we can move where we can be happy." She bit her tongue. "Who's to say? Maybe we will be happy in Boomer. We all love Father Tom so much. He's a real plus."

Her parents agreed to allow the Burkes to move in. Indeed, they were overjoyed at the prospect that the house would be a home again. They had left Boomer and friends for economic reasons. Bob and Ellie would be fun to visit in the place of so many memories. The inn would be a base from whence the Burtons could visit good friends in the old town.

Dr. Burke informed the clinic he would leave Mayo. They granted him permission to terminate at his earliest convenience. He needed time to clear the laboratory, where he had spent so many hours. With the clinic's blessing he was allowed all his files and logs. They allowed that the "fruit of his labors" belonged entirely to him. They were convinced his work, to the moment, was in vain.

The following Saturday morning, Dr. Robert Burke was in Boomer deciding which room could best serve as the laboratory and which would make the best office. That night he called Ellie from Father Tom's booth. He needed Ellie's input.

He hired a woman, recommended by the Burtons, to clean the house thoroughly. When she finished, he began to assemble his laboratory.

Meanwhile, Ellie selected furniture for the office. It was placed in the van with their other belongings, and suddenly the Burkes were the newest residents of Boomer. Mrs. Burke prayed fervently that their presence would be very temporary.

Boomer rejoiced. It had a doctor again. Since so many residents were elderly, Dr. Burke was quite certain of their loyalty, as it was not easy for them to go elsewhere for medical attention. He would have sufficient patients.

Dr. Bob asked Ellie if it would be all right with her if a research doctor from Rochester came each Wednesday to act as his assistant. She consented. With the exception of Dr. Philip Hurley, Bob's Wednesday help, Ellie became his sole helper. She was sec-

170

retary, bookkeeper, and, above all else, his beautiful, efficient nurse. She appreciated the many extra moments they were now able to share. She was happier than she had been in her entire life. They were grateful spouses and happy parents.

As a dedicated wife, Ellie wrote what she considered a necessary letter. The envelope was addressed to Becky Carpenter, 2112 Park Street, Washington, D.C.:

Dear Becky,

I was very blessed on Dr. Burke's and my honeymoon to have met you in our nation's capital. Bob often lets me know how much he appreciates what a faithful friend you were to his mother and the financial aid you gave him to cover his costs at the University of Minnesota School of Medicine.

Only last week did we discover that you provided the grant moneys necessary for AIDS research at the Mayo Clinic. As you probably know, to do medical research it is necessary that the researchers have an M.D. and a Ph.C. The clinic allowed Dr. Burke the privilege of using the clinic laboratory because he worked with a researcher who was qualified with the necessary degrees. When the other doctor decided in favor of practice rather than continued research in AIDS, it was necessary to terminate Dr. Bob. It is my husband's intention to continue his research on his own. Presently, he is setting up his own laboratory in our home. I am acting as his nurse and secretary. His office is also in our home. He has secured the help of a qualified researcher who will be helping him each Wednesday. This doctor comes from Mayo in Rochester.

Boomer, where we now live with our beautiful daughter, has too few people to support a doctor, let alone the research for the discovery of the final solution to AIDS.

My husband does not know I am writing this letter. I know he thinks he owes you more than he can thank you for sufficiently. I have no idea what moneys are needed for his research but am hopeful you might continue helping him in his mission.

Any consideration will be most appreciated.

> Sincerely,
> Ellie Burke
> Box 12
> Boomer, MN

Transforming her wifely image, she donned her nursing cap

and secretary's pin and walked into his ill-equipped lab. She placed the letter in front of him.

He read it slowly and carefully. Then he handed it back to her. The doctor wasn't sure how he should react. He knew he needed the help the letter sought.

"Well," said Ellie, "I'm not telling her a lie. You didn't know I was writing the letter. Do we leave it just as it is or do you want to write the message yourself?"

"You've said it as well as it can be said. Becky can guess how much money is needed as well as we can. And, let's face it, the decision is totally up to her. Whatever she sends, if she sends anything at all, we sure are in need," responded Burke.

Ellie folded the letter and placed it in the envelope. "I'll get a stamp from the office, walk downtown, and mail this immediately."

That night at dinner, Ellie was on a high. "Isn't it exciting? No matter what Becky decides, somehow we'll make it. I called Father Tom and asked him to pray for our intention at Mass tomorrow morning. We'll be there, won't we?"

The husband smiled. "We'll be there. Who would have thought in our deacon year at Roland Park that my best friend, Tom Burns, would one day be my pastor?"

"He's a great priest, Bob. He will make Boomer a happier place for our family, a happier place for everyone. I hope he is happy here," said Ellie. "I pray it with all my heart."

Chapter 15

Within the first month of the Burkes' having settled in Boomer, a letter arrived from the nation's capital. Ellie presumed it was a response to the letter she had sent Becky Carpenter concerning moneys for continuing research. She anxiously opened it and handed it to her husband. As he began reading its contents, his face became ashen and taut. Gradually he relaxed and his expression moved from surprise to amazement.

> Saint Veronica's AIDS Center
> Washington, D.C.

Dr. Robert Burke
Box 12
Boomer, MN

Dr. Burke,

I have just reconciled myself with God at the feet of your dear friend Fr. James O'Donnell. I bared my soul to him concerning my many sins against you. Part of my penance is being realized in the words I address to you now.

Throughout your years as a seminarian, you were not only at the head of the class; you were in a class all by yourself. You were the model seminarian, and I know now you would have been a model priest.

When Father O'Donnell informed me your mother had AIDS, I was relieved to know I could refuse you ordination because you left the seminary without my permission. This even though you had satisfied all the seminary requirements, as the rector clearly indicated.

My actions displayed duplicity rather than courage. I had the arrogance which fosters ignorance. If I had a problem with ordaining a person whose mother had died from AIDS, what would my priests have thought? The people of the diocese? What about any parishioners assigned to his pastoral care?

Without any consultation, I refused you ordination even though you volunteered a priesthood that would be dedicated to the AIDS ministry.

The bishop of Winona asked permission to ordain you in his diocese. I sent him your records with the permission. When he asked for your address, I pleaded ignorance when I knew Father O'Donnell would certainly have it.

To salve my conscience, I promised to fund a diocesan center for AIDS victims. You and Father O'Donnell forced my hand.

You asked for diocesan funding for medical school. Again I refused you.

Your honesty and humility disarmed me. You told me a visit from me to your mother during her last days would have meant the world to you and your mother. Next to the Eucharist it would have been her greatest comfort.

I didn't want to hear what you said, but you gave me no choice. You were right when you said all the money I spent wasn't nearly as important as one visit to the guests at Saint Veronica's. To visit the sick is a work of mercy for all Christians, but especially for our leaders, from whom we have a right to expect a good example.

I bristled when you said those words, not because you said them in an accusing manner, but because you spoke humbly and because you were right. All the arguments I could have used, such as a busy schedule or whatever, carried no weight, not even with myself.

I knew you were right, but the necessary grace seemed beyond me. To know what is right and to do what is right sometimes seem to lack any connection.

You left my office that day but never my mind. You still pursue the ambitious goal of finding the solution for AIDS. Your singleness of purpose I deeply admire, and I pray for your success.

Meanwhile, I finally forced myself to visit Saint Veronica's AIDS Center. I stopped in Father O'Donnell's office, praying all the while that my visit might be just an exchange of pleasantries with him and then a quick return to some kind of official business.

I thank God that wasn't the case. A volunteer told me Father was giving a talk to some new guests. I was asked to come and listen to his words and help greet the newcomers.

When I came to the door, Father interrupted his message. He beckoned me in and introduced me to the newest arrivals. He motioned me to be seated next to his podium and continued his talk.

As he spoke, I studied the faces of the new arrivals. They seemed to reflect every human emotion from joy to bitterness. I tried, at first, not to meet anyone's glance, but unwittingly they were forcing nonverbal communication.

Father Jim asked if I would say a few words of official welcome in the name of the diocese. Never before had I seen people listen more intently. Every person's eyes seemed filled with simultaneous hope and despair. It was as though their salvation or damnation hinged on my every word. I have never experienced so much power and weakness in my being. I could feel tears seeking their own level down my cheeks.

The listeners moved toward me. All voiced the same sentiment: "Bishop, we are so happy to be here. Thanks much for your heartfelt kindness."

I asked myself an all-important question: Did I have heartfelt kindness or was I merely acting? I held out a stiff hand on the end of a stiff arm. I would shake hands, but I would not put myself at any risk.

They moved past my defenses and each, hardly waiting for his turn, embraced me. Then, like Damien of Molokai or Francis of Assisi, I found myself returning the embraces with my whole heart and soul.

In an instant, I knew I wasn't acting. I was genuine. By my consecration to the episcopacy, I knew I was a successor of the Apostles; I knew I shared the fullness of Christ's priesthood. Now, for the first time in my life, I felt the fullness of Christ's person.

With the guests I wept over the city of Jerusalem. With them I wept in the Agony of the Garden of Gethsemane. Together we stripped away all fear, even though we knew there was so much suffering to come.

Robert Burke, you have done more for my ministry than any other person. Your words led me to Saint Veronica's. You spoke of the privilege I could have afforded your mother with one single visit. As the scales left my eyes there was the realization that I had robbed myself of the privilege and joy of visiting her in her moments of suffering.

Minutes before, I had feared the guests. Now I loved them with an indescribable joy. As we walked back to Father O'Donnell's office, I commented, "This place is properly called Saint Veronica's. I have seen the image of the face of Christ in every person!"

I asked Father to hear my confession. He allowed me to pour out my soul as I had never done before. Father has learned kindness and compassion from serving his guests. I was wonderfully transported by this Christ-like person.

I asked my confessor if you were still interested in the priesthood. My injustice to you must cry to heaven. I want to make amends.

He told me you are a doctor now, married to a wonderful woman, and you have a beautiful daughter. Any interest in the priesthood now would be of little relevance.

Twice in my life I have passed judgment on you, Dr. Burke. Both times I was wrong. I made my decisions out of the worst kind of ignorance, that of prejudice. Prejudice is especially destructive because it is insidious. A prejudiced person isn't aware of his condition.

The word *prejudice* comes from "to prejudge." It means one doesn't have all the facts. One of the principal roles of the Apostles was to teach. As a successor of the Apostles, I had the obligation to teach my priests and my people about AIDS. I presumed they had my prejudice when I refused you ordination. Through you, I have found I should have assumed my role as teacher to remove prejudice, to remove ignorance.

These words are not written with the hope that you can excuse me. I seek not being excused; I seek forgiveness for my sins against you.

At the end of this year I will retire as the Ordinary of this diocese. It is my intention to visit Saint Veronica's one day a week in the meantime.

I have asked Father O'Donnell if I can move in as his associate when my time as the head of the diocese is ended. He has graciously consented. It is my intention to spend the rest of my life sharing his ministry.

Each day at Mass, I pray for your success. It is my hope that you will find the solution to the terrible disease of AIDS.

You know and understand my faults and shortcomings, especially my sins of omission, better than I. In this letter I ask you, to whom I refused ordination, the forgiveness I seek.

May the healing Christ bless you, your wife, your daughter, and the thousands of persons suffering from AIDS. I pray your knowledge and skill in the area of research will give relief to the world even as I pray for the relief of your forgiveness, which I earnestly seek.

With prayers and humility,
E. B. Messick, Archbishop

When Bob concluded reading, he returned the letter to Ellie. "I can't believe it," he said. "It is something I never thought could or would happen. I'm so surprised I don't know how to react. I have never questioned the possibility of miracles, but the bishop's conversion is one I never thought possible. If God can work such wonders, there is no reason we cannot find the answer to AIDS.

"I must sit down immediately and respond to the letter. How can I not forgive someone who seems so serious about the need? He grievously offended me. All the more does he seek forgiveness.

"There is so much he can do for the guests at Saint Veronica's and for the diocese. We know we can use his prayers in our apostolate to the AIDS victims."

Chapter 16

Iota Burke knew the best and the worst of nearly two centuries of progress. The Amish allowed her to view firsthand exactly how life had been before the Elliots had left the safety of Ohio.

The one element missing was the presence of the Native Americans in the early settlement of Elliota. Otherwise, the horse-and-buggy days were always visible. The hitching posts were once again in evidence in every part of town.

Men wore bib overalls and bonneted women's skirts reached to the ground. Little girls' faces were protected by visors from the sun, the wind, and the view of strangers.

The countryside was filled with groaning windmills, and kerosene lamps cast eerie shadows in rooms heated by crackling wood stoves.

Fence lines were in abundance, not merely for the separation of fields, but for the nests of quail, rabbits, and mice. Ever-alert hawks soared in the clouds watching for the next meal from the protection provided prey in the hedgerows.

Long-abandoned country schools had reopened their doors and pumps were once more being primed and stacks of firewood awaited chilly days.

Chic sale specials of two and three holes stood side by side, one for the girls and one for the boys. The only thing betraying modernity was the absence of Sears-Roebuck and Montgomery Ward catalogs. And the Amish children needed no instruction or direction as to their purpose, since each braved the weather at home to relieve the necessity of bodily elimination.

From her earliest recollection, Iota knew of the Amish coming to her dad as patients. They were of no special interest because they had always been there. They didn't always deal in cash, so the quilts in the house, some of the furniture, and many home-baked pies and breads were all part of the little girl's existence.

There were seldom any house calls to the Amish homesteads. When the occasional one occurred, Dr. Burke brought his daughter along. It had been a long time since he had needed to explain to her why the people had no electricity and no running water. Iota had once said, "They sure do everything the hard way, don't they, Dad?" His answer, as was so often the case, was a smile.

Given a choice, under ordinary circumstances, the elderly of Boomer would have preferred a house call from the doctor, but the extraordinary circumstance was the presence of his little girl in the office. Iota called each one of them Grandma or Grandpa and would add their first name to her greeting.

Ellie would watch her daughter crawl from lap to lap. Each in turn would read to the precocious child until his or her moment to enter the doctor's examining room. All patients were told to bring no candy or toys and were assured the parents were doing more than was necessary to spoil Iota.

It became a Burke custom to invite Father Tom for an evening meal at least once a week. The priest and Iota became great friends. Whenever Dr. Burke and Ellie left town for a day of shopping or medical meetings, their daughter let it be known she wanted to stay at Carolan's with the pastor.

Whenever a parishioner needed some of Father Burns's time at his office in booth number one, DOC would quickly volunteer his baby-sitting skills in booth number three. DOC would use such opportunities to challenge the child's mind and found her brilliantly receptive. No matter what else he had in his booth for educational purposes, there was always a recent edition for Iota.

It wasn't long before the charming child was asking the weekly boarder, Father Tom, why he hadn't brought his friend along also. As a result, DOC was soon sharing the fare at the Burkes'.

Iota wanted to know where the priest lived. On entering and leaving the church on Sunday morning, Ellie pointed to the rectory as the priest's residence.

On one occasion, when Iota had wandered down to Carolan's

to visit her friends, she was unnoticed and unable to open the front door. Determined to see her friend, she approached the rectory to find him. Bridget answered the door.

"Who are you?" asked Iota.

"I'm the housekeeper," answered Bridget.

"Does that mean you are Father Tom's mother?"

"No, I'm his sister."

"Do you live here?"

"Of course I live here."

"Can I come in and see Father?"

"He isn't here."

"Sometimes, when I visit people, they give me cookies."

"I don't have any cookies."

"Why don't you bake some?"

"I don't know how."

"That's too bad. Father and I love cookies."

With that, Iota, at this time five years of age, strolled back home. She entered the office and spoke to Ellie. "Mom, is it hard to make cookies?"

"Some kinds are real easy; some kinds aren't."

"Do the easy kind taste good?"

"I think all cookies taste good."

"Can we make some easy ones today?"

"Sure, sweetheart. I'll show you how."

After the cookies were made and had cooled, Ellie and Iota tasted the results. Both were happy with the product. Ellie excused herself and returned to the office. Iota placed four cookies in a paper napkin and returned to the rectory. Again she knocked on the door.

"Do you have a name?"

"My name is Bridget. Bridget Burns."

"Well, Bridget, I made some cookies for you. Two for you and two for Father Tom."

Bridget was speechless as she motioned the child into the house, took the napkin, and unfolded it very carefully. "You made these yourself?"

"Mom helped."

"Could you make some more?"

180

"Sure. Mom taught me how."

"I'd sure like to meet your mother," said Bridget.

"I know her phone number. Should I call her?"

Bridget hesitated a moment, then asked for the number and dialed the phone. Ellie answered, "Dr. Burke's office. May I help you?"

"Hi, Mom. This is Iota."

"For heaven's sake, where are you?"

"I'm with Bridget at Father Tom's house."

"Is Father Tom there?"

"No, we are alone, just Bridget and I."

"What are you doing there?"

"Well, Mom, she didn't have any cookies and didn't know how to make them, so I brought some over for her and Father."

"Honey, do you want me to come and get you?"

"No, I want you to come over here and show Bridget how to make cookies. She doesn't know how."

"Put Bridget on the phone."

"Okay. Mom wants to talk to you, Bridget."

"This is Bridget."

"Is Iota bothering you?"

"In fact, she's quite lovable. But yes, she is bothering me."

"I'll be right over."

Ellie told Dr. Burke she needed to go out for a minute and would be back shortly. She hopped in the car and hurried to the rectory. Bridget was waiting at the door. Iota was sitting in the porch swing.

"I am sorry Iota is bothering you. I didn't even know she had left the house," Ellie apologized.

"Please don't be upset with her. She really opened my eyes."

"What do you mean, Bridget?"

"She came earlier and couldn't believe there were no cookies in the house. Two hours later she came back with four of them. She said you taught her how to make them. If you could teach your little girl, is it possible you could teach me?" asked Bridget.

Ellie looked at the housekeeper's countenance. Tears were streaming down her face.

"Did I make her cry, Mommy?"

"She's crying for happy, honey, for happy.

"Bridget," continued Ellie, "I'd love to teach you and Iota to bake cookies and cake or whatever you want. We'll set a special time one morning a week. What morning is best?"

"Makes no difference to me. Anytime except Sunday, I guess."

"Wednesdays it will be, if it is all right with you, Bridget. May we come to the rectory?"

"Of course. What do I need?"

"Let's check your kitchen right now for pots and pans and supplies."

"It's kind of a mess, Ellie. This is the first time it has made any difference," admitted Bridget.

Ellie quickly surveyed the situation. She advised Bridget to clean out the refrigerator and discard all its contents and replace her kitchen utensils.

"I'll talk to the ladies at the next women's meeting. They can refurbish the kitchen with what is needed. Next Wednesday, the three of us will clean the rectory from top to bottom. Then the officers of the women's group can tour the place and decide what is needed," said a determined Ellie.

"What about Father Tom? How will he take what we're doing?"

"You let me handle him, Bridget. Next Thursday, you, Father Tom, Iota, and I will go grocery shopping. All he has to do is pay the bill!"

So it was the rectory was cleaned. Mrs. Burke explained that no one spends more time learning how to make beds than nurses, unless they are in the military. It just takes practice and more practice. So Bridget spent time on that Wednesday of purgation making beds.

When Ellie and Iota left in the late afternoon, a very happy Bridget embraced them both. As they departed, she said quietly and sincerely, "I can hardly wait until next Wednesday."

"Don't forget tomorrow, Bridget. Remember, we are all going shopping with Father Tom."

True to the plan, every ensuing Wednesday morning was a learning experience for Bridget and Iota. Even though the house-keeper was anxious to get into the food preparation, the first weeks were spent cleaning the house, washing the clothes, doing the dishes, washing the windows, and doing things most house-keepers do well.

The doctor's wife finally started teaching baking and cooking. "If it is all the same with you, Bridget, let us start with breakfast. Look at page 1 in this cookbook. One has to learn measurements first."

So it began with Bridget's amazement that a large *T* meant tablespoon and a small *t* meant teaspoon. It was difficult for her to grasp that *lb.* meant pound, but she was happy to learn from a kind and patient teacher.

Setting the table came easy after the initial shock. "You mean there is a right and a wrong place to put the silverware? I never knew that before," said Bridget.

Ellie would laugh happily at the housekeeper. For the first time in her life, the Burns girl was beginning to laugh, not only with people instead of at people but, most important, at herself.

"Let's start with the silverware," taught Ellie. "There are four letters in the word *fork*, the word *left* has four letters, too, so put the fork on the left. The words *knife* and *spoon* have five letters, as does the word *right*. They both go to the right of the plate."

Sometimes Iota would ask questions that brought forth laughter. Often she could answer Bridget's queries, and sometimes Bridget could respond to hers. All three were beginning to enjoy Wednesday mornings at the rectory.

On one occasion, Ellie, after the usual Wednesday, called Bridget. "Bridget, it is beginning to bother me somewhat that Iota is calling you by your first name. There seems to be a certain lack of respect in that. Does it bother you?"

"Heavens, no, Ellie. In fact, I've never given it a thought."

"Maybe it shouldn't bother me either, but it does," admitted Ellie.

"What else could she call me? I much prefer being called Bridget to being called Miss Burns."

"She calls all Dr. Bob's patients, at least the elderly ones, Grandma or Grandpa. How would it be if she called you Aunt Bridget?"

"That would be wonderful. She is closer to me than any of my nephews and nieces. If that would be all right with you and Iota, I'd really be honored." Bridget smiled.

"I'll talk with Iota. If she starts calling you Aunt Bridget, you'll know she wants to. Bye-bye now," concluded Ellie.

A few weeks later, Iota and Aunt Bridget were baking cookies at the rectory. Ellie was in the dining room polishing the silver. She was amazed at the ensuing conversation.

"Aunt Bridget, do you have a mother?" quizzed Iota.

"Everyone has a mother," responded Bridget.

"But I never see your mother. Doesn't she ever visit you?"

"My mother is in heaven," said Bridget.

"You mean she is dead?" asked the little girl.

"Yes, she died. Father Tom had the funeral," stated the housekeeper.

"I just knew you didn't have a live mommy," continued Iota.

"How did you just know?" queried Bridget.

"Because mothers buy special dresses for their girls and comb their hair so it is beautiful like mine is," stated Iota. "You need your mother."

Ellie was frozen in her place. Should she pretend she hadn't heard? Should she interrupt before Bridget was more embarrassed? Ellie couldn't believe Iota's questions. At the same time, she was proud and ashamed of her offspring. She had to interrupt.

"Bridget," she called from the adjoining room, "don't you think it is time for a break? Coffee? Orange juice? Cookies? Something?"

"I suspect you're right," responded the housekeeper.

"Iota, honey, will you run home and get me the cookbook from the kitchen table?"

"Sure, Mommy. Right away."

As soon as she left, Ellie began apologizing for her daughter.

"Don't you worry about her, Ellie. She is the best friend I have. She says it like she sees it. And she sees it right. My mother was never really honest with me. When I couldn't make a bed, she said it didn't make any difference. She should have worked on me until I could. She told me I didn't need to cook or sew or bake. She didn't have the patience or the honesty to teach me. Iota saw right away that I couldn't bake cookies. She knew something was wrong. She told me so and you have taught us both.

"The same with my appearance. No one ever told me that clothes and hairstyle might make a difference, but Iota had the honesty to suggest it.

"Last Wednesday, after you left, your daughter and I had a heart-to-heart talk. She explained that she had told DOC she was calling me Aunt Bridget. He told her that wasn't fair unless Iota started calling him Uncle DOC.

"Then she told me that Uncle DOC asked her how I was doing. She told him she was afraid some people thought I was not beautiful, but she thought I was. Do you know what DOC told her?" Bridget asked.

"I'm sure I could never guess," answered Ellie.

"He told Iota that up to a certain age, like thirty or so, a woman is supposed to have a beautiful face and figure to be attractive. But that is all on the outside. Inside, every woman can be beautiful. Then Iota told me I was beautiful, very beautiful, on the inside," stated Bridget emphatically.

With that the breathless daughter reentered the kitchen. The orange juice and cookies were on the table. They all bowed their heads in silent prayer.

Then, with an infectious smile, Iota turned to her mother. "Mom, Aunt Bridget doesn't have a mother to help her."

"How do you know?" questioned Ellie.

"She told me," answered the girl. "I told her how mothers pick nice dresses and know how to comb hair so it looks beautiful."

Bridget sat stoically, uncertain as to where the conversation was leading. She looked at Iota, then at Ellie, and then began passing the cookies.

"Anyway, Mommy, because she doesn't have a mother, you taught her to cook and clean. I think you are like a mother to her like you are to me," said Iota thoughtfully and happily.

"I think Bridget and I need to talk," said Ellie.

"Anything you can do for this old shoe would be appreciated," concluded the housekeeper.

The following Wednesday afternoon, Ellie and her two daughters proceeded to Rochester to visit a beautician. Iota was ecstatic as she saw Aunt Bridget transformed before her happy eyes.

Ellie's choice for the housekeeper's garb was as fortuitous as the hairstylist was. Iota's statement when they went for lunch said it all: "Aren't you happy, Aunt Bridget, that I told you how much mothers can do for you?"

Father Tom was the happy recipient of the good news of Aunt

Bridget's becoming a whole person. At first, she mentioned that he might want to have breakfast tomorrow morning. He shuddered but was reassured when told the sweet rolls were the result of Ellie and Iota's kindness.

As Bridget ventured into new menus, her brother became a regular at her morning table. He knew it wasn't an answer to his prayers. Even though he believed in miracles, he had surer bets for other results than her culinary conquests.

He complimented her on the clean house, the freshly made beds, and her nice table settings. He hesitated inviting fellow priests to visit his rectory, lest everything was a temporary conquest. He was positive he wouldn't jeopardize the bishop's health and sanity.

Eventually, the Bridget breakfast grew into the packed lunch and finally a grand dinner that satisfied Father "Doubting Thomas" Burns.

To that momentous dinner were invited Dr. Robert Burke, Ellie, Iota, and Uncle DOC. The priest sat proudly at the head of the beautiful table.

Ellie remained in place throughout the dinner. Aunt Bridget and Iota did all the serving and graced the feast with their presence at the table. Everyone was proud of Bridget and let her know it. Proudest of all was the housekeeper, now in game as well as in name.

After the meal, everyone moved to the parlor for quiet music and easy conversation. Ellie suggested that Aunt Bridget and Father Tom could do the dishes after the company's departure. Meanwhile, Iota could remove the plates to the kitchen.

Uncle DOC apologized for directing the conversation. "It seems to me that everyone loves Iota. It seems further that she is a most brilliant little girl. She is related by friendship to all in Boomer. Everyone is her grandfather, grandmother, uncle, or aunt, including me," he began.

"You all know that Carolan's is the social center of town. It's where the elderly come to chat, play cards, or whatever. Sometimes there is a need for another person to form a foursome in bridge or five hundred. With your permission, Dr. Bob and Ellie, I'd like to teach Iota how to play bridge."

"Are you serious?" questioned Bob.

"Of course I am. Most of cards is a matter of mathematics and luck. I can teach her the mathematics. For luck, Iota is on her own," chuckled DOC.

"What I mean, Uncle DOC, is would it be a proper place for a little girl?" asked Bob.

"Come on down and see for yourself. All your clientele is there nearly every evening. Father Tom and I have our offices there in the daytime and sometimes into the night," boasted DOC.

"You know, I have wanted to come to Carolan's for some time now. I've convinced myself I'm too busy. It must be a three-ring circus. A priest hearing confessions, a professor teaching a class on Shakespeare in the 'University of Booth Number Three,' the elderly having tea and crumpets, and the volunteer fire department playing pinochle in booth number six, the booth they refer to as the 'bull pen,' " chuckled Dr. Burke.

"When will you make the time?" asked Ellie.

"Fact, is, I don't have to make or find time at the present. I just had word this afternoon that Becky Carpenter died last Monday. There is no money in her will for a continuation of AIDS research. Next Wednesday will be the last day we can afford the assistance of Dr. Hurley. So now I'll find time to check out Carolan's," reported Dr. Bob.

Ellie gasped, "What will happen to the research?"

The doctor assured everyone that the money wouldn't be missed and there would be no change in his plans. He was pleased to announce that he would have more time for church, family, and community. Maybe there would be a booth for him at Carolan's in which to teach biology, chemistry, or physics!

"In fact," the doctor concluded, "you have my permission to teach Iota bridge and also to sharpen my skill with the cardboards."

"That's great, Dr. Burke. She already knows the value of each card. I'll start out sitting her on a stool beside me while I play. Gradually, she can take over," asserted DOC.

"By the way, Dr. Bob, if my hearing doesn't deceive me, you have volunteered to be a lector at Masses," stated Father Tom.

"As a medical man and friend, I would say your hearing is perfect," chuckled the doctor.

"You understand Iota will be in first grade next year. She won't have as much time to spend at Carolan's after that, so you'd better begin the bridge instructions soon," urged Ellie.

"She is having an interesting childhood," mused Uncle DOC. "She lives with the Amish, who are in the nineteenth century. She has grandmas and grandpas who speak only of the twentieth century. Now, when she will be a full-time student, she can enter with her classmates into the present century, the twenty-first.

"I suspect that is the case. Even though she lives in a home where her dad is working on twenty-first-century medicine, it doesn't affect her that much," agreed Ellie.

"No matter what century she finds herself in, she will survive. She is a beautiful, bright child. Doctor, you and Ellie have every right to be proud of her," concluded DOC as Iota entered the parlor.

So it was that Iota began her grade school career. DOC was her constant friend and tutor when it came to studies. He taught her many things but, most important, a love for learning. Her first-grade teacher accepted the child as the brilliant youngster she was. It was her fear, however, that Iota might develop into a spoiled person. On one occasion she asked her, "Iota, are you spoiled?"

The youngster pondered the question and then offered her response: "I may be. I'm not sure. If I am, I didn't do it!"

Chapter 17

It seemed to Iota that her world was crumbling. She was finishing her sixth year in school, and in September she would be starting junior high school. That meant a different school in a different town. The teacher had warned the entire class that the adjustment isn't always easy.

The girl knew that Father Tom was completing his second six-year term as pastor and his move was inevitable. It was certain that Aunt Bridget would accompany him wherever the Spirit would direct them.

There was talk also that Uncle DOC might be moving on. The number of youngsters in Boomer was dwindling, so his challenges were diminished.

In the years of her schooling, Iota had lost many grandmas and grandpas. She missed them and they weren't being replaced. That meant there weren't as many settings for bridge as there once were. People felt once Father Tom vacated booth number one DOC might abandon booth number three.

Iota had some real concerns about the future. Would her parents want to leave Boomer also? For nearly six years her father had spent less and less time in the research laboratory and more and more time in parish and community work. Ellie seemed restless to her daughter, and the girl heard more and more about the early days of their marriage in Rochester, where there was so much to do compared to Boomer.

On May 30, the anniversary of his mother's funeral and the wedding anniversary of Dr. and Ellie Burke, there was a loud knock at the door at four o'clock in the afternoon.

Ellie answered the door and stood aside as the sheriff brushed past her. "Is Dr. Robert Burke at home?"

"Yes, he is. Do you wish to speak to him?"

Many times the sheriff had come to their home, for any number of reasons. This time, however, he was tense and distraught. "I have a warrant for his arrest. Would you call him please?"

"There has to be some mistake. Of course I'll call him." Ellie called, and the doctor sauntered into the room.

"Hello, Sheriff. What can I do for you today?"

"If you would accompany me please, I have a warrant here for your arrest."

"On what charges, Officer?"

"First, I'll read you your rights." The sheriff read them slowly and clearly, then continued, "To answer your question, Dr. Burke, the warrant states you have possessed the cure for AIDS for the past six years and have not shared it with the human race."

Robert Burke looked at his wife.

"There must be an easy explanation for all this," Ellie said as she turned to the sheriff. "This is an awful mistake. This is our wedding anniversary. You can't be serious."

"Mrs. Burke, a sheriff's work is generally serious and I've never been more serious than I am right now."

"Do I need to take anything with me? Toothbrush? Anything?"

"It's all furnished, Doctor."

"Ellie, you have to wait here until Iota comes home from school. Let's hope the mistake can be corrected and I'll be home tonight." He held his wife in his arms and kissed her for just a moment on the lips. Then he followed the sheriff. Ellie collapsed in the chair next to the door.

Father Tom was at a clergy conference in Albert Lea. He wouldn't be home until late in the evening. Like an automaton, Ellie walked to the phone and called Bridget.

"Assumption Rectory. Bridget speaking."

"Bridget, this is Ellie. I know Father is out of town. No matter how late he comes home tonight, would you please have him call me?"

"Sure, Ellie. Is there anything I can do?"

"Yes, there is. Pray for the family as you've never prayed before!"

"Yes, I will. God bless."

"Good-bye, Bridget."

There is no need for a newspaper in a town the size of Boomer unless one is interested in the outside world. Secrets are things you tell one person at a time. News is when the secret is generally known.

It was dutifully reported at Carolan's about the sheriff's stop at Dr. Burke's. Eyewitnesses saw them leave together. Because such had happened before, there wasn't any editorializing.

The guessing began when one of the locals, who drew his employment check from the county courthouse, reported that the sheriff had placed Dr. Burke in jail.

There were actually two jails at the county seat. One was much larger than the other. It was where prisoners were kept after the judge or the jury had found them guilty in a court of law.

The smaller jail was an innovation in Minnesota. If a person is considered innocent until proven guilty, why should such a person be confined with anyone whose guilt has been established? So the new jail had two nice cells, not stiff and cold like the big place. It was built right onto the courtroom and the judge's chambers. Everything was convenient that way. One of the deputies was on guard whenever anyone was incarcerated. That way the confined person was given more visitors' privileges than at the big place.

Anyway, the word was official right from a courthouse employee that Dr. Burke was in the small jail. Why, of course, was any body's guess. And as a citizen of Boomer, everyone had a right to any number of guesses.

Ryan Patterson and Michael Clancy entered Carolan's in search of Father Burns. The sign at his office had indicated the priest was out for the day.

The two interrupted DOC in his reading. "Isn't that the way it always is, DOC? Father is never on hand when he is needed," said Clancy in a demanding voice.

"What is your need?" responded DOC.

"Oh, it isn't us. We don't have any needs of our own. It's just that we want justice done," spoke Michael Clancy in his usual abrasive manner.

"And what justice is your concern?" asked DOC.

"No less than the injustice being done Dr. Burke. Don't tell me you are unaware of his arrest?" bleated Clancy.

"You know everything else. You must know about our good and deserving doctor. He is a model for the whole town. Can't imagine him doing anything wrong," added Patterson.

"I know he has been arrested. I know he is in jail. I, too, believe in his innocence. We are a nation of laws, and justice will have its way and day," said DOC.

"That's easy for you to say," rasped Clancy. "You're here nice and relaxed while our doctor is in jail."

"I think Father Tom will appreciate your concern. Why don't you leave him a note telling him?" suggested Dominic O. Crotty.

"Will you write it if we tell you what to say?" asked Patterson.

"Certainly."

"Father, Dr. Burke being in jail ain't right. We want you to know we will do anything necessary to spring him." They signed: "Michael Clancy" and "Ryan Patterson."

"DOC," commented Patterson, "it's important that Father and the town of Boomer know we are men of action. Dr. Burke can count on us."

The two activists left Carolan's happy to have volunteered themselves so unselfishly.

DOC took his CLOSED sign and hung it on booth number three. Unobtrusively he walked out of Carolan's. He knew Father Tom was out of town, so he sauntered over to Ellie's to offer assistance.

Iota ran to her uncle and threw her arms around him.

"They have Daddy in jail, Uncle DOC."

"I know. I know."

"Mommy can't stop crying."

"I see. I see."

DOC pulled a straight-backed chair next to Ellie's easy chair. He placed a gentle hand on her shoulder. She touched his hand and thanked him for his presence.

"I'm sure Father Tom will come as soon as he gets home. I called Bridget, and she'll have him call."

"I'm sure he will. I'm sure he will," said DOC.

Iota came to her mother. She sat half on the armrest, half on her mother's leg. They embraced and said nothing. DOC studied the carpet first, then the wallpaper. He stood and began to walk back and forth. He knew he would do anything for Ellie and Iota; he also knew he could do nothing.

"Have you had dinner?" asked DOC, knowing that the question was irrelevant but necessary to break the silence.

"No, Uncle DOC, and I'm a little hungry," answered Iota.

"We were on our way to Rochester to celebrate our twelfth anniversary. Then we were going to a concert at the Mayo Civic Center." Ellie spoke almost inaudibly.

DOC didn't want to pursue Ellie's line of thinking. The facts were bad enough. The circumstances made them unbearable and DOC wasn't up to discussing the unbearable, so he moved on with Iota's answer.

"There must be some food in the kitchen . . . something we can manufacture in a hurry without too much difficulty," he suggested.

"Nothing. We were going out for dinner," continued Ellie. "We were going out for dinner."

"Let's investigate the kitchen, Iota," continued DOC. "Maybe we can find something and surprise Ellie."

"I've already had enough surprises today. I've had enough surprises to last the rest of my life." Ellie spoke to the lamp. Uncle DOC and Iota were rummaging in the refrigerator.

Father Tom's welcome call came just after ten-thirty. Uncle DOC had suggested earlier that Iota retire for the evening, and her mother had agreed.

DOC, who had answered the phone, asked the priest to come over. The late hour was inconsequential. "Don't knock. Come right in."

Father Tom's appearance caused Ellie to do what was most necessary. She fell totally apart. She placed her head on the pastor's chest and sobbed incoherent words into his heart. Father Burns put his huge arms around her shuddering frame.

DOC stood beside them. "About four o'clock this afternoon the sheriff arrested Dr. Bob. I came over as soon as I heard. There is coffee in the pot and some cookies in the dish on the counter. Would you prefer I stay or leave?"

The priest nodded his head toward the door. A much relieved DOC spoke over his shoulder as he left. "Ellie, let me know if there is anything I can do . . . anything."

She lifted her head slightly, "Thanks, DOC. Thanks for coming. Thanks for everything. Iota and I love you."

Gradually the priest's strength produced a calm for Ellie's spirits. She described the sheriff's coming and the arrest and tried to express her shock and disbelief to Father Tom. Her inability to describe her emotions allowed him a perfect barometer of her feelings.

"Ellie, I'm sure you want to visit Bob, but I know the visiting hours are over for today. I have a schedule for visiting hours at the jail in the rectory and at Carolan's. I'll call you right after Mass in the morning. Your family will be my special intention. You probably won't get any sleep tonight, but the body still needs to rest."

"Will you see him tomorrow, Father Tom? If it's all a mistake, maybe we won't have to worry about visiting."

"I hope you are right, Ellie. In any case, I'll see him in the morning. Pastors generally have unlimited visiting privileges."

"Thanks, Father, for being so understanding."

"Sure, and add me to DOC's list. If there is anything I can do at any time, just let me know. Good night now and God bless. Tell Iota I was here and will see her tomorrow."

And Boomer was asleep. Dr. Burke had been discussed in the business establishments and other workplaces. Conclusions were brought home to husbands, wives, and children. Freedom of speech was never a problem in the village.

The ten o'clock news added little knowledge. It merely reported: "Dr. Robert Burke has been arrested and the indictment will be handed down tomorrow." They showed his picture and it was good to know there was total agreement in Boomer that it didn't do him justice.

As the prisoner stared at the dark ceiling, he had a similar question: *Will the court do me justice?*

194

Chapter 18

Immediately after Mass, Father Tom called Ellie. "The hearing begins at ten. Do you want to attend?"

"Are you going?" asked Ellie.

"Yes. Do you want to accompany me?"

"I'll be ready whenever you say," answered Ellie.

At nine-thirty they left Boomer for the courthouse.

"Father, did Bob ever tell you he had the final solution?"

"Never so much as a hint. What about you?"

"Nothing. I can't believe he wouldn't tell me," thought Ellie aloud.

"Fact is, I never asked him about any process or progress. I wouldn't have understood. It seems he would have said something to you rather than to me," pondered the priest.

"Remember the first party we had at the rectory when we produced the new Bridget?" Ellie asked tentatively.

"Yes."

"He dropped several bombs that night," continued the wife.

"For instance?"

"He announced the death of Becky Carpenter and that her will allowed no more funding."

"I remember."

"Then he announced, quite matter-of-fact-like, that Dr. Hurley would no longer be helping."

"I thought that was because of the lack of funds," responded the priest.

"At the time, so did I. Now, as I recall, the real surprise was his intention to spend less time in his research lab. To spend more time with Iota and me, with the church, and in the community," continued Ellie.

"He even gave me an affirmative when I asked if he would be a lector," agreed the pastor.

"That was nearly six years ago. Is it possible, Father, that he has had the final solution for that long and he never even told me and I never suspected it?"

"That doesn't seem possible."

"Not to me anyway. We have never had any secrets in our marriage."

"Ellie, I guess our questions may or may not be answered in a short time. I'm totally baffled by everything that has happened the past few hours."

When they entered the courtroom it was quite empty. Present were a reporter from the *Rochester Post Bulletin*, some court officers, and a person who turned out to be the prosecutor.

Dr. Burke entered the courtroom in the company of a deputy sheriff. He spotted his wife and pastor and walked over to where they were seated. As they stood, he embraced Ellie, then shook his friend's hand. It was as though the doctor had entered the house after a day visiting patients.

Then the judge entered as everyone stood. He was announced as Judge Robert Nelson. When he sat, all were asked to do the same.

"Would you read the indictment, please?" the judge asked.

"If it please the court, Dr. Robert Burke, here present, is hereby accused of possessing the cure for the disease of AIDS. He is further accused of not sharing said cure with the world."

Father Tom leaned toward Ellie. "Judge Nelson is really a fine man. I don't think he is forty-five yet. He is just and as fair as any judge I know."

Ellie nodded with pleasure as she looked at Judge Nelson. He was a fair-haired, clean-shaven Scandinavian. His blue eyes gave more hint of compassion than one might expect of his office. He seemed tall while he was standing, but she conjectured that his legs must account for most of his height, because he was of average size when seated.

"Dr. Burke," he said to the defendant, "did you have your

rights read to you at the time of your arrest?"

"I did, Your Honor."

"You have a right to counsel."

"I want to forgo that, Your Honor."

"You want to represent yourself?"

"I do."

"Do you know anything about law?"

"No, sir. This is the first time I've ever been arrested. There has been no need."

"Don't you think you need a lawyer? One will be provided if you cannot afford the expense," offered the judge.

"Your Honor, I know nothing of procedure. I hope that isn't too troublesome for you. Any time I'm out of line, you can correct me. You seem friendly enough."

"If you change your mind, let me know. Meanwhile, how do you plead to the charges?"

"I don't plead," answered the doctor. "It seems to me there are two possibilities: I have the cure or I don't have the cure. If I don't have it, there is no case. If I do have it, then that speaks for itself. If I have it, it is mine. In either situation, I'm not sure why I am here."

"You must make a plea of innocent or guilty."

"I am an innocent man," said Burke with finality.

"It is the burden of the court to find you innocent or guilty. Let us move on to jury selection."

"Your Honor, if it please the court, I don't want a jury. I trust you. If I have one man I trust, why should I have a dozen or so that I don't even know?"

"You have a right to a jury," said the judge, somewhat perturbed.

"At the risk of sounding proud, Your Honor, I have a right to a jury of my peers. This is a case that pertains to medicine, where I have few peers," suggested the doctor.

"This is how the selection process goes," continued the judge, explaining everything in great detail.

The selection process began. Of each prospective juror Dr. Burke asked just one question: "Do you have a close relative or friend who has AIDS?" One after another answered the question the same way. Not a single negative answer. Without emotion, Dr.

Burke turned to the judge. "With all due respect, Your Honor, we'll never get a jury that can be objective. I trust you as my judge."

The judge was clearly uncomfortable. "I've lost two brothers to AIDS, Doctor. Can you trust me?"

"Judge, you are trained to be objective. If I can't trust your ability to rise above your emotions, whom can I trust?"

"Dr. Burke, would you give me until ten o'clock tomorrow morning to make my decision?"

"Certainly, and I hope you decide to be my judge."

"Doctor, as you could see by the failure to select a jury, AIDS is a volatile subject. I believe it is for your own protection that you remain in jail until this case is resolved."

"Thank you, Your Honor. At ten then."

The judge rapped his gavel and called the recess. Ellie and Father Tom came forward to talk with the prisoner. Neither of them asked the questions burning within them. After a few minutes, the jailer motioned in the direction of the jail.

Any questions concerning visits for that afternoon or evening were settled with finality with the words Dr. Burke spoke as he left the courtroom: "Thanks to both of you for coming. I hope to see you tomorrow at ten."

On the return to Boomer, Ellie wept softly. "He doesn't even want us to visit him, his wife and best friend."

Father Burns was quiet. To himself he kept saying, *Dr. Bob, what is going on? What is going on?*

As he stopped the car in front of the house he was invited in for coffee. He declined. He had been gone for two days now and he should at least check the mail. In his heart he knew he couldn't face Iota with all her probable sensible questions.

The following morning the pastor stopped again for his parishioner. He had been correct. Iota was full of questions for her mother, and Ellie felt trapped by each of them. How could a loving wife not have answers about a loving husband? How could a good mother not have the truth for her daughter? It wasn't acceptable, to Iota or herself, that she didn't have the answers.

The courtroom was a busy place. The *Post Bulletin* coverage had made national news. The media was present in great numbers. Curiosity seekers filled every available space.

The court recorder met the two at the door. If it was all right with them, it was all right with Judge Nelson if they sat next to Dr. Burke where the defense lawyer would ordinarily be.

They readily consented to the offer and took their places. Soon thereafter Dr. Burke entered. Again he embraced his wife, shook Father Tom's hand, and was seated. Opposite them was the prosecuting attorney, Bill Canton. Beside him was seated Dr. Hurley.

"It looks like Judge Nelson is not going to step aside from the case, dear. It was his suggestion we sit here," said Ellie to her husband.

"That is good news. I really like him," responded the defendant.

With that, all the formalities of the bench and the judge's entrance were accomplished. The indictment was read again to the crowded assembly.

"I understand," Judge Nelson began, "we have a goodly number of the media present today. In my judgment, since we have no jury, one and only one reporter from each newspaper or television station may be seated in the jury box. Is that all right with the prosecuting attorney?"

"Yes, it is, Your Honor," he responded.

"Is it all right with you, Dr. Burke?"

Dr. Burke arose for the answer. "At the risk of serious frivolity, I would suggest it is very fitting. After all, the media has been judge and jury of nearly everything in the country since the police action in Korea in the middle of the last century."

"Thank you both. Would the media then take places in the jury box until the conclusion of these proceedings?" After the changing of seats was accomplished, Judge Nelson again rapped his gavel. "Would the prosecution please introduce your first witness?"

Dr. Hurley came forward and was sworn in.

"What is your name?" asked the attorney.

"I am Dr. Philip Hurley."

"Doctor, what do you do?"

"I am a research scientist at the Mayo Clinic."

"Do you know the defendant: Dr. Robert Burke?"

"Yes, I do."

"How long have you known him?"

"Over fifteen years."

"Please tell the court how you know him."

"Some years ago, fifteen or more, the Clinic was given grant money to be used in AIDS research. The grantor stipulated that the grant was available on the condition that Dr. Robert Burke, who had just finished his internship, head the research.

"It is required in research that the researcher have a Ph.C. or a Ph.D., as well as an M.D. Dr. Burke did not have the former. Because I did, it was necessary for me to be present during his research or at least available during the study.

"Mayo wasn't comfortable with the arrangement. They asked me if any real progress had taken place. My appraisal was in the negative.

"Dr. Burke was released by the Clinic. As a result, the grant was terminated. At that time he moved his family, laboratory, and office to Boomer.

"He appreciated my help over the years. Since the grant money was now given to him personally and he still didn't have his Ph.D., he used part of the grant money to pay for me to spend one day a week in his laboratory.

"Mayo had no objection, so I accepted the offer. Six years ago, his benefactor died, leaving no money for further research. At that time, my role in his work was terminated."

"Let me make certain I have the facts correct," prodded Canton. "The entire time you worked with Dr. Burke it was in AIDS research?"

"Yes, it was," answered Dr. Hurley.

"You mentioned there was no progress in the time at Mayo?"

"During those nearly six years, that was my assessment. Once we were in Boomer, though, everything began falling in place. All his theories became verified," Hurley replied.

"Are you convinced, at the present time, that Dr. Burke has the final solution for AIDS?" inquired Bill Canton.

"Completely convinced."

"On what do you base your judgment?"

"Before the grant money was gone, while we were still working together, we cured AIDS several times," asserted Dr. Hurley.

The crowd started as one person. Excited conversation filled the room. The members of the media were hurriedly scratching on their notepads. Father Tom and Ellie looked at each other in dumbfounded amazement.

Judge Nelson fumbled for his gavel and rapped sharply. "There will be order in the court or all spectators will be removed."

Everyone's eyes were focused on Dr. Burke. An eerie calm had settled in. The defendant sat as though he were not a party to the proceedings. His countenance was that of a person who was listening to classical music.

"Proceed," ordered the judge.

"You have seen cures from AIDS with your own eyes?" asked Canton.

"On different occasions. On infected mice, infected rabbits, infected rats, infected dogs and cats," Hurley asserted.

"That will be all the questions for this witness, Your Honor."

"Dr. Burke," queried the judge, "do you wish to examine the witness?"

"Thanks, Your Honor, I do." Then he moved forward a bit and faced his former compatriot in research. "Dr. Phil, has anyone with whom you ever labored exacted an oath from you?"

"Yes," answered Dr. Hurley. "You did."

"And what was that oath?"

"I swore I would never reveal, in any way, anything that might result from our research," spoke Hurley.

"You are under oath in this courtroom. Does an oath have any importance in your life?" pushed Burke.

"Indeed it does. My appearance here is not without much soul-searching. As doctors, we all take the Hippocratic oath. My dilemma has been that my oath to you contradicts the oath I took as a doctor."

"The Hippocratic oath binds you to do all that is in your power to save lives. It doesn't bind you to what is not in your power. If there is a final solution, it is in my power, not yours," Dr. Burke said with unbelievable control.

Then he continued, "Dr. Hurley, you have mentioned numerous occasions on which laboratory animals have been cured of AIDS. Do you know of any human cures?"

"No, but what value is the use of animals if one can't infer the same results will occur with humans?" argued Dr. Hurley.

"The only reason for using animals is to save humans from

experimentation," explained the defendant.

"Dr. Burke, anyone with AIDS would welcome any opportunity for healing, no matter how experimental," countered Dr. Hurley passionately.

"There is really only one question I want to ask, and it has nothing to do with conjecture. Are you aware of any human healing as a result of using what you refer to as the final solution?" insisted Dr. Burke.

"No."

"No more questions," concluded Burke.

"The witness may step down," directed the judge. "Mr. Canton, do you have any further witnesses at this time?"

"Your Honor, I have none present. I do, however, have two more witnesses who should be heard."

"When can they be here?"

"Tomorrow."

"That being the case, we will recess until tomorrow morning at ten o'clock."

All stood as the judge returned to his chambers. The media rushed toward Dr. Burke, who leaned over to Ellie with the request, "Would you visit with me for a while in my cell? Just you, not Father Tom."

"I'll follow you right now. Father Tom, would you mind if I talk to Bob alone? . . . Thanks." She followed the jailer and her husband.

Once they were alone, Ellie turned on her husband. "Why have you never confided any of this to me? Do I mean nothing? Why have you spent all these years in research and now keep the results to yourself?"

"I wish I had answers as obvious as your questions. I don't. I am not positive what I'm doing is right or wrong intellectually, but in the area of feelings I'm convinced," he responded.

"Feelings? Why don't you think about my feelings? I have been used." Ellie said quietly. "I am worse than a streetwalker or a prostitute. The only difference is that they are paid.

"You forced me back to Boomer when I was happy in Rochester. The time you've spent in research has been an absolute waste.

"You have used me. You have used my parents for free rent.

202

You have used your mother's friend Becky Carpenter—she gave you funds so people could be cured of AIDS, and you took all the money under false pretenses. You have lied to everyone who I thought was near and dear to you.

"The Archbishop prays daily for your success." Ellie's voice was beginning to crescendo. "You've made a mockery of him and Father O'Donnell.

"Is there anyone in the world who agrees with you? Any doctor? Any theologian? Certainly not the Archbishop. You have spent too much time searching through a microscope. Open your eyes to the real world. Do you, with your test tubes, think you are God?

"We could be living the good life. You have chosen a life of squalor. You've made the choice without consulting family or friends.

"In your moment of success in the seminary, you complained because the bishop shot you down. Now in a moment of success in which you could remove the final sickness from the world, you shoot yourself down.

"You don't need my support. You need a psychiatrist. I'm the one who needs support, and you just aren't present for me or for your daughter.

"I always have been open and honest with you. I've taken the words of the wedding ceremony seriously. I have done all in my power to be 'one in mind,' to always tell you the truth. I have always wanted to be 'one in heart.' I have never refused you anything, regardless of the cost. As to 'one in affection,' where is your affection?

"You say you aren't sure whether what you're doing is right or wrong. I'm telling you that you are dead wrong! There is no one in the world who would agree with you."

"Ellie," Dr. Burke said humbly, "remember the conversation we had concerning pain and sacrifice before we married. You started me thinking at that time about the role of suffering in the world.

"Somehow, my mother never seemed lovable until she had AIDS. The archbishop was a distant man until he visited Saint Veronica's. Pain seems to have some value."

"If God wants pain in the world, he can always allow the devil to invent it. Besides, isn't there enough pain with broken bones, blisters, slivers, and the like? Pain doesn't have to take lives."

"I need time."

"You have had much time and may not have much more."

"I am truly sorry about the way you feel."

"But not sorry enough to do something."

"I can't. I just can't."

"In other words, your plan is to remain secretive, even with me."

"At present, I don't seem to have any choice. Your questions indicate that no answer would be adequate," he said.

"And what about Iota? She has lost every friend in school. She cries herself to sleep at night. She just plays with her food. What am I supposed to tell her?" demanded Ellie.

"At the risk of sounding flippant, tell her how you feel. Tell her you don't understand. Tell her that maybe Dad is sick. Tell her whatever you think is the truth," Bob said in a matter-of-fact manner.

"Aren't you concerned about her?"

"Of course I am. I'm concerned about you both. I love you both."

"Then why are you putting us through this nightmare?" she insisted.

"I can't answer your questions. I can only answer that I love you both. There are only two more days of school. Why don't you keep Iota out so her friends can't hurt her?" suggested Burke.

"With her parents in court, should she remain alone at home?"

"Aunt Bridget would be happy for her company while this trial continues. They love each other very much," Burke reassured Ellie.

"I can't take any more of this. I'm leaving." Ellie called to the jailer. She allowed her husband no embrace, no kiss, no sign of affection.

The doctor slumped in his chair. "Would you ask Father Tom to come in for a minute?"

Ellie gave no answer, but in a few moments Burke's pastor was being ushered into the cell.

"Thanks for coming, Father."

"Ellie is very angry, Bob. You have to be aware of it."

"Indeed, I am. For herself, for Iota, and because of me."

"I'm not sure what I am supposed to do or say. Is there any way I can help?" inquired the priest.

"From my point of view, I appreciate the fact that you're not asking questions about my sanity or my reasoning." Burke smiled.

"I have held you in awe since our first days in the seminary. You must have some reason for what is or isn't happening. When you want to discuss it, I'll be there," assured Father Burke.

"Right now my main concern is Iota. What she is enduring shouldn't happen to anyone, let alone an eleven-year-old child. I'm asking you for a miracle. Will you talk with her? All her friends have not only abandoned her, but are taunting her without mercy. Maybe you and Uncle DOC can both talk with her."

"I'll take care of it as soon as we get home," said the pastor.

"This cell is getting smaller all the time. I know the walls are stationary, but the square footage is diminishing. It is nearly as large as my laboratory, but that was always expanding. Freedom is a wonderful thing. Whenever we went to the Bay in Baltimore, I used to admire the gulls. They seemed free in the air, on the water, and on the land."

"You always admired them, didn't you?" said Father Tom wistfully.

"I admired all birds but especially the gulls. They seemed so capable of making the most of everything. In fact, as I was thinking about my imprisonment last night they came to mind. Would you like to hear the poem I wrote concerning them?" asked Burke.

"You wrote a poem about sea gulls last night?" the priest asked incredulously.

"I'll read it to you:

" 'You mount to heights not known by lesser birds
Or in the calm you hover listlessly,
With lusty cry alarm your fellow gulls
To food, to peril, or to simple play,
And in your weightless flight arrest man's soul . . .
Distract his frantic mind to idle thoughts.'

"You know, Tom, I haven't had time for idle thoughts, and

that's unfortunate. Take it with you. I have it memorized. You mustn't keep Ellie waiting," concluded the doctor.

What manner of man is this who has the final cure at his disposal, who is facing heaven knows how much time in jail, and is praising the importance of idle thought? asked the priest of himself. He placed the poem carefully in his billfold, walked to the car where Ellie was waiting, and once again headed for Boomer.

"He's concerned about Iota."

"Not concerned enough to do anything," she said acidly.

"He asked me if DOC and I would talk with her. Is that all right with you?" asked Father Tom.

"I guess so. Where do you want to do it?" asked the mother.

"Would she feel most comfortable at home or in the rectory?"

"Do you want to contact DOC?" she asked.

"Sure. Why don't we talk in the rectory? If you would bring Iota over, DOC and I will talk with her. When we are through we will call you to join us at Bridget's table."

Father Burns called DOC from the rectory to explain the situation. DOC was very understanding and left booth number three immediately. Bridget had already begun dinner when the confused girl of eleven was delivered.

Father Tom began, "DOC and I want you to know how much we love you. If there is any way we can make life happier for you, please let us know."

"Father," began Iota, "I have no friends. No one talks to me anymore. I'm so lonely. I miss my dad."

"Your daddy is lonesome too, Iota. He wishes he could hug you and let you know that everything will be all right," explained the priest.

"All Daddy has to do is give the people what they want. He has chosen his loneliness. I haven't chosen mine," she pleaded.

"Daddy is alone and lonely. At least you aren't alone," the priest responded.

"He is just thinking of himself. He is selfish," shot back the girl.

"I guess we're all a little bit selfish. When I was a young priest in Mankato, there was a little boy of eight who was completely happy with all his Christmas gifts. He was invited to his friend's house to see his gifts. Among those presents was a beautiful new

206

bicycle. He came home and complained to his parents that his friend Andy got a bike for Christmas and he didn't."

The priest continued the story, "The mother said, 'Just because Andy does something it doesn't mean you do. If Andy were to put his head in a bucket of cold water, would you?' The boy answered, 'No.' 'And if Andy threw his marbles away, would you?' 'No.' Then the mother continued, 'If Andy jumped off the high bridge, would you?' The boy thought for a moment before replying, 'If Andy jumps off the bridge, can I have his bicycle?'

"Iota, we all think we know what we want and what we need. If the children in school turn their backs on you, does that mean you have no friends? You have many other friends. We all know you have other friends because we know you have us. If you want, though, you can say, like the little boy in Mankato, 'I have no toys because I have no bicycle.' Only you are saying, 'I have no friends because the people in school aren't friends.'"

"But, Father," she protested, "all my friends are important."

"My child, there are two major problems in raising children: obedience and popularity. You are always obedient, so that isn't a problem," began the priest.

"You mean it's wrong to be popular?" interrupted the girl.

"Heavens, no! Your parents want you to be popular. They want you to be the head of the class. They want you to be always beautiful. They want you to be good," continued the priest.

"Then I don't understand," she said.

"Sometimes, to be popular, people want us to compromise, to do things we know we shouldn't. It may be they ask us to drink or do drugs. We know better, but they can tell us to do it or we won't be popular. It may be an act of impurity is requested. The reward: Popularity! Friends!"

"But people aren't asking me to do anything!" protested Iota.

"Perhaps they don't realize it. Perhaps you may not. But aren't they telling you to quit loving your dad? Isn't that the price being asked?" said the pastor.

He continued, "Popularity is wonderful. I suspect, though, when your mother and dad met they were much more concerned about goodness than popularity."

"I think I understand what you're saying, but I'm not sure if I agree," persisted Iota.

The priest held out his arms and embraced his little friend. "Iota, we all love you very much. Would you like to talk with Uncle DOC for a bit?"

"I'm not sure," responded Iota all too honestly.

Father Burns walked toward the kitchen, where he surprised an intent Bridget eavesdropping at the door. Any embarrassment on her part was not followed by an apology. In fact, after a quick check on the food's progress she returned to her listening position.

Uncle DOC turned to his favorite person. "Iota, I wouldn't want you hurt for anything. Above all else, I don't want to hurt you."

"I know that. We are really good friends."

"Any time a person wants to be loved, it has to start with loving herself. When you start losing friends you have to start wondering if you're lovable. Is that how you feel?" asked DOC.

"I guess so. If nobody loves me, how can I love myself?"

"Iota, would you trade places with anyone in the world?" he inquired. "Think about each of your classmates. Would you rather be yourself or any one of them?"

Thoughtfully the girl began to process each of her "friends." She was coming to no conclusion.

DOC continued, "You might think someone else lives in a nicer house. You might know that some girls have better clothes. There are several whose parents are probably richer.

"But, Iota, God gives each one of us something very wonderful. He lets each person know he or she is most special. I don't think you would want to be anyone but yourself. Your folks think you're special. Father Tom thinks you're special. Aunt Bridget thinks you're special. I know you're special, and God knows you're special. It's all up to you, my wonderful friend. Don't you think you are special?"

Iota moved over to where Uncle DOC was seated. She crawled up on his knees, then bent forward and threw her arms around his neck. "I love you, Uncle DOC, but I miss my daddy so much."

Bridget turned to her brother, who had remained in the kitchen. "Call Ellie. Tell her everything will be ready in half an hour. Iota and I are going over to the church."

She took her friend by the hand and they entered the church together. Bridget was never neutral. She may not have been famil-

208

iar with Revelation, but with her everything was black or white, never gray, hot or cold, never lukewarm, unless it was the greasy soup she used to serve Father Tom.

They walked to the front of the church and sat in the front pew. For a while all was silent. Then Aunt Bridget began. "Iota, I was listening when Father Tom and Uncle DOC talked to you. I wasn't nosy. I was and am interested.

"My little friend, you know that is Jesus hanging on the cross. He had twelve Apostles. One betrayed him. One denied him and nine fled when he was arrested. All through the night he was alone without a friend.

"When they nailed him on the cross and raised him between two thieves to die, only one Apostle remained true. There were three women at the foot of the cross: Mary, his mother, Mary Magdalene, and Mary, the mother of James and John.

"When I was a little girl, Iota, I didn't have a single friend. My parents didn't take the time to let me know whether or not I was loved. My three brothers were ashamed of me.

"I came to live with Father Tom because no one else would have me. He put up with me because he is a priest. He had everything, and I had nothing. I became his judge, jury, mother, sister, confessor, spiritual director, and jailer.

"He moved his office to Carolan's to escape me, and then I was truly alone. But not like Christ. I was alone because I was mean and wanted to get even with the world. Christ was alone because he loved the world and wanted to save it.

"Then, Iota, you came into my world. The Bible says 'a child will lead.' You have led me into self-respect and caring for others. You are the best friend I have in all the world.

"Father Tom and Uncle DOC and I want so much to help you, but we are just three old relics who hardly remember our own childhood with all its problems.

"Just know one thing. As you look at the crucifix, it looks like Christ is alone. But John and the three Marys are there. And we are here also.

"So no matter how alone you may feel, you have Mom and Dad, Father Tom, Uncle DOC, me, and God knows how many other friends who want to lift you from the cross, kiss and heal all your wounds, and protect you from all harm.

"Saint Paul says somewhere that when he was a child, he thought as a child, spoke and acted as a child. Then he said he became an adult and put away the things of a child and did everything as an adult.

"Father and DOC want you to think, act, and be like a grown-up. They have forgotten the importance of childhood. They solve problems as adults. They expect you to do the same.

"Young people who smoke, use drugs, or have sex will tell you out of envy, 'Be an adult—smoke; have a drink; have sex. Be an adult.' They are really saying, 'We have forsaken our childhood. You're no better than we are. Do these things and prove it.'

"Once you asked me if I had a mother. I said she was dead. You knew I needed a mother, someone to love me.

"My mother never really loved me. She protected me. She pitied me. She never loved me. She robbed me of my childhood.

"Because I was merely pitied, I became more pitiable. If I had been loved, I would have become more lovable.

"Iota, you were the first person who ever loved me. You shared your most precious gift with me: your mother and her love. Christ shared his mother from his cross.

"Because of you, I now have many friends. I am no longer an object of pity. Because of you, I am enjoying my first childhood. I want it to last as long as it can.

"We are friends. That is a beautiful word. You and I are friends no matter what might happen.

"The word *friend* means many, many things. People are most obviously friends in times of trouble. Friends stick together through any and every hardship and heartache.

"We don't have to say 'loving friends' or 'happy friends' or 'special friends.' The word *friend* all by itself implies all the other words.

"So you see, Iota, because we are friends we are lovable, we are special, we are happy. The truth is, unless you are happy I cannot be happy.

"What Father Tom and Uncle DOC said to you was all true. There are times children have to hear the adult truth from adults and have to accept it. But that doesn't mean the youngster has to compromise or surrender the joys of being a child or forgo the happiness and innocence of youth.

210

"I know I am being selfish, Iota. I know the day you put away the things of a child, my own childhood is ended.

"I think most parents never want their children to really grow up. It is through their offspring they can continually see life with all its wonder through the eyes of a child.

"I have been able to experience a wonderful world through you. God knows, Iota, when you become an adult, I may be nothing more than your dear old Aunt Bridget.

"Let's spend a few moments now in silent prayer. Then we can go back to the rectory."

Chapter 19

Ellie decided she would not attend court the following day. She thought it best to remain at home with Iota. After Mass and breakfast, the pastor journeyed again to the county seat. As he had the day before, he sat beside the defendant.

There was nothing one could ascertain concerning Dr. Burke's emotional state. He seemed less excited than most of the other people in the room. He and the priest exchanged pleasantries. Father Tom explained Ellie's absence.

The first witness introduced by the prosecuting attorney was a middle-aged woman named Elizabeth Norton. She was not especially attractive, but her good grooming forced an observer to take a second look.

She was nervous, but her determined demeanor gave her an appearance of practical calm. She was duly sworn in and seated herself in the witness chair.

Canton began his interrogation, "Mrs. Norton, why are you here?"

"To testify against the defendant: Dr. Robert Burke."

"Do you know Dr. Burke?" asked the prosecutor.

"Only indirectly. My daughter, Evelyn Norton, requested his help. She was an AIDS victim."

"Where is your daughter now?"

"She is dead. He would not treat her and she died."

"Are you sure your daughter sought Dr. Burke specifically?"

"Absolutely positive."

"No more questions, Your Honor," concluded Canton.

"Do you wish to ask any questions, Dr. Burke?"

"Yes, Your Honor." Then to Elizabeth Norton, "Are you from Minneapolis?"

"I am. I've lived there all my life," answered the witness.

"And your daughter came from Minneapolis to Boomer for my help? Are there no doctors in the Twin Cities?"

"None with your expertise on the disease of AIDS."

"Mrs. Norton, while you were responding to the prosecutor's question I was racking my memory as to where I had heard your name before. Were you in a Hennepin County court about twenty years ago?"

"I was," she answered.

"You may very well be the same Elizabeth Norton whose case was so often discussed at the University Medical School. Did you approach a doctor in the Twin Cities for an abortion?"

"That's right."

"And he refused to accept you as his patient?"

"Right."

"You were driving to consult with another doctor with the same request in mind when you had a serious automobile accident?"

"Correct."

"You were taken, unconscious, by ambulance to a hospital?"

"Correct."

"And in the emergency room, your baby was delivered prematurely but very much alive?"

"Where is this getting us?" she asked.

"To the next question. Are my facts correct?"

"Yes."

"And you sued the hospital for its action . . . for saving the baby?"

"True."

"Did you win the case?" asked the defendant.

"No, I didn't."

"It doesn't surprise me that you or your daughter might not have sought medical help in Minneapolis. Mrs. Norton, I believe every person is intended to be a temple of love and life. If some prefer themselves as temples of death and destruction, they shouldn't be surprised if a given doctor won't cooperate."

213

Dr. Burke continued, "A doctor said no to you before the accident. I, another doctor, said no to your daughter. A daughter on account of whom you sued the hospital for bringing her into the world.

"Except under extreme circumstances, I believe a doctor can refuse a client for any number of reasons." Then to the judge, "Your Honor, I have no further questions."

Elizabeth Norton stepped down. Bill Canton called the next witness, Randy Schmitz. Mr. Schmitz was a young man, apparently in his twenties. He was clean-shaven. He stood about six feet, two inches in height and had an athletic appearance and quite striking features. He was placed under oath and took his place in the witness chair.

The prosecuting attorney stood in place and then, instead of asking questions, said to the witness, "You have asked to be a witness here today. I'll try not to interrupt. Say what you have to say."

Mr. Schmitz cleared his throat, took a deep breath, exhaled, and began.

"My name is Randy Schmitz. I am from Minnetonka. Three years ago I contracted AIDS. I went to several doctors and clinics in the Twin Cities. None gave me any hope.

"Fortunately, one I eventually approached informed me of a classmate he had at the university medical school. He said his classmate was dedicating his life in the hope of finding a cure for AIDS.

"He asked if I was interested. If so, he would locate the doctor. He went through the directory for doctors and found that Dr. Robert Burke was doing research in a small town in southeastern Minnesota called Boomer.

"I took down Dr. Burke's phone number and address. The same day, I placed the call to Boomer. He indicated he had medication that might or might not heal. Would I want to experiment?

"I had nothing to lose and asked how much it would cost. He said he had some conditions and if I filled the conditions there would be no cost.

"What were the conditions? I would grow a beard and mustache, I would wear dark glasses, and under no conditions would I ever reveal the results of the experiment.

"He wanted it to be a real beard, which meant several weeks' delay. He did not want to know anything about my identity. I would respond to the name John Doe.

"I was to get in touch with him when the beard was full. He didn't want to know my phone number or address. He cautioned me that the experiment would take place only if I promised never to report the results.

"Three times we met. Each time there was immediate improvement. One week after the third visit, he examined me and declared I was totally healed.

"That, in a nutshell, is what I wanted to tell today," concluded Randy Schmitz, alias John Doe.

The members of the media ran for the exit as Randy Schmitz finished his statement. They wanted to get the scoop to the various news sources immediately. Those remaining in the courtroom were all talking in animated conversation. Judge Nelson rapped his gavel sharply.

The judge turned to Bill Canton. "Any questions?"

"No, Your Honor."

Then he turned to Dr. Burke. "Do you wish to cross-examine the witness, Doctor?"

"Yes, Your Honor," responded Dr. Burke. Slowly he rose to his feet, then addressed Randy Schmitz. "In your testimony, you indicate you made a promise not to reveal your cure and its source."

"Yes, Doctor, I made such a promise to you."

"If you don't keep your word in your promise, of what value is your word? Is the court to believe the word of one who openly admits to lies?" asked the defendant.

"The entire narrative is accurate as I spoke it!"

"Presuming that to be the case, how can you testify against the very person responsible for saving your life?" pursued Burke.

"Because life without my fiancée is no life at all."

"And who is your fiancée?"

"The daughter of the previous witness, Elizabeth Norton: Evelyn Norton! The young woman who came to you at my direction. You refused to accept her as your patient," retorted Schmitz.

"No further questions, Your Honor," said the doctor as he slumped in his chair.

"This has been a frantic afternoon for everyone here. The witness is dismissed. Do I hear any objections to a recess? . . . As I hear none, the court stands in recess until tomorrow at ten o'clock." The judge rapped the gavel; all stood as he retired.

Father Tom followed Dr. Burke and the jailer to the welcome relief of the cell. For the first time, the defendant was obviously shaken.

"John Doe really did me in, didn't he?" Dr. Burke exhaled a deep sigh.

"You've certainly had better days, Bob. Now what?"

"Would you mind, my friend, if we just sat in silence for a few moments? A few moments of reflection?"

Father Tom nodded assent. Dr. Robert Burke closed his eyes and spoke inaudibly to his God and Creator, his Brother and Redeemer, his Spirit of Love and Hope.

After several minutes, the doctor opened his eyes and began to smile at his friend. "Father Tom, you've given many good sermons. Would you run through a couple of them with me now?"

"I don't have your memory, Dr. Bob, but I'll try."

"Remember the one about the elderly woman who was dying from skin cancer?"

"I will never forget Mrs. Pendergast. Her whole countenance was like very red hamburger placed thinly over her skull. There were holes where the nostrils and eyes had been. Her teeth were all in place. It took me several visits before I could stand the smell."

"Please, go on."

"She suffered much but never complained. To the very end she maintained her sense of humor. I remember preparing her funeral sermon. I wasn't ordained a year at the time. I was sure she was in heaven, as she was truly a person of deep faith and hope. Anyway, I was wondering how she might look in heaven. Was she as beautiful as she was in her high school graduation picture? That was my first conclusion. Then I thought of Jesus at the Resurrection. He carried all the marks of his suffering. He insisted that Thomas place his finger in the nail wounds and his hand into His side.

"I decided that Mrs. Pendergast was in heaven carrying all her wounds that she accepted as a blessing without complaint.

The saints in heaven say of her, 'Look how she suffered without loss of faith, hope, and love.'

"At the time, I also thought perhaps if she had died in all the beauty of her youth, she may not have attained heaven. Maybe lost souls could curse her beauty for all eternity."

"I really appreciated that sermon, Father Tom. The other you will recall. It was concerning the Parade of the Sick at Lourdes," the doctor said hopefully.

"We were on a trip to Europe on the occasion of my fifth anniversary as a priest. At Lourdes, they have a candlelight procession each night. Pilgrims gather in groups according to country and language. Each person carries a lighted candle and everyone sings the Lourdes Hymn in his or her own tongue. It is quite moving.

"The 'parade' is in the afternoon. People gather around a very large field. They are on crutches, in wheelchairs, use canes, or are carried on litters. The bishop of the day processes with the Blessed Sacrament, blessing the sick as he moves along.

"Anyway, I was standing next to an American who was in his wheelchair. He seemed to be in a great deal of pain. I asked him how long he had been at Lourdes. He told me he had been at Lourdes for two weeks and was going home tomorrow.

"Then I asked if he had washed in the 'baths' and he said he had. I questioned him as to whether he had come to Lourdes expecting a miracle on his behalf, and he admitted as much.

"Then I said he must be very upset to have spent two weeks praying for a miracle and nothing had happened. His answer surprised me.

"He said, 'I prayed for the miracle of healing, but God has blessed me with something much more wonderful. He gave me the wonderful miracle of acceptance.'

"Dr. Bob, I'll never forget that man at that moment," concluded the priest.

"Father Tom, I was thinking about those two people who became a part of you. Both must have affected you greatly, since your telling of them affected me. I've written a poem along those lines. It is on this piece of paper. Would you read it aloud to me?" asked the doctor anxiously.

The priest took the folded sheet of paper from an envelope. Then he began reading it to the author:

" 'If we could choose one moment
From that life in which
He would live and live no other . . .
What moment would we choose?

" 'Would we want to share
The warmth of Bethlehem
With shepherds and Magi
In ignorant adoration . . .
Or rejoice at two and ten
In the mother's embrace
of the child found in Zion's Temple
Deep steeped in teaching?

" 'Moments of grandeur
Of miracles and praise . . .
Concerning these we would hesitate
Briefly . . . and move to Calvary.' "

Father Burns refolded the poem and replaced it in the envelope. He made a gesture to return it to his friend.

"Bob, that really is a fine poem."

"Thanks, Tom. Would you keep it? I want you to have it. Someday you might want to show it to Ellie and Iota.

"Psalm 119 keeps coming to my mind:

" 'Before I was afflicted, I went astray
but now I hold to your promise.
It is good for me that I have been
afflicted, that I may learn your statutes.' "

"Dr. Bob, you scare me a little. Do you understand the seriousness of your situation?"

"Father Tom, does it bother you how I speak and how I act? If I were to know I have only ten minutes left in life, I would talk of God. We shouldn't flee Him.

218

"The Old Testament is not a history of searching for God so much as it is a history of fleeing from God. Our history is often the same.

"God searches for us. We must be 'findable.' The Lord speaks of hen and chicks. No sparrow falls but what the Father's heart goes out to it. And we, we are worth much more.

"We are the center of His search. The question we must answer is whether He is the Center of ours. The question is not merely: What is truth? But rather, Does life have any meaning?

"Christ has shown us from the cross that there is nothing so whole as a broken heart." The doctor paused.

"I hate to admit that the difference between us is that you use the Scripture for life and I use it for sermon material," said the pastor thoughtfully.

"Father, I suspect Ellie has heard from various sources what happened in court today. She must need you now. At the risk of being selfish, could I ask you to come back tonight with the Eucharist?"

Father Burns called for the jailer and as he left promised he would do as requested. "See you later." Again he found himself on that all too familiar road back to Boomer.

He stopped at Ellie's. There was no information he could give that she didn't possess. He had stopped along the way to purchase a broiled chicken and a prepared salad. They and Iota ate it as they discussed the weather and had other unhurtful conversation.

"He asked me to bring him Communion tonight," the priest said as he was leaving. "Would you care to come along?"

"No, I really wouldn't. He knows I disagree with the decisions he has made without even consulting me. I think there is greater likelihood that he will come to his senses in my absence than in my presence," she conjectured.

"If your lights are still on when I get back, I'll stop in. Especially, if there is any report on any new happenings," and the pastor departed.

On his return to the cell he was warmly welcomed by his old friend. They spent the necessary moments in preparation and administration of the Eucharist. Then Dr. Bob spent several minutes in silent thanksgiving.

"Did you see Ellie and Iota?" he finally ventured.

"As a matter of fact, we had dinner together."

"How is Ellie looking, Father Tom?" he asked.

"To be honest with you, Doc, if she weren't so angry, I could say she is in deep mourning," answered the pastor.

"And Iota?"

"Quiet. Quiet and withdrawn. There is so much she can't understand, Bob," said the cleric.

"And I suppose because you can't understand either, you can't explain anything to her," said the doctor, shaking his head.

"I have never understood you, Bob. I never understood you before because of your superior brilliance. Now, I just don't understand," admitted Father Tom in all honesty.

"Do you think I'm wrong in what I am doing?" queried the doctor.

"Bob, I've never been a judgmental person. I'm not sure if it is because the Lord says to 'judge not lest you be judged' or if it is just part of my lazy nature, wanting to avoid conflict at any cost," he pondered.

The priest thought he was leaving a door open for further discussion. Should he have said more about Ellie and Iota? Should he have given his feelings concerning his friend's situation?

"This afternoon, Father, you repeated two sermons you gave in the past. Would you indulge me with another?"

"Bob, I really appreciate how you remember some of my sermons. No one knows how much time I spent in their preparation. I've never entered the pulpit without a well-thought-out homily.

"That doesn't mean it is a good sermon. Sometimes I really strike out. But it is never due to lack of effort.

"Strange as it may seem, the real inspiration for working on every sermon came from an educational psychology class at Saint Mary's University.

"The professor said, 'Don't think for one minute that if you come to teach a one-hour class without preparation and there are thirty students in the class you have wasted an hour; you have wasted thirty hours.'

"So I concluded if I preach a poor ten-minute sermon, I haven't wasted ten minutes. I must multiply the number of parishioners by ten to judge the time wasted," said Father Tom.

"My apology for the digression. Getting back to your request,

Dr. Bob, just give me a clue and I will try to recall the sermon you want."

"I can recall every word of it, but I want to hear it again. It doesn't have to be the sermon, just the facts and circumstances," commented Burke.

"What was it about?"

"It was about the woman who came for the Sacrament of Reconciliation at the request of her nephew."

"That I remember as vividly as if it were yesterday. It was during the Lenten season and we were celebrating communal penance.

"This woman came to me and she was having a great deal of difficulty getting started. I presumed her problem was the enormity of her offenses.

"Consequently, I asked her if there was anything I could say to make it easier. She shook her head but couldn't get control of herself.

"I was about to go through the commandments as an aid, but she assured me it wouldn't be of any assistance.

"Finally, she gained some control of her emotions and began to tell me the problem. This was some time ago before the last cancer cure had been found. Anyway, through her veil of tears, she explained that her nephew was dying of that dreaded disease.

"At his insistence, his parents called all the relatives together so he could talk with them. He lay in his bed, a mere skeleton of his former self, and looked at each of them in turn.

"This is what he said: 'I am dying and all of you will miss me. You are my dearest friends. The priest was here last night. He heard my sins, administered the Sacrament of Healing, and gave me Holy Eucharist.

" 'I am ready to die except for one thing. I asked you to come here so I can encourage each of you to attend Communal Penance this afternoon or tonight.

" 'Please make every effort for a worthy reception of the sacrament. It is my hope that one day soon all of you, my relatives and friends, will be with me forever with Christ.'

"Then she confessed her sins, received absolution, and was gone. Dr. Bob, I'll never forget that moment and it looks like you haven't either," concluded the priest.

"Father Tom, I have always believed in God with all my heart. I so wanted to be a priest so I could dedicate my life to some growth in His kingdom. I was denied the priesthood because of my saintly mother.

"I hated the god I had created because he was a false god. He didn't produce when I prayed. I asked for bread and he handed me a stone. The more I hated God, the more I was forced to accept reality. It would be unrealistic to hate a nonexistent God.

"I don't think God wills pain, but God does will that it will bring us closer to him. There is so much contradiction. We know the role of the missionary is not merely producing bread-and-butter Christians.

"We get angry at God when we hunger or thirst, yet at the same time it draws us to him. It must be impossible to satisfy a starving person with a sermon.

"No, God doesn't allow pain merely so we will be drawn to Him. I believe this purpose is much more noble. He wants us to have oneness with him in his Son.

"In our country, slaves were often denied the things of society except faith. It was as though they were being told, 'Take our God, but nothing else.' Often they accepted that God even though their 'masters' may have deserted him long ago.'

"That is why every black spiritual is sacred. The African-American was able to identify with the prophets of old who came forth in times of adversity."

"Dr. Bob, what does all that have to do with the sermon you wanted me to repeat?" asked Father Tom.

"Everything. My family, Ellie and Iota, wants me to share family pleasures that are temporary. I want us to be together forever. Father Tom, be honest with me. Let me know who your very best friends are. As you read off their names, you are forced to admit they became friends in times of adversity," stated Bob.

"It has been a long day for both of us. I'm tired and you must be also. This was not an easy twenty-four hours and tomorrow could be worse," said the pastor.

"Thanks for bringing me the Eucharist. Thanks for your visit. It is only a friend such as you who would let me ramble so. It may not seem that way to you, but I'm at least making sense to myself," Dr. Burke said, half in gratitude, half in need of assurance.

"Get your sleep now. I'll give you my blessing before I leave."

"Isn't it incredible, Father Tom, that a person who for just a moment was called John Doe would be my undoing?"

"That's right, Bob. Never again trust a man named John Doe."

The pastor again called the jailer and departed. When he drove past Ellie's house it was dark. He breathed a silent prayer that she was resting peacefully and proceeded home. There was a note from Bridget by the telephone: "Ellie wants to go with you tomorrow." The priest slept fitfully. He wondered over and over what was ahead for the doctor, his wife, and their daughter.

Chapter 20

Immediately after Mass and breakfast, Father Tom made his fourth journey to court in the same number of days. It was Friday, and he guessed the court would not be in session again until Monday.

Much to his surprise, he found he had a full car of people. Iota wanted to go with her mother. Also, Uncle DOC and Bridget were on the passenger list.

There weren't enough chairs next to the doctor's in the courtroom, and since the last seat was filled within seconds of opening the doors, the judge allowed extra chairs for DOC and Bridget as well as Ellie, Iota, and Father Tom.

After the court was called to order, Judge Nelson asked Bill Canton if he had any more witnesses. The response was in the positive. "The prosecution would like to call to the stand the defendant: Dr. Robert Burke."

The doctor had suspected he would be called to testify but hadn't expected it so soon. He looked at his wife and daughter, whom he was pleased to see again. He smiled at Bridget and DOC. Then he shook hands with Father Tom as though it would be the last time. Then, as if in a trance, he move forward to take the oath. He took the stand.

"Dr. Burke," began Canton, "it has been established, at least to my satisfaction, that you have discovered or manufactured, or whatever the correct verb might be, a cure for AIDS. At the present time, are you prepared to make the final solution to that known sickness available to the world?"

"The answer to your question is no," responded Burke.

"Is it because you fear for the medical profession, that there would be no more need for doctors?"

"Not at all. I think, however, that doctors would all have to become psychiatrists rather than physicians."

"Dr. Burke," continued the attorney, "you have spent your medical career searching for the cure. Why and how did you become so interested and dedicated?"

"My mother died of AIDS. I watched her suffer. I decided if it were in my power, I would erase AIDS from the face of the earth," answered the defendant.

"Something changed your mind?" pursued Canton.

"Not all at once. One day I realized that even though my mother suffered much from AIDS, she also had become a much more loving and caring person," offered the defendant.

"You think pain is good?"

"I don't think it is necessarily evil. I believe it is by the suffering and death of Christ that we are redeemed. Once there was a seminary rector who would tell the future priests that no one should be ordained until he had spent at least six months in a hospital bed. Then he might have some of the compassion of Christ."

"Compassion?"

"Yes, two good Latin words, *cum* and *passio*, meaning 'to suffer with.' How can I suffer with anyone if I don't know about pain?"

"Does that mean you will never release the cure?"

"If I may have the court's indulgence, in Boomer there is a little three-year-old girl named Annie. She has an aunt named Tish. Tish has a cat called Greta.

"On a regular basis, nearly daily, Annie calls Aunt Tish and asks to talk to Greta. Tish then pretends she is Greta and listens to all Annie's woes and joys. Annie loves Greta.

"But whenever Annie comes to her Aunt Tish's house, Greta hides. No amount of coaxing can bring Greta out from under the sofa or bed.

"One time, on the phone, Annie admonished Greta, 'Why do you always hide when I come to visit you? Why won't you talk with me? You don't even know that I'm a cute little blonde with beautiful blue eyes.'

"The human race, like Greta, has become many selfish individuals who aren't taking the time to look into the eyes of others or study faces.

"We all say, 'If only the deer would let me pet them. If only the eagle would perch at my window.' People aren't decent to animals or to one another. Francis of Assisi referred to 'Brother Wolf.' He preached to the fish. Not because he was mental, but because he had a message and people wouldn't listen. They didn't understand him. His own father had him arrested.

"People are happy to have Francis in their gardens but not in their hearts. When the whole world accepts the Lord's message and becomes as Francis, then we will have no further need of pain.

"But even then we must remember that the man from Assisi carried the wounds of Christ's passion on his person."

"Dr. Burke, have you, then, wasted your life?" asked Canton.

"I don't know. History will decide," answered the witness.

"Would you take the final solution were you to find you have AIDS?"

"No," he answered without hesitation.

"Doctor, if your wife or daughter contracted AIDS, would you administer the cure to either of them?"

"That is the most difficult question I have had to face. You would never believe the prayers I have directed to God over that question. I love my wife and my daughter more than myself . . ." He bowed his head as though needing to pray one more time.

For a moment he looked at his family, seated between Aunt Bridget and Uncle DOC. Both Ellie and Iota were also praying fervently.

God heard these words from Ellie: *Please, Lord, make him say, "Yes." I have given this man everything that I am. Don't let me suffer the embarrassment, the indignity, of denial.*

God heard these words from Iota: *Please, Lord, I want my friends back. Make Dad say, "No," so everyone will know I am no different than they are and I'll be accepted again.*

The doctor cleared his throat with great difficulty. Then in a husky whisper he spoke. "I love them with all my heart, but I wouldn't give them the medicine."

As though raised from the chair by some unseen power, Ellie rose to her full stature, and her husband, through tear-filled eyes, watched her march down the aisle to the exit. Behind her hurried Uncle DOC.

Iota had arisen beside her mother, but instead of following her out of the courtroom, she raced up to her dad and embraced him. "Daddy, I love you. I love you."

Then she saw the tears streaming down his face. She took the handkerchief from his coat pocket and tried to dry his tears. Dr. Robert Burke threw his arms around his most priceless possession. "Iota, I love you so much. You and your mother will never know how much I love you both."

It all happened so fast that everyone was caught off guard. Bill Canton was sorry he had asked the mean question. The judge knew that order had left his court and that, for the first time in his career, the heavy gavel was not the answer.

Father Tom motioned to his sister, Bridget. She in turn moved slowly to Iota, who was now crying uncontrollably.

"Come on, Iota; let's go home," urged Bridget.

"Daddy, why don't you come home, too? I miss you so much." And Iota and Aunt Bridget were gone.

During the commotion, the sheriff, accompanied by Dr. Philip Hurley, had entered the court. The sheriff handed a file to the prosecuting attorney.

After Iota and Bridget left the room, Canton came to the judge's bench.

"Your Honor, your search warrant has produced the desired effect. In this file is the mystery of the final solution. According to Dr. Hurley, it seems intact."

"The warrant specifically stated that you were not to look at the contents. Did you follow my instructions?"

Canton turned to the sheriff, who responded, "Your instructions were followed. Dr. Hurley does not know any more than he knew before except that this is complete. The index on the cover indicates as much."

A voice from the media spoke out. "We have the final solution. We don't need Dr. Burke anymore."

The judge looked sternly at the newsman. Then he spoke to the sheriff. "Arrest that man for contempt of court. Take him to your office and charge him. His case will be at nine o'clock on Monday morning. Except as a defendant, he is not to return to this courtroom. Let me tell this court we will not have a repeat of such conduct."

Then he turned to Canton. "Do you have more questions? If so, please proceed."

"Dr. Burke, in view of the fact that the materials needed for the final solution are in the possession of the court, is it possible, since you did not destroy the evidence, that you planned eventually to give it to the world?"

"There is always the possibility that a person may change his mind, but at the present, I would have to say the possibility was absolutely remote at best," answered Burke.

"Why, then, did you not destroy the evidence?" asked Canton.

"There are really two reasons. First, that folder represents years of arduous work of which I am proud and for which I am grateful. Second, I never thought of it as evidence. To me, it was my own private property. In fact, I am dumbfounded that Judge Nelson would sign the search warrant for its procurement," responded the defendant.

"I have no further questions of the defendant, Your Honor."

The judge had been so intent on listening to the conversation that its abrupt termination caught him somewhat off guard. For a moment he stumbled for words. "Dr. Burke," he began, "it was not easy to sign that warrant. The consideration against signing was your last statement. It is your personal property.

"The consideration in favor," he continued, "is whether the evidence is not a matter of life and death as much as any murder weapon. After all, your refusal to allow the use of the final solution has cost thousands, if not millions, of lives.

"Further, it must be determined who really owns the evidence. Is it yours as you believe it is? Does it, in part at least, belong to the Mayo Clinic or perhaps to the heirs of Becky Carpenter?" pondered the judge.

"Your Honor," responded Burke, "on page 14 in the file on your bench is a disclaimer from the Mayo Clinic.

"Becky Carpenter never married. She has no living relatives. That is one of the reasons she was good to me and my work. My mother and I were her family.

"Dr. Hurley worked for a salary. He admitted under oath in this court that he had no idea what all the ingredients were in the final solution.

"The final solution exists solely because of my dedication. Without that, it wouldn't exist," concluded the doctor.

"Dr. Burke, I tend to agree with all you have just said. Do you not think the common good is at stake here?" asked the judge.

"Indeed I do. That is my very point. However, I'm surprised to hear the 'common good' mentioned in court. *Common good* pertains to what is moral rather than to what is legal," claimed Dr. Burke.

"What do you mean by that?" queried the judge.

"Slavery was legal at one time in the United States. It was never moral. Prohibition was legal but, most would agree, not moral. The fact that abortion is legal doesn't make it moral. In all three issues, the common good was not the issue," responded Burke.

"How does all this pertain to you and what is happening here?"

"Your Honor, the court will find me guilty because the charges are unfair. I am guilty of all the charges but am an innocent man."

"Dr. Burke, you were charged with possessing the final solution."

"Right. And I do possess it," said the defendant.

"And you are charged with not sharing it."

"Right again. I have said from the beginning that if I have it, it is mine. I can do what I want with it," responded Burke.

"Dr. Burke, I tend to agree with you. However, I still feel a need to discover who really owns the final solution. In the mind of this court, I declare you guilty of the charges, but since the charges are illegal, I declare you innocent."

"You mean I am a free man? That I can leave?"

"I mean no such thing. You are guilty of breaking a most serious law. When you administered the final solution to Randy Schmitz, you were using a medication never approved by the Federal Drug Administration. It is interesting that our legislature has no mandatory sentence for the offense. I will make that decision myself."

"You mean, Your Honor, that I came into this court accused of not using the drug but I'm being convicted for the one and only time I did?" asked the doctor.

"That is correct," continued the judge. "I will pronounce the sentence on Monday morning. Meanwhile, since I have much to ponder, might I ask you one more question? . . . Doctor, what do you think your sentence should be?"

"Your Honor, you asked me for an opinion. I would rather respond with a wish. I do not believe in capital punishment. I believe all life is sacred. Because of that, I would like a life sentence," said the doctor calmly.

"Why?"

"I believe that sanctity of life is more important than quality of life. With quality of life, one tends to think of self. With sanctity of life, one has to consider others.

"Parents generally tend to want their children to have what they didn't have. That's not all bad. What is bad is when they fail to give them what they did have. They sometimes exchange the child's sanctity of life for quality of life," said Burke.

"No, no. Doctor Burke, why would you want a life sentence?"

"Your Honor, I don't think I want to live in a world such as I and my medications would produce. Many years ago I was approached to develop a means whereby anyone could run one hundred meters in seven seconds. I succeeded even though I was angered by the waste of time.

"What were the results? Everyone who went out for track became a robot. Six or so sprinters would get into the blocks, the gun would go off, all the runners would start simultaneously, run stride for stride, and hit the tape at the same time . . . like robots. The same thing became true for all the running events. The result you know too well. There is no more track.

"The same thing is true of basketball. With the ability of all to jump the same height, basketball players became no more than robots.

"When pain is no longer a part of human existence, what will happen to emotions? Without emotion, we all become nothing more than robots. God created a wonderful world. The world people want today is not," concluded Dr. Burke.

"Dr. Burke, do you have anything else to say before we

recess?" asked Judge Nelson. "We will resume here on Monday at one o'clock in the afternoon for sentencing. I assure you, it will not be for life.

"Also, the file I possess concerning the final solution will be kept safe in my chambers until ownership is determined once and for all. If neither the prosecuting attorney nor the defendant has a question, we are recessed until Monday." The judge rapped his gavel.

Dr. Burke turned to his pastor. "Father Tom, I know you have to take your passengers home. Will you do me a favor? After dinner tonight, please bring the oils for the Sacrament of Healing and the Eucharist."

"Sure, Bob, whatever you ask."

The jailer led the prisoner to his cell.

Father Tom wasn't sure what to expect when he arrived at his car. He was relieved to see Ellie was quite angry. Iota was happy, much to her mother's distress.

"God certainly is asking much of all of us at this time, isn't he?" suggested the priest.

"Much more than is humanly possible," responded Ellie.

"We have to believe that God is reasonable. A reasonable God does not ask the impossible," pondered the pastor aloud.

Once at home, Uncle DOC asked Iota for a moment's chat. She consented. They walked up the street toward the school.

"Iota, remember the discussion we had on popularity?" questioned DOC.

"That was a terrible night. Only Aunt Bridget made sense."

"I apologize for that. Now I want to say that what you did for your dad today was wonderful. He needs your support, understanding, and love. He has a right to it. These are hard times for him. Your dad loves you. If you understand nothing else, understand that," said Uncle DOC.

Chapter 21

Father Burns walked into his friend's cell. As requested, he had brought the Eucharist and the oils.

"Please, Tom," said the prisoner, "you will give me the Sacrament of Healing, won't you?"

"Bob, what is this sudden pessimism? It isn't your nature to look for the dark side of anything. Besides, I'm not sure what Canon Law would say about this. You look healthy to me, except for the lack of color."

"Neither one of us ever cared for Canon Law. And I am not a pessimist. The fact is, as an optimist, I want total preparation for the kingdom of God. I have a feeling this is my last night on earth.

"I'm not anxious to die, but I want to be prepared. Somehow, I have always known there is suffering ahead for me. Two Scripture quotes make it bearable. They keep me able to proceed with some courage.

"The first is Romans 8:18: 'I reckon that the sufferings of the present time are not worthy to be compared with the glory to come that will be revealed to us. For the eager longing of creation awaits the revelation of the sons of God. For creation was made subject to vanity, not by its own will but by reason of him who made it subject, in hope, because creation itself also will be delivered from its slavery to corruption into the freedom of the glory of the sons of God. For we know that all creation groans and travails in pain until now.'

"The second is Colossians 1:24: 'I rejoice now in the sufferings

I bear for your sake; and what is lacking in the sufferings of Christ I fill up in my flesh for His body which is the church.'

"These two Scriptures are part of why I didn't share the final solution and are the cause of my courage.

"I can't explain it. I just know it. Prepare me for my death. It may be only my old self that will die tonight. In any case, tomorrow will have brought a new life."

The priest gave the doctor a quizzical look.

The doctor continued, "I have tried to the best of my ability to forgive all who have ever hurt me. It hasn't always been easy. Some people are always so right it makes forgiving them very difficult.

"As a child, I resented my mother when she was right. Whether she was right or wrong, though, made no difference. I always loved her more when she was understanding. She became most understanding after she was diagnosed as having AIDS.

"My bishop was very right, in his own mind, when he refused to ordain me, but he was not understanding. I pray often that I have truly forgiven him. More important for him and for me, I know God has forgiven him.

"You know I became a doctor so I could work toward a curing medication for AIDS. I resented the time and energy the NCAA stole from me when I was forced to respond to its whims. I'm not sure if one can forgive stupidity. If so, I have forgiven them.

"Mayo was kind to me. They agreed with my attitude toward finding the solution. They expected faster results. I did all I could within the time frame allowed. Again, they were right, but not understanding.

"They allowed me ownership of the results of my labors. I could take it with me when I left. They have been the easiest to forgive.

"Father Tom, I don't know of anyone on this earth I haven't forgiven. There has been one forgiving that has been most difficult. I have wrestled much about forgiving God."

The priest suddenly became completely attentive. He was no longer a passive listener. His leaning forward encouraged his friend to proceed.

"How could God have taken Dad from me? How could he allow my mother such terrible physical and emotional pain? I never prayed so much before or since as when I prayed that God would spare her.

"How could God allow me to be top of the class all through college and the seminary and then refuse me when the Church was pleading desperately for vocations to the priesthood?

"The day you were ordained, Tom, I seemed so totally alone. No parents, no relatives, except for Father Jim no friends, and, it seemed to me, no God! I was unable to identify with anyone. I was lonely as a soul damned to hell without any possibility of love.

"With whom could I identify? Job seemed the only person, and he was so fictional. There must be someone, but whom? Then it came to me. Thousands and thousands suffering from AIDS knew what I was enduring.

"Like Saint Damien, I could say 'we lepers.' Spiritually and psychologically I had AIDS. But I have forgiven God. The bishop didn't know what he was doing, so I forgave him. God knew completely and I forgave him, too.

"If he is God, he must be right even though I don't understand. But because he is God, he is understanding. I forgave him."

Half-joking, half seriously, the priest murmured, "I'm sure God appreciates that!"

"I sometimes recall a college English class I once attended," continued Burke, ignoring the priest. "The prof was talking about 'hero motif.' He explained that initially, the hero was in a comfortable situation. He would be invited to depart from comfort to some ordeal. The ordeal was handled well, all problems overcome, and the hero would be elevated to a high place in society because he had overcome adversity.

"Jung explained the words *departure, ordeal,* and *return* with the terms *separation, initiation,* and *transformation.*

"The unborn child enjoys swimming in the mother's womb. The temperature is always correct, and the food is usually adequate. Then there is the birth, when the infant is cast forth where one has to cry for the bottle and the diaper service is not always perfect.

"Eventually, the infant becomes the child, the child a teenager, and the teenager an adult. If the person survives each initiation, his transformation will never want a return to any previous situation.

234

"The Apostle Peter, from the comfort of his boat, recognized Christ walking on the water. Jesus asked Peter to come to him. The Apostle left the safety of the boat to walk on the water.

"We know, of course, that he began to sink. The Lord lifted him up, and they were at the shore. The Peter of increased faith would never be quite the same as before.

"I had the comfort of the seminary. That comfort and its future were destroyed. I'm not a priest, but I am a better person for having survived.

"I lost the friendship of parents and friends. At the University of Minnesota it seemed no one loved me. Then I met Ellie, and my life has been love-filled ever since.

"Christ understands all this. All one needs to do is open the Scripture to the second chapter of Philippians. The pertinent part begins with verse 5: 'The attitude you should have is the one that Jesus Christ had. He always had the nature of God but he did not think that by force he should try to become equal with God. Instead of this, of his own free will, he gave up all he had and took the nature of a servant. He became like man and appeared in human likeness. He was humble and walked the path of obedience all the way to his death, his death on the cross. For this reason God raised him to the highest place above and gave him the name that is greater than any other name. And so, in honor of the name of Jesus, all beings in heaven, on earth and in the world below will fall on their knees and will openly proclaim that Jesus Christ is Lord, to the glory of God the Father.'

"Christ lived the separation, the initiation, and the transformation," continued Burke. "We merely need to understand that he invites us to share with him.

"I have moved from success to trial to greater success over and over again. Now is the final time. My success is behind me. The trial is concluded. Death is ahead. Then the reward," spoke Burke quietly.

"Father Tom, I have forgiven everyone. Please forgive me. Give me Christ. Prepare me for the final healing."

Tears moved down the face of the priest. His choked words were hardly audible. He blessed and absolved. He placed the Healer into the hand of the doctor and anointed his friend.

There was much time spent in silent thanksgiving. After the

moments of gratitude Dr. Burke looked pleadingly at his pastor. "You have been generous with the time you have spent with me this week, and I am deeply appreciative. Could we visit a bit more?"

"As long as you like, Bob." The priest smiled.

"People don't understand me, Father Tom. Am I such a mystery?"

"Everyone is a mystery. The average person wants to maintain that element. Any time a husband is foolish enough to tell his wife he has her totally figured out, he is merely fooling himself. A wife who suspects her husband has her figured out is a wife who will quickly change," laughed Father Tom.

"What you say is true, but I want people to understand me."

"Why can't a genius be flattered by the fact that ordinary people don't understand him rather than perplexed by it? It is easy for you to plead that people don't understand you, because basically they never have and never will," said the priest.

"You know," he continued, "my mother and dad always got along, but they didn't always understand one another."

"You loved your parents, didn't you, Father Tom? You speak of them in such a way that one can't think otherwise. You know, I think it would be a good idea to put a chuckle in our conversation. Will you tell me the story of your mom and dad and the fur coat?" asked the prisoner.

"I love that story," chuckled Father Tom, "but you've heard it often enough so you could tell it to me."

However, Father Burns hurriedly proceeded with the tale lest the doctor deprive him of the podium.

"Well, the folks had gone through some bad times such as farmers often share. My mother had come from money and was lace-curtain Irish. She'd never allow any possibility that we be dependent on charity.

"Dad came from money, too, but he was shanty Irish. Her pride was adequate for them both. One day, coming from no place at all, she said, 'John Burns, I want a new fur coat.' Dad looked at her with dismay and unbelief. 'Hannah, I can't afford to buy you a coat, let alone a fur coat!'

"His answer was no surprise to her, but she was not about to let the matter drop so easily. She turned on him. 'If I were like

236

you, we'd be living in a tent!' Dad turned to her. 'And if you were like me, you'd be happy in a tent!' "

"That is a great story, Tom. And all the better because it is true!" Dr. Burke exclaimed.

Then a great silence ensued. It was like the story wasn't really appropriate no matter how needed it was. The silence was almost as uncomfortable as it would have been to break it. Finally, Dr. Burke cleared his throat as though words, any words, would be acceptable.

"Curses and blessings seem easily identified as disparate, yet they often interchange. Augustine refers to the disobedience of Adam and Eve as 'Oh happy fault that would cause the Son of God to become man.'

"In Eden, our first parents were free from death, suffering, and having to earn a living by the sweat of their brows. Those blessings turned to curses. They soon witnessed death when Cain killed Abel not too long after Eve had suffered the pains of childbirth.

"They also lost the gift of grace. They no longer walked face to face with God in the Garden. Instead of experiencing constant love, they experienced hatred within their own family.

"When Jesus came into the world he accepted all the curses. He suffered the bloody sweat in the Agony of the Garden. He was subjected to the hatred of the mob. He was punished with the Scourging at the Pillar. He was crowned with thorns. He carried the cross and was nailed to it. He died a terrible death.

"By means of Christ's acceptance of the curses, we were saved. The curses begun in the Garden of Eden were reversed in the Garden of Olives. The curses became blessings. They are the means of our salvation.

"So I question myself, 'Is the final solution which I have in my power a blessing or a curse?' I ask God for the answer in prayer, and he tells me what I already know. I know faith is reasonable. I have faith. I have reason. But I don't know whether the human race without pain would consider itself blessed or cursed.

"It seems like the world is concerned about last frontiers all the time. The last frontier in medicine was to be the final solution to AIDS. I suppose I thought that was the case."

"That makes some sense, but society often looks to outer space or the ocean depths as the last frontier," responded Father Tom.

"I suppose that is because we tend to be materialistic," reflected Dr. Bob.

"All right, my genius friend, what is your concept of the last frontier?" joked the priest.

"The last frontier is really the first one. It all began in the story of Adam and Eve."

"How so, Bob?"

"Cain and Abel were brothers, and Cain killed his brother. God asked him where Abel was, and Cain responded with the question: 'Am I my brother's keeper?'

"Ellie had an ancestor whose name was Ezra Elliot. He was looked upon as a frontiersman. Actually, he was just plain antisocial," commented the doctor.

"Where is this going?" asked the priest.

"I guess back to today's courtroom scene. The last frontier will be hurdled when Cain recognizes that Abel is his brother, not in the Book of Genesis, but the book titled *The Twenty-first Century*. When we all are able to take the time to care lovingly for one another. The last frontier will be present when we all keep the great commandment to love God above all things and our neighbor as ourselves," the doctor said triumphantly.

"Remember the priest who taught us Old Testament in the seminary? Remember the remark he made as he introduced us to the prophet Jonah?" asked the prisoner.

"I hate to admit that I don't, but I have a feeling you are about to refresh my memory." The priest smiled.

"Right. He said that whenever a person hears the name of Jonah, the first instinct is to ask the question, 'Can a whale actually swallow a man or is that more than a man can swallow?' " the doctor reminded his friend.

"Yes, I remember it now," admitted Father Burns.

"Once a person asks that question, the whole story of Jonah becomes biological rather than theological and the message is lost," continued Burke.

"That's what he said. He was a good teacher. He covered the material, which was most serious, but never lost his sense of humor," chuckled the pastor.

"God had a definite task for Jonah: to preach repentance to the powerful Ninevites. It was hardly an enviable task to preach to the enemy. Jonah did all he could to escape his mission.

"He hid in a ship that found itself in a terrible storm. The sailors jettisoned the cargo. They examined their own consciences to find if any one of them was guilty. Then lo and behold, they found Jonah in the hold of the ship.

"They pleaded with him, 'We have prayed to our gods; now you pray to your God and save us.' Jonah, however, was still in control of his destiny, so they cast him into the sea.

"He had no idea where the shore was. He knew not the directions, but he trusted his ability to swim. He was being very human.

"Then he suddenly discovered himself in the whale's belly. There was no longer any alternative. He turned to God. It was then that the whale spit him forth on the shore and he proceeded to preach successfully to the Ninevites. He accomplished with God's help what he had feared to attempt on his own.

"All through my childhood, in college, in the seminary, I was Jonah, in total control of my destiny. I thought I was praying, but I suspect I was only going through all the motions.

"When I stood at my mother's deathbed I was, for the first time, in the belly of the whale. By myself I was powerless, so I turned to God.

"God said no to my prayer then. He said no to my prayer that the bishop would ordain me. He said no when I asked the diocese for funding for medical school.

"God kept saying no to me all the time I was in the belly of the whale. I thought he wasn't answering my prayers. Since we have had Iota, I know as a parent that *no* is an answer.

"Jonah had the advantage of knowing exactly what his mission was. God made the message clear. Most of us merely have our consciences to tell us. Yet Holy Scripture tells us the law of God is written in the heart. Our task is to make certain we don't have hearts of stone.

"This week, in this cell, I find myself once more in the whale's belly. The sailors asked Jonah to pray to his God. That same God has said no to me many times.

"So this week I've asked God what he wants me to do. What he wants me to be. All at once, I knew there was something I could ask for and he would not deny me.

"I knelt beside this cot and I made my petition: "Please, God, make me a saint.' I believe He has answered me. I am not afraid."

"Bob, for heaven's sake, how can you be so sure that you are about to die?" asked Father Tom.

"When I say I'm not afraid, it means I'm not afraid to die. It also means I'm not afraid to live. Under the circumstances, there is less to fear in death. My premonition is that my time is very limited," said Burke resolutely.

"What can I do?" questioned the priest.

"I fell in love with a prayer I learned in the seminary. It is attributed to Pope Clement XI. I've recited it often. I use it as my final night prayer. Would you pray it with me now?"

"Yes, of course," said the pastor.

" 'Lord, I believe in you; increase my faith.
I trust in you; strengthen my trust.
I love you; let me love you more and more.
I am sorry for my sins; deepen my sorrow.

" 'I worship you as my first beginning.
I long for you as my last end.
I praise you as my constant helper
And call on you as my loving protector.

" 'Guide me by your wisdom.
Correct me with your justice.
Comfort me with your mercy.
Protect me with your power.

" 'I offer you, Lord, my thoughts to be fixed on you,
My words to have you for their theme,
My actions to reflect my love for you,
My sufferings to be endured for your greater glory.

" 'I want to do what you ask of me,
In the way you ask,

For as long as you ask,
Because you ask it.

" 'Lord, enlighten my understanding,
Strengthen my will,
Purify my heart,
And make me holy.
Help me to repent of my past sins and
To resist temptation in the future.
Help me to rise above my human weaknesses
And to grow stronger as a Christian.

" 'Let me love you, my Lord and my God,
And see myself as I really am,
A pilgrim in this world,
A Christian called to respect and love
All those whose lives I touch,
Those in authority over me
Or those under my authority,
My friends and my enemies.

" 'Help me to conquer anger by gentleness,
Greed by generosity,
Apathy by fervor.
Help me to forget myself
And reach out toward others.

" 'Make me prudent in planning,
Courageous in taking risks.
Make me patient in suffering and
Unassuming in prosperity.

" 'Keep me, Lord, attentive at prayer,
Temperate in food and drink,
Diligent in my work,
Firm in my good intentions.

" 'Let my conscience be clear,
My conduct without fault,

My speech blameless,
My life well ordered.

" 'Put me on guard against my human weaknesses;
Let me cherish your love for me,
Keep your law,
And come at last to your salvation.

" 'Teach me to realize that this world is passing,
That my true future is the happiness of heaven,
That life is short
And life to come eternal.

" 'Help me to prepare for death
With a proper fear of judgment
But a greater trust in your goodness.
Lead me safely through death
To the endless joy of heaven. Amen.' "

"That is a beautiful prayer. It is so inclusive," said the priest.

"Father Tom, one final favor. In court, the prosecuting attorney asked if I would give Ellie and Iota the final solution if they had AIDS. That moment was the worst in my life.

"Never have I been so deep in the belly of the whale. I so wanted to lie and say, 'Yes,' for Ellie's sake. I have never lied in my life, but I wanted to then.

"When Iota rushed forward and embraced me, I was so filled with mixed emotions. The daughter I had said no to told me she loved me and pleaded with me to come home. Her touch was so beautiful, so innocent, so needed. May Christ grant her and Ellie peace.

"Ellie brought me back to life. She brought me back to love. She returned me to Christ and the church. I owe her everything.

"The look on her face when I said no to her haunts me constantly. It is as though I have killed the person I love more than myself. Only God knows how much I love her.

"I will never see her again. Even if I should, I couldn't tell her how much I love her. If I can't, there is no way I could expect you to do it for me. I love her. Maybe, with God's grace, you can help her understand.

"During dinnertime I wrote her a note. Take it with you. At least I want her to know I am thinking of her in my last hours," pleaded the doctor.

Father Tom wanted to blurt out something like: "You don't know what you're saying . . . you're crazy. Don't talk such stupidity." Instead, he merely responded, "If the moment arrives that what you are expecting comes to pass, I'll give her this envelope and, with God's help, do what I can for Ellie and Iota."

The two silently embraced each other as the friends they were.

"Now, Father Tom, I need some time to be alone with Christ." He gripped the priest's hand. "Thanks."

The priest picked up his Bible and his book on pastoral care of the sick and was gone.

A short distance from Boomer he met a parade of cars being driven carelessly. He commented to himself, "The way those people are driving, someone could be killed."

Chapter 22

The people of Boomer gathered at Carolan's. Something had to be done to assure adequate punishment for the doctor.

"It looks as though Judge Nelson might not give him any sentence at all!" shouted Michael Clancy.

"None at all. None at all!" sang out Ryan Patterson. "But what can we do about it?"

DOC stood on the bench in booth number three and demanded attention. "You are right, absolutely right. There is nothing you can do about it. You have no right to take the law into your own hands. The whole thing is in the proper hands, and we need some civility here.

"Don't be led into being a mob. A mob has no logic, no reason, no conscience. There is a heavy price to pay for acting merely out of emotion. Go home and let justice take its course," demanded DOC.

"That's easy for you to say," shouted the irate, red-faced Clancy. "Did you ever lose a family member to AIDS?"

"You're becoming unreasonable," retorted DOC, standing as a monumental figure over the crowd.

"Unreasonable, are we? And you, with all your education, know it all, I suppose. Get out of your ivory tower into the real world!" screamed Patterson.

"What right do you, an outsider, have to tell us what is right and what is wrong?" rejoined Clancy.

"Things' being right or wrong don't depend on where you're from. No matter where you are in this country, it is wrong to take the law into your own hands!" shouted Dominic O. Crotty, not to be outdone.

"One more word out of you, DOC, and you'll be just a warm-up for what we have to do to Burke."

DOC took his chances. "Can't you at least wait for Father Tom to come back to town? He always stops in here before returning to the rectory. You can at least wait that long."

"Father Burns? Sure and don't we know where his mind is on this matter. Look at the sign in his office in booth one: GONE FOR THE DAY. That sign has been there all week. And where is he gone to? We all know he is in court in the day and in jail at night," clamored Clancy.

DOC looked about the room. He searched for just one person to join his minority and found none. He sagged against the wall and slid slowly to a sitting position in the booth. In a hardly audible voice he muttered, "You are stupid. Go home. Don't do anything you'll regret. Sleep on it. Let's meet here again tomorrow night."

Immediately, as though to pick up the torch, Sean Carolan began to bang the heel of his shoe against the bar hard. "DOC is right. Whatever you might want to do tonight can wait until tomorrow night. Can't you wait that long before doing anything?"

For a moment that seemed like an eternity, the room was in absolute silence. Sean had never spoken out on any issue. He had never taken sides. He was never judgmental. Everyone was in shock, not by what he said but that he had said anything at all. And, further, this was his court.

Most surprised was Sean himself. He couldn't comprehend where he had found the courage to hit his heel on the bar, let alone pronounce his feelings.

He realized that every eye was glued on him. All waited for him to say more. He knew he owned the building. Now they were giving him the floor.

Under these horrible circumstances, his mind blanked. His knees seemed incapable of supporting his tall, lean frame. He lowered his eyes, then his head, and seized the bar in front of him rather than the moment.

His lips formed the only words that would come to him: "Everybody, everybody, step forward. Drinks are on the house!"

Patterson broke the spell. He lifted his huge hulk up on the bar. His head nearly touched the ceiling. He placed himself directly in front of Sean, almost as though he was trying to protect Carolan from any attack for having uttered his words of protest.

Patterson spoke deliberately through clenched teeth. His fists flailed the air in a show of horrendous power. "We all know that Father Burns has stayed neutral. This is no time for neutrality. This is a time for action. We are all in this together."

All the anger stored for generations against God for all human ills was suddenly unleashed against Dr. Robert Burke. All the suffering experienced by every AIDS victim known by the citizens of Boomer was now wished on the man whose original intention was to remove all pain from the face of the earth.

Frustration from having watched loved ones die removed individuality. Each surrendered his own personality and character. Without personality and character, reason dies and from the ashes of abandoned consciences there is the terrifying existence of a mob.

"I have a fine length of rope here!" yelled Clancy. "It should be used for Burke's necktie, but if Sean and DOC want to remain out of this, let's make sure they do."

He motioned the mob to make room in the center of the floor. "Bring them here and let them sit back to back on these two chairs. We'll tie them to the chairs and to one another."

Once the rope was in place, obliging hands taped the mouths of law and order shut. The mob smashed most of the lights and moved out.

"We know what has to be done!" shouted Patterson. "This is no time for the weak." Then he urged, "Let's form a caravan to the county jail. I'll lead. Let anyone with the courage follow me!"

The caravan thundered in low gear up and down Main Street three times. Each time the mob's resolve seemed to increase. Then the procession went north on the highway leading to the county seat. All was quiet in Boomer.

Sean and DOC sat motionless in the semidarkened room, knowing that any movement might be of more hindrance than help. Both knew that Father Tom should return at any moment. For two people unaccustomed to prayer there was a sincere bombardment of heaven for themselves, for Dr. Burke, and for the mob. All three objects of prayer depended on an early return by the priest.

Colleen Carolan had heard the noise from next door. She had

watched the cars move back and forth on Main Street. Then all was quiet. She moved cautiously down the stairs to investigate the situation.

Father Burns experienced an eerie sensation as he turned from the highway to Main Street. The town was devoid of cars. The neon lights in Carolan's front windows were on, but it was too dark inside. He had considered skipping Carolan's to go directly to the rectory and bed when he spotted Colleen coming on to the street. Now he was compelled to investigate.

He and Colleen peered in the window. He tried the door and it opened. As their eyes adjusted, they saw the forms in the center of the room. Somehow Father Burns sensed he was in no danger and quickly moved toward Sean and DOC.

Once he identified them, he pulled the tapes from their mouths and unbound their fetters. "For heaven's sake, what is going on?" asked the priest.

"We've no time to talk, Father. Let me call the sheriff while DOC fills you in," said Sean.

DOC hurriedly gave Father Burns the story, sparing him the details. Meanwhile, Sean dialed the phone. No answer. The phone had been pulled from the wall, as had the phones in booths one and three.

"Colleen," Father instructed, "go to your apartment and call the sheriff. Tell him the situation and advise him to get help."

Then he turned to his friends. "Let's go." And they were speeding frantically in the direction of the county seat, fifteen miles away.

"They have a big head start," Sean murmured.

The sky ahead was a brilliant crimson. "My God in heaven, help!" said the priest, half to God and half to his passengers. Then they drove on in silence.

The mob had performed its task well. The sheriff had been called to the big jail, and no one was on guard. Kerosene was poured all around the building that adjoined the courtroom. Then kerosene was thrown into the windows of the jail.

As Patterson ignited the kerosene, Clancy shouted into the jail, "Burn, Burke, burn here and in the hereafter! We have the final solution. We don't need you!"

247

Once the fire had worked its destruction, the mob dissipated into the darkness. Lest they be identified with the night's work, the various mob members chose different ways to return to Boomer.

Father Tom hurried over to the sheriff. "Was anyone hurt?" he questioned, quite afraid of the answer.

"He never had a chance, Father. Dr. Burke is dead. I'm truly sorry. Believe me," answered the sheriff as he studied the embers.

"Was anyone else hurt?" inquired DOC.

"Yes," responded the sheriff. "When the fire broke out, Dr. Philip Hurley was just leaving the restaurant up on the hill. He hurried down to save the portfolio containing the formula for the final solution.

"He knew where it was in the judge's chambers. Even though the area was already ablaze, he broke a window to rescue the portfolio. He knew where the judge had placed it.

"Dr. Hurley didn't make it out again. He and the final solution are both gone," the sheriff concluded.

"The remains. Are there any remains?" asked Father Tom.

"Father, I think it would be best for Dr. Burke's wife if we finished the cremation process begun by the mob. For sure, there won't be any reviewal. Of course, that's her decision, whether or not she wants cremation or a coffin," responded the lawman.

"Thanks, Sheriff. I appreciate the information." Then he turned to his friends. "Come on; let's go home."

The streets of Boomer were dark and deserted. The pastor parked in front of Carolan's, and the three entered. So much had happened since they were there hardly an hour before.

The trio sat in booth number three. "There isn't any coffee made," Sean remarked. "Would you like some?"

"No thanks," responded DOC. "I just want to sit for a moment."

"I think I'll call it a day then," Sean said as he moved to the door. "Colleen must wonder what has happened. Turn off this switch when you leave. Stay as long as you want and don't worry about locking the door."

"Good night, Sean," both said in unison and he was gone.

Neither cared to discuss the events of the night. DOC's attention was drawn, as was so often the case, to the booth top where the heart and the initials were perfectly carved.

"This might sound funny coming from me, but regardless of who the original 'J.C.' was, I think the initials refer to Jesus Christ," began DOC.

"Why should that sound funny coming from you? I listened from the kitchen when you discussed popularity with Iota. You talked to her about God," said the priest.

"Anyway," continued DOC, quite ignoring Father Tom's statement, "it says Jesus Christ loves. I've thought about it quite a bit this week. I think the letters *m-e* should be added.

"'Jesus Christ loves me'. Also, I thought perhaps the letters added should be *u-s*. That is less selfish. What do you think? 'Jesus Christ loves us'?" said Dominic, looking for affirmation.

"Have you thought about carving the letters *a-l-l*?"

"Great," said Dominic with enthusiasm. "'J.C. loves *all*'! I'll carve it in right now."

"No, not yet," protested the priest. "There has to be an arrow drawn through the heart. The heart of Christ was pierced with a lance. Dr. Bob said it to me: 'There is nothing as whole as a heart that is broken.' Don't you think the arrow is needed?"

"Yes, I do. I'll get right at it," responded DOC.

"DOC, you're no artist. Get it done right. Tomorrow, okay? Tomorrow, DOC. Now I have to leave," said the priest. He stood up as erect as possible. He stretched his back like an imaginary football injury was recurring. Then he took a long deep breath and exhaled. "Say a little prayer for me, DOC. I'm going over to see Ellie now."

DOC stared after him and spoke softly to himself. "I've never prayed before in my life until tonight. I didn't even know I knew how. But, Lord, I've talked to you so much this night, we are on a first-name basis.

"Right now, Jesus, I would much rather talk with you than with Ellie. Lord, I don't envy that priest for what is ahead of him. Please be with him. Help him."

Then Dominic O. Crotty stood and moved out the open door to the street. Burns had made a U-turn just past where the tracks used to be and was coming back on his way to the Burkes'.

DOC waved him to a stop, ran to the passenger side, and crawled in. "If it's okay with you, Father, I want to go along."

Father put the lights on dim and eased to the curb. He didn't want to waken any neighbors at that hour of the night. He and DOC closed the car doors quietly and proceeded to the porch. They touched the doorbell once.

Both were surprised when the door was immediately opened for them. Ellie greeted them, "I can't explain this, but I knew you were coming tonight, Father. I'm pleased you can be here also, Uncle DOC. Bob is dead, isn't he?"

They were both taken by such surprise they could only nod their answer. "I have the coffee and some of Iota's favorite cookies ready. I decided to stay up tonight until you brought me the news," she said.

Father and DOC sat at the kitchen table while she filled their cups. She continued, "I thought I might catch the door so the bell wouldn't disturb Iota's rest. She needs all she can get." She poured her own coffee, replaced the pot, and passed the cookies. "How was he killed? Were you there?"

DOC responded, "A group of locals fired the jail. He didn't have a chance."

"I had the strangest feeling he was in trouble. Where were you, Father?" she asked slowly.

"I was with him until nearly ten o'clock. I brought him the oils of healing, accepted his reconciliation, and gave him Eucharist. Then we talked at great length."

"I am so happy you were there for him, Father Tom."

"When I came to Carolan's they had tied up Sean and DOC so they couldn't alert anyone. We hurried right back to the jail, but it was too late.

"Dr. Hurley died also. He tried to save Bob's files from the fire. They were in the judge's chambers. The files are gone, too," commented Father Tom.

"I'm not sure but what that may have made Bob happy," she guessed.

"Just before I left last night, Bob gave me this note for you. He had had a premonition of his death. Here it is." He took it from his coat pocket and handed it to her.

"Uncle DOC, would you please read it for me? I don't think either Father or I could handle it," she stated.

DOC took the envelope, opened it, and read: " 'My dear Ellie,

The first time I met you, I felt you were too good to be true. Our marriage has been so wonderful from the beginning that I knew it was too perfect to last.

" 'You have provided me with the happiest moments of my life. The love we have shared the last twelve years has brought me temporal joy and now eternal happiness. I cherish every moment God had given us as a loving couple.

" 'Please let Iota know that she was conceived in love, born in joy, and is in our constant prayers as she goes through her life. No one ever had a more wonderful wife and daughter than I have. I pray Iota may always share our tradition of love.

" 'Despite the fact that I am the richest man in the world, I have no money to leave you. However, I am certain the judge will decide in your favor for the final solution.

" 'I have never kept any secrets from you except its existence. It caused me such problems I didn't want to force you to share the anxiety. The judge may decide that the cure must be distributed for the good of the human race. If that be the case, you will be rich financially and be spared the agony of the decision.

" 'If his judgment is that you must make the decision, know that whatever you decide, it will be the correct thing.

" 'You will use the money for many good things. I trust you completely.

" 'My life may seem to others as a terrible failure. I worked so many years to be a priest and was denied. I spent the last years in nearly constant research for the AIDS cure and benefited only one person.

" 'Because of you, my darling, I am not a failure. God himself promises us nothing more important than happiness born out of love.

" 'You have given me such a wondrous love that I have already shared untold happiness. The happiness of heaven began for me the first time I met you.

" 'Your whole person has introduced me to God. The words come alive with you: "God is love and he who abides in love abides in God and God in him."

" 'If I have failed you in any way, I am truly sorry. This night I begin my watch over you from heaven, from where I will send you his strength.

" 'I will always love you with all my heart and soul. Your loving husband, Bob.' "

When Uncle DOC finished reading the letter, he folded it, replaced it in the envelope, and handed it to Ellie.

"Thanks," she said quite simply. "Bob and I really had only one problem: I never totally understood him."

"If people had understood him, he'd still be alive," responded Father Tom. "I never understood him."

"Father Tom," asked Ellie, "should we awaken Iota now while you are here or should we wait until morning?"

"Whatever you say, Ellie," he answered.

Ellie moved toward the staircase. As she began the ascent, she looked up. On the top step, with face in her hands, sat Iota sobbing softly.

"Come down, honey. We have something to tell you," said a surprised mother.

"I know, Mom. I heard the doorbell ring. I heard everything you said in the kitchen." She crawled onto her mother's lap and said in a reassuring voice, "Daddy loved us, Mom. And we loved him. Nothing can ever change that."

Chapter 23

The whole town of Boomer was like a morgue awaiting the remains of Dr. Burke.

The door stood ajar at Carolan's. It might be recalled that the week it had opened with the Courtneys as owners, their son, Jim, had been crushed to death. The half-finished carving in booth number three symbolized his half-lived life. His death had been too much for his parents. They moved to Rochester and never returned.

Now, as the curiosity seekers paused for a moment to peer through the open door, they viewed the two chairs and length of rope in the center of the room.

Sean and Colleen never entered the building again. Colleen called the various suppliers, and in turn the unused commodities were removed. The bank agreed to remove anything of value and have an auction.

Sean walked to the rectory to inform the priest of his intention. Father Tom agreed to talk to DOC. They would vacate their offices on Monday morning.

Aunt Bridget was grief-stricken with the news of Dr. Burke's death. It wasn't that she had felt so close to him. Her closeness to Iota and seeing her without a dad left Bridget totally devastated.

Ellie decided the remains of her husband should be cremated. She also decided the funeral should be on Sunday afternoon at one o'clock at Assumption Catholic Church in Boomer. There would be no announcement in the newspapers. Only the family would be present.

Because Father Tom no longer had a phone at Carolan's, the rectory telephone was ringing constantly. Bridget answered. The caller invariably had the same question. "When and where is the funeral?"

The response was always the same: "The funeral Mass will be at one o'clock on Sunday at Assumption. Only the family is expected."

Father Burns had suggested there be no homily. He wasn't sure if he could deliver one for his very best friend. Also, anything he would want to say to the wife and daughter could be better said in private.

The remains were placed in front of the altar for the celebration of the memorial Mass. While Father Tom was vesting, the church began to fill. When he came from the sacristy he was totally surprised. Ellie and Iota, Uncle DOC and Aunt Bridget, Sean and Colleen sat together in the front pew. They shared the pastor's amazement when they found so many friends present.

At the conclusion of the Mass, Father Tom asked if there was anyone present who wanted to say anything on the occasion. A beautiful elderly woman, Mrs. Gertrude Johnson, rose to her feet. The priest asked her to come forward.

Mrs. Johnson spoke with gratitude and humility. "When any of us called concerning arrangements for the funeral, Bridget gave all of us the same message. 'The funeral Mass will be at one o'clock on Sunday at Assumption. Only the family is expected.'

"Ellie, you notice that we are the elderly of Boomer. Your husband's expertise made it possible for us to remain in our own homes. As his secretary and bookkeeper, you know he charged us nothing or a very minimal amount for his services.

"His concern and care were the most important element in our lives. He always treated us with dignity and respect. He loved us, and we loved him.

"We are family. Iota, you call every one of us Grandma or Grandpa. None of us has a grandchild we love any more than we love you.

"After the completion of this memorial, we want you to eat with us in the parish hall. We know that potluck isn't always the greatest food in the world, but that is all we can do. Please honor us with your presence."

Father Tom thanked those in attendance and assured them of his participation in the meal. Then he added, "Ellie and Iota will appreciate this opportunity to thank everyone.

"I presume," he continued, "that Gertrude has spoken for all of you. Ellie and I decided there would be no homily. Gertrude, what you have said is more important than any words of mine.

"As I celebrate this moment with all of you, two significant thoughts come to me. The trial of Dr. Burke unearthed the hatred in Boomer. The funeral of Dr. Burke has illuminated the love in Boomer."

Everyone appreciated the potluck. Ellie suddenly understood her husband better than she ever had before. Iota was given an unmistakable message: she had many wonderful friends. Uncle DOC was thanked not only for so often being the fourth hand in bridge, but also because of the hours he had spent with the youth of Boomer.

For many, it was an introduction to Bridget Burns. Her brother, Father Tom, was appreciative that the church had been filled with members of other denominations as well as Catholics. "You know," one of the Protestants said, "I'm not sure a pastor's office should be in a place like Carolan's, but for me you were much more accessible than if you'd stayed in the rectory."

Chapter 24

The next morning, DOC and Father Tom met in front of Carolan's. The door was still open, so they entered together to officially evacuate their offices.

As they placed their office belongings in their cars, the moving van parked in front of the old hardware store. They went up the stairs to Carolan's apartment to enjoy a last cup of coffee with Sean and Colleen.

They stood and watched as the chairs and table joined the easy chair in its final descent. In a short time, the last of the furniture was on the truck. As they departed the store, they noted that the Amish were preparing for the final destruction of Carolan's.

DOC pleaded, "Sean, I don't know what plans the Amish might have for the table in booth number three, but if you could see your way to let me have it, I would be most grateful. In fact, I want to have professional work done on the heart."

"If they have any designs on it, I'm not aware of it. If you want it in a well-preserved state, just tell that young man over there you will give him a twenty-dollar bill if he will remove it without so much as a scratch on it." Sean smiled.

DOC did as he was advised. The top was not only rescued for that price, but it was placed carefully in the back of DOC's van. He turned again to Sean. "I plan to have a coffee table made of it. I'll cover it with glass and take good care of it. It has been my office furniture for nearly twelve years now, and I thank you for it."

"Father Tom," spoke Colleen, "have you seen this editorial from the *Saint Paul Pioneer Press*?"

"No, I haven't."

"Read it," said Colleen. "It is about Dr. Bob. You might want to share it with Ellie."

There was a quiet embrace with no promise for the future, and suddenly the priest and DOC stood alone. The Carolans were returning to Saint Paul.

Several wagons gathered in front of Carolan's like camels awaiting their burdens. Methodically the roof was stripped and lowered, board by board, to the ground.

The walls lost their outer sidings. Then the horizontal boards, nailed for so many years to the upright two-by-eight studs, were removed. The interior walls were torn asunder until only the dimension lumber marked the spot where the building had stood for over a hundred years. Square nails and ax-fashioned joints spoke of antiquity.

As each wagon creaked and groaned out of sight, another would return with its insatiable appetite. By nightfall, even the huge rocks serving as the foundation would be removed and nature could begin her reclamation.

The following dawn, like busy ants, the Amish would begin the same board-by-board removal of the hardware store. It was the oldest building in town except for the structure that was originally the Stage Coach Inn of Elliota. The inn was successively the Boomer House, the Elliot descendants' home, and most recently the home, office, and research laboratory of Dr. Robert Burke.

Elliota had been leveled within a few months. Boomer's demise was much slower but, nonetheless, inexorable. HOME FOR SALE signs were in evidence on every street.

People could live without a grocery store in town. They can survive if youngsters have to be transported to the next town for schooling. If one has to drive thirty miles to the movies, he can do the same for church, clothing, and even gas.

Every town wants a doctor. When the majority are senior citizens, a doctor is essential. After all, humans suffer physically, psychologically, and spiritually.

We generally think we have plenty of time before we will meet our God and Judge. An appointment with a psychiatrist can be delayed, but for physical pain we want immediate attention.

And so HOME FOR SALE in Boomer was the sign of the times, because Boomer had no doctor.

"DOC," suggested Father Tom, "why don't we go to the rectory? I want to share this editorial with Ellie. Maybe we can persuade Bridget to prepare a snack."

"The answer is yes, a quick yes, before you change your mind," responded an agreeable friend.

When they arrived, they were pleased to discover that Bridget had already invited Ellie and Iota for the same purpose. The five enjoyed a light brunch as Father Burns read the newspaper article: " 'Anyone who perpetrates violence needs to know that violence has no parameters. It is like a rock dropped into the pond. The individual who drops it may have the intention of merely creating a splash. It has to be noted that after the splash, the ripples move irrevocably to the shore until the entire body of water is affected.

" 'It is not hard to pass judgment on the mob which destroyed Dr. Burke. It is hard to forgive them. Having attended the trial and seen the doctor in the courtroom, I know that he forgives them because he was, in my mind, always Christlike.

" 'I have no obligation to pass judgment on his decision not to share his cure for AIDS with society. His contention was that a violent society has no right to be free of pain.

" 'His entire life was spent in bringing kindness and peace to the world in such a way that pain would no longer be required.

" 'A violent society is incapable of understanding a mind such as his. I sincerely believe that Burke's thinking was very simple. If the human race, with all its suffering, could not understand what Christ endured for them, how could it possibly fathom, without pain, how deep his love is for everyone?

" 'A mob has no soul. It refuses responsibility. No one seems at fault, because everyone is. But violence takes place.

" 'The gentle doctor was not ultimately responsible for keeping his secret from society. The just and objective Judge Nelson was not responsible.

" 'The mob's action destroyed the only person who knew the

secret. It destroyed his coworker, Dr. Philip Hurley, who knew most of the secret. It destroyed the folder containing the secret itself.

" 'The mob's final solution destroyed the final solution to AIDS and much more. The ripple caused by the mob covered the entire pond of human suffering.' "

"That is a good editorial," said Ellie. "I must get some copies for myself, the archbishop, and Father O'Donnell."

"I'll get you ten copies of today's *Pioneer Press*. That should be adequate," responded DOC.

"It says a lot of things I would have talked about at the memorial service, but I couldn't say anything," said Father Burke. "Also, it says it better than I could say it."

"There is a kind of finality and closure to the whole incident at the jail. The question we must face now is where do we go from here?" asked DOC.

"Well," said Father Tom, "I don't get to vote. I go wherever the bishop sends me on July 1. As of now, I haven't a clue."

"Ellie, what about you and Iota?" queried DOC.

"I don't know. There is nothing left in Boomer. I suppose I could take some refresher courses and be a nurse in Rochester. I still have good friends there. Lourdes is a good high school, and I think Bob would want Iota to attend there.

"If I didn't need money for Iota's education, I'd like to volunteer to work with the Archbishop and Father O'Donnell."

"Aunt Bridget, it's your turn," suggested DOC.

"I guess I could go with Father Tom. Thanks to Ellie and Iota, I'm a fairly capable housekeeper. If I could do what I really would like most, I would go with Ellie and Iota. I could keep house while Ellie works. I could care for Iota when the need arises. I've never loved anyone like I love Iota."

Iota moved over to her friend. "Let's go over to the church and pray we all make the right decision, Aunt Bridget."

"And what about you, DOC? You must have been making some plans, too," said Father Tom.

"I've loved my time in Boomer. It has allowed me great friends and many wonderful moments. When I first came, the natives thought I was important, but eventually I was just different."

DOC grimaced. "As of today, my office has been rendered into oblivion. That is except for my tabletop, which I will guard with my life.

"I have a feeling Boomer has 'busted.' The few people remaining aren't sure how to interact anymore. It has fast become a ghost town.

"Initially, my undesignated purpose was working with the young to further their intellectual prowess. The trouble is the young are a vanishing minority.

"Gradually, I've become little more than a fourth for bridge when someone couldn't find his glasses or teeth. The whole place was becoming an elder hostel.

"I remember being told at Brown University, by a professor in educational psychology, that if I wanted to stay young, I should work with the young. If I wanted to get old, I should try to keep up with them.

"I strongly suspect I need a new challenge. With the demise of Carolan's, it won't be found here. Where I am going, I know not and care very little. Father, I'm back to testing where the winds blow!"

Father Tom laughed. He remembered their conversation.

"But to continue with the future. Ellie, I'm glad Iota is over at the church with Aunt Bridget. You see, I'm a person of means. I have a mansion on the ocean in New Jersey. I'm rarely there. Yet I maintain a butler, a maid, and a cook there at all times.

"Like Bridget, I'm smitten with Iota. You two could move into the mansion tomorrow. The only added expense would be food, and I can handle that. If you and Bridget decide her fate is with you, all three of you are welcome.

"Regardless of what you decide, I want to ensure Iota's education for high school, college, and whatever. Think about it, Ellie."

"That is really a generous offer, Uncle DOC. I am going to have to pray over this a great deal," responded Ellie.

"I know what you mean, Ellie, and I can't help you. I know what you will think about and pray over: what Bob would want you to do."

"I am positive what he wants me to do. In fact, he told me in the letter you delivered from his cell the night he was killed," remarked Ellie.

"What did he say?"

"He said, 'Whatever you decide, it will be the correct thing.'"

Ellie continued, "I know we can't stay here. Boomer isn't big enough. I'm not talking about blocks and buildings and streets. It's big enough that way. What I mean is for some people, their hearts aren't big enough.

"The people who killed Bob and destroyed the final solution are all good people, every one of them. It was passion, the passion of anger, that transformed them.

"There lies within the soul of the sinner something more terrible than anger, and that something is guilt.

"Sometimes guilt is removed by a jail sentence and we call it restitution. Sometimes the transgressed is Christian enough to forgive. Sometimes one goes to Christ personally or through his sacrament.

"Sometimes, people just conceal it as well as possible, as though nothing really happened, or they invent excusing circumstances.

"But in Boomer, everyone who dies of AIDS will be a reminder of mindless destruction. Every unsolved case of AIDS will resurrect the buried guilt.

"Even worse for us and for Boomer, every time we walk down the street some people will be reminded of their guilt.

"So I say to you, my friends, unless we remove ourselves from our roots, our home, our town, even though Dr. Bob has forgiven, even though we have forgiven, unless we remove ourselves, we will be removed.

"The world, which has never understood Jesus, teaches that the Church controls through guilt. The truth is that Christ established the Church to remove guilt.

"The cross is the instrument of forgiveness, not a perpetuating of guilt. The cross is the ultimate proof of God's love for humanity. My husband understood that.

"He also knew that except for his refusal to respect my view in regard to sharing the final solution, I was always in charge.

"I disposed. I proposed. I didn't want to come back to Boomer, but finances dictated otherwise. Bob trusted my judgment. He knew I was the strength in our family."